NOSFERATU WENT OUT THROUGH
the heavy wooden door, swinging it shut behind
him. He walked down stone steps, deeper into his
lair. Nosferatu came to a steel door. On one side was
a retinal scanner and he pressed his eyes to it. When
the computer recognized his pattern, the door's
bolts withdrew and it slowly swung open.

The room he walked into was a crypt. In the center was a raised platform upon which rested a black
metal tube. Surrounding the tube were dozens of
plants and small trees, a veritable oasis of greenery
underground.

Nosferatu went up to the tube, placing his hands
gently on the lid. He leaned forward until his head
was next to the front. Inside was the fourth Undead
at haven.

"Soon, my love," he whispered. "Soon we will finally be together forever."

◆ ◆ ◆

ALSO FROM ROBERT DOHERTY

The Rock
Area 51
Area 51: The Reply
Area 51: The Mission
Area 51: The Sphinx
Area 51: The Grail
Area 51: Excalibur
Area 51: The Truth

Psychic Warrior
Psychic Warrior: Project Aura

AVAILABLE FROM DELL

ROBERT DOHERTY

AREA 51
NOSFERATU

A DELL BOOK

AREA 51: NOSFERATU
A Dell Book / July 2003

Published by Bantam Dell
A Division of Random House, Inc.
New York, New York

ISBN 0-440-23724-6

Manufactured in the United States of America
Published simultaneously in Canada

OPM 10 9 8 7 6 5 4 3 2

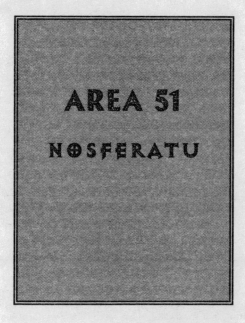

AREA 51

NOSFERATU

PROLOGUE

THE PRESENT
The Skeleton Coast, West Africa

THE ROOM WAS DIMLY LIT BY A
single low-wattage bulb set beneath the tattered shade of
an old lamp sitting in the center of the large, oaken table
that dominated the room. The table was oval, stretching
ten feet in length and five in width, and its top was
marked and scarred by centuries of use. Four large wing
armchairs were spaced evenly around the table. They
were cushioned and covered in well-worn black leather.
The curved outer wall was smoothly cut sandstone,
breached only by a single door made of thick planks of
weathered wood, bound with iron spikes to a diagonal
crossbeam.

Three figures occupied chairs, leaving one empty.
There were no papers in front of them, no laptops, hand-
helds, or any other electronic device in the room other
than the single light and a large flat-screen display set in
front of the empty chair, facing the other three. The faces
of the three were hidden in the shadows of their high-
backed chairs and the only way for each to determine
who was speaking was from accent and direction.

"Gentlemen, I welcome you to the Haven." The voice
was low yet powerful, easily carrying from the chair opposite the door across the polished oak tabletop from the

others. The accent was indeterminate, an amalgamation of numerous languages warped over the ages into speaking English.

The voice continued. "We have waited a long time, a very long time, for this day. The Airlia have been defeated by the humans. Both sides. The two alien leaders, Aspasia and Artad, are dead. Quite remarkable and more fortuitous than I had ever hoped. They who made us and hate us are gone. It is our time now."

The man leaned forward, revealing a narrow face, white hair, and dark eyes with the slightest hint of red in them. When the dim light struck them a certain way the pupils appeared to be slightly elongated. Despite the white hair, his skin was smooth and alabaster, as if it had never seen the light of day or the grim hand of time. He wore a flowing robe of soft gray cloth.

His voice deepened as he spoke. "I was made Nosferatu in the First Age of Egypt, before the dawn of history as recorded by the humans, the child of Horus the Airlia and a human High Consort. I have lived for over ten millennia waiting for the time when those who made us would be defeated and we would not have to live in fear of them." He looked around the table. "This is the first time the three of us have been together in the same place at the same time. I thank you for answering my summons. With the Airlia gone we are the eldest and most powerful species on the planet."

Nosferatu paused, the words sinking into the sandstone, replaced by utter silence. Nosferatu indicated that the man to the screen's right should speak next.

The voice spoke English like a song, the Chinese background unmistakable. "I am Tian Dao Lin." He leaned forward, revealing Oriental features and a bald, liver-spotted scalp. He wore a black silk robe with a single red dragon embroidered on each loose sleeve. "I was made underneath the great mountain tomb Qian-Ling by Artad himself in consort with a sacrificial girl well before even the dynasty of ShiHuangdi, the first true Emperor of the Middle Kingdom." He turned toward Nosferatu. "We met many, many years ago, a most fascinating story that I will tell you if you wish"—he glanced at the third occupant of the room—"but at another time and place as we are here for business." Tian Dao Lin leaned back in his seat.

The third person in the room waited a few seconds before speaking. Then he stood, a formidable figure, over six and a half feet in height and as erect as a soldier on parade. His skin was pale, his face perfectly smooth and unlined except for a single scar down the left side from the edge of the eye to the edge of his mouth. He had a prominent nose, giving him the appearance of a hunting hawk. His eyes were slanted, though not as much as Tian Dao Lin's, and his long red hair flowed over his shoulders. He was dressed in black pants and shirt made of some soft material that absorbed what little light there was in the room.

"I too was made by Artad in consort with a human girl, but long after you, Tian Dao Lin. The name I choose others to know me as now is Adrik. I have—as have both of you—been called by many other names over the years. I am here to find out this business that the Eldest, Nosferatu, proposes."

Adrik retook his seat.

Nosferatu placed his fingers lightly on the edge of the table as if keeping himself balanced. "As you both know, we have a stronger genetic link with the humans than with the Airlia. We look like them and can even pass as human. It is our blood—the Airlia blood that runs through our veins—that makes us different from humans and has kept us alive through the ages."

Nosferatu continued. "The Airlia are gone. The Ones Who Wait—who were in a way brethren to us but under the thrall of Artad and manufactured, not bred—are also gone as far as can be determined. Aspasia's Shadow, who meddled many times with us, is dead and his guides ineffective since the humans took over and destroyed the Master Guardian, effectively shutting down all the subordinate Guardian computers upon which the Guides relied.

"It is a new age."

Nosferatu paused and looked around the table, waiting. He knew there were different agendas here and he wanted to know what they were before he got to his.

Tian Dao Lin was the first to speak. "A new age, but the humans believe it is *their* age now. I do not think they will treat us any better than the Airlia or their minions did. We may look like them but we are most definitely not the same. And what we have had to do over the many years to remain alive—while there are small cults that worship the vampire legend, the majority of humans fear and despise even our myth. I think their reaction to the reality if it is revealed will be much more severe and unforgiving."

"That is why I changed my manner of feeding many years ago," Nosferatu noted. "I do not kill anymore to get my sustenance."

Adrik dissented. "We are superior to humans. It is the natural order that we feed from them. Your distinction means nothing."

It meant something to the victim, Nosferatu thought, but he didn't give voice to the words.

"We have all done well over the years," Tian Dao Lin continued, ignoring the Russian. "Each of us controls vast wealth and power from the shadows. Why should we do anything differently?"

"Because the world is a different place now," Nosferatu said. "Even the two of you acknowledge that by coming to this meeting, something we have never done before. There are new opportunities now. And new dangers."

"Why did Vampyr not come here then?" Adrik demanded. "Did you not invite him?"

"I invited him," Nosferatu replied.

"Then why is he not here?" Adrik asked once more.

"You seem quite concerned about Vampyr," Nosferatu said. "Do you fear him?"

Adrik leapt to his feet. "I fear no one."

"Please sit." Nosferatu glanced at the Chinese, who was watching Adrik closely. "I meant you no disrespect. I am the Eldest and *I* fear Vampyr. He is powerful and dangerous."

"You said new opportunities," Tian Dao Lin said. "Do you mean the Grail and immortality?"

"It would be most fortuitous to get the Grail," Nosferatu said. "However, my sources tell me it was destroyed when the mothership was crashed into the array on Mars by Dr. Duncan. Whom I met many years ago under a different name."

"Donnchadh." Adrik spit the name out like a curse. "Lisa Duncan, most recently. Among the many aliases she used in her reincarnations over the years. A troublesome human if ever there was one."

"She freed me from the Airlia long ago," Nosferatu noted.

"For her own reasons, I am sure," Adrik said.

"But are you certain the Grail was destroyed?" Tian Dao Lin pressed, cutting off Adrik. "My sources believe the same thing, but I have heard that those from Area 51 brought some artifacts back from Mars on board Donnchadh's spaceship."

"It is slightly possible," Nosferatu granted, "that they brought the Grail back, but I very much doubt it."

Tian Dao Lin lapsed into silence, waiting.

Adrik spoke up. "I agree with Nosferatu, the Eldest, on one key point. I do not think we will be accepted by the humans. Therefore, I propose we do not ask to be accepted by the humans." He crossed his arms across his chest. "I propose we rule them."

There were several moments of silence following Adrik's proposal. Finally, Nosferatu voiced the objection he knew Tian Dao Lin was thinking. "Ruling would force us into the open. Even with the great power and influence we have amassed over the years, we would still be vulnerable. We have all seen great and powerful rulers over the ages who were destroyed. We have just witnessed the humans defeat the Airlia, something I would not have thought possible. We should not underestimate them. And there have been attempts by Undead, particularly Vampyr, and you"—he stared at Adrik—"to rule before and all have failed."

"It depends on what you mean by failure," Adrik argued. "I had magnificent successes in many places. Names I have used are in the human history books as great leaders."

"But you could never maintain your kingdoms; nor could Vampyr," Nosferatu noted.

"So you say we stay in the shadows still?" Adrik demanded. "Let our fortunes and fates go with the flow of mankind? At least when the Airlia ruled through their minions we had some degree of assurance that there would be a world left for us to live in. Humans, on their own"—he shook his head—"they will destroy themselves, and us with them. We are wiser, more experienced. It would be in their interest for us to dictate their course."

"And when we feed?" Tian Dao Lin quietly asked. "If we could have partaken of the Grail and become immortal without the need to drink blood, then I would say perhaps we could rule. But without that, do you think the humans would be so obliging as to give us bodies to feed on?"

Adrik shrugged. "They could give us their worst criminals—the humans kill thousands themselves in punishment. Your own China chops off how many heads each year? And for those who feel the kill is not necessary"—he glanced disdainfully toward Nosferatu—"there is always a way to get blood without killing."

"We are only a handful," Tian Dao Lin said. "Even with our money and influence . . ." He trailed off into silence.

"Why have you brought us here then?" Adrik demanded of Nosferatu. "Surely you had a reason."

Nosferatu nodded. "I had two reasons. I called you here to discuss what we should do first before we can accomplish anything else, including trying to rule the humans."

Nosferatu got to his feet and walked over to an ancient armoire, opening its wooden doors to reveal a small stainless-steel door. He slid it up and removed three flasks also made of unmarked steel resting in specially made cradles that kept the contents warm. He carried them back to the table, placing one in front of each man before taking his seat with the third. He unscrewed the lid and lifted it to his lips, tilting the flask and drinking deeply for several seconds before putting it back on the table. There was a faint trace of red on his lips, which he dabbed away with a silk handkerchief. When he was done his face was flushed, his eyes glittering with increased power.

He indicated the other flasks. "It's tested: clean, pure, relatively fresh, and kept at body temperature. Imbibe, my friends. There is much I have to talk to you about."

The other two drank and Nosferatu waited until they were done. Then he tapped the flask. "This is our sustenance and it is our greatest weakness. We are half-breeds. We have some Airlia blood, but not enough to sustain us without constant nourishment of human blood for it. We drink human blood because we have to in order to stay alive."

"You tell us what we have all known since the beginning," Adrik grumbled.

"You knew it from the beginning?" Nosferatu challenged him. "I was entombed for much longer than you by the Airlia Gods themselves, and knew practically nothing. I've known about the Grail and the promise of immortality from the beginning, but I didn't know exactly how it gave eternal life. It is only because the science of the humans has advanced so far that we have an idea of how we have managed to live so long."

He placed one finger against the engorged vein on his wrist. "We have a virus in our blood. An Airlia virus. It helps our cells regenerate when they should die. However, we're half-breeds. So we don't have enough of the virus for it to be self-sustaining. Thus, we must"—he reached forward and plinked a fingernail against the steel flask—"drink human blood to feed and sustain the Airlia virus. The Grail—if we had it—would purify our blood, injecting the Airlia virus, making the virus dominant and self-sustaining just as it is—or was—in the Airlia themselves. We would no longer need to drink human blood for sustenance."

Nosferatu waited. As he expected, Tian Dao Lin, with his obsession for the Grail, was the first to grasp the significance of this. "If we had more of the virus . . ."

Nosferatu nodded. "If we could somehow—without the lost Grail—cross the threshold to where the virus is self-sustaining, we would be, in effect, immortal. We would not need to drink human blood anymore and we would have the benefits of the Airlia virus's ability to replicate, which means even if killed, we would come back to life as it quickly regenerated us."

"But there are no more Airlia," Tian Dao Lin said. "You started this meeting saying that. So there is no more virus except what we already have in our veins."

Nosferatu shook his head. "The Airlia are gone, but there are sources of Airlia virus we can recover."

" 'We'?" Adrik repeated. "Why do you need us?"

A good question, Nosferatu thought. One he knew that Tian Dao Lin was thinking but had not voiced. "Because we would not be the only ones trying to get this blood."

"Vampyr." Tian Dao Lin said it as a statement, not a question.

Nosferatu pressed a button under the tabletop and the screen came alive with an image. The man pictured was similar in appearance to Nosferatu, but his hair was dyed jet-black and he wore a pair of sleek sunglasses that hid his eyes. He wore an expensive suit of black, with a black shirt and tie completing the image. He was standing on the wide stairs of some building, perhaps a symphony hall, looking out over the night crowd.

"I have known him a long time," Nosferatu said, staring at the screen. "He was made Vampyr, also in the First Age of Egypt, the son of the Airlia Amun and a High Consort, along with his twin sister Lilith. She died most horribly at the hands of the Airlia while Vampyr and I watched. He swore revenge then against both Airlia and humans, who so blindly followed them and helped kill her."

"He is very powerful," Tian Dao Lin said.

Nosferatu nodded. "He too has gone by many names

over the years and has wielded much power from the shadows. We have met several times, even as allies long ago. But now that the Airlia are gone, I fear what he will do next."

"You fear or you know?" Tian Dao Lin asked.

"I have had some reports," Nosferatu acknowledged vaguely. He stared at the image on the screen. "I have known Vampyr for millennia, from the first day he swore vengeance, and his rage has not abated over the years, but rather grown. He has done many terrible things through the ages and"—Nosferatu paused, then reluctantly continued—"now that the constraint of the Airlia and their minions is gone the only real threat he has is in this room."

"So that is why you brought us here," Tian Dao Lin said. "You need allies against Vampyr."

"Yes," Nosferatu said, "but also remember that *we* are sources of the Airlia virus also, and I have no doubt Vampyr has plans to gather our blood also."

"He would kill his own?" Adrik asked.

"Vampyr does what he wills, whenever he wants," Nosferatu said. "If he decides he wants our blood, he will let nothing stand in his way."

"But you would not take his blood," Tian Dao Lin noted. "So what other sources of Airlia blood are there?"

Nosferatu leaned back in his chair. He glanced at Adrik. "As you are well aware, the SS screened vast amounts of blood in their concentration camps, searching for any that might be special, although they didn't know exactly what was special about it. The SS was corrupted by the Mission and Aspasia's Shadow, who were seeking traces of the Airlia blood as he finally knew why it was important. He used a blood ceremony for initiation into the SS. During that ceremony, top members of the SS received minute portions of the virus, most likely that which Aspasia's Shadow recovered from the Ones Who Wait, whom he killed.

"That is why Dr. Von Seeckt, who eventually ended up on the American Majestic-12 committee, managed to live so long and survive his illness as long as he did. As did other Nazis who escaped after the war."

"I know of what you speak," Adrik said. "But I lost track of that blood at the end of the war. For a while I thought the Mission moved it to South America via the Odessa link."

Nosferatu shook his head. "No. The ceremony was held at the SS castle at Wevelsburg in Bavaria and the blood was stored there. As the Americans closed in on it at the end of the Second World War, it was your Russians who sent in a parachute team to recover what they could. They brought everything they found back to Moscow, including the blood.

"Not only that," Nosferatu continued, "but a part of Section IV from the KGB—the Russian equivalent of America's Majestic-12—knew from the Nazi documents that a particular strain of blood was important and began to see if it could find more. Deep under Moscow, there is a chamber that contains what Aspasia's Shadow brought to the SS and what was scavenged out of the concentration camps by the SS and by the KGB during the Cold War from prisoners at Lubyanka and in the Gulags. If you agree, it will be your job"—he inclined his head toward Adrik—"to use your resources to recover this. I believe you have the power to do it."

Adrik made no commitment, waiting to see what else the Eldest had to propose.

"Two." Nosferatu held up another finger. "The Ones Who Wait. They were like us—half-human, half-Airlia—

except cloned. They had some of the virus, which accounted for their extended lives. I know where we can find some of their bodies. Intact and preserved." He turned to Tian Dao Lin. "This will be your responsibility, my old friend."

"And where would I find these preserved bodies?" Tian Dao Lin quietly asked.

"Mount Everest. Where Merlin took the great sword Excalibur so many years ago. Several Ones Who Wait were recently sent by Artad to recover the sword and failed. Their bodies are still up there. Frozen. Three of them."

Tian Dao Lin steepled his fingers as he considered this.

"And the third source?" Adrik asked.

"That is most important and most difficult to get to," Nosferatu said. "Pure Airlia blood. Preserved. Waiting to be harvested."

"Where?" Tian Dao Lin was leaning forward, his interest obvious. Adrik was also edging forward in his chair.

Nosferatu pointed up. "The first mothership from Area 51. Aspasia's. The one the human soldier Turcotte destroyed when Aspasia tried to return to Earth from Mars aboard his Talon spacecraft."

"How will one get to that?" Adrik asked. "The American shuttle fleet was devastated during the recent war and it is not likely they would kindly allow us to use one anyway. Russia's ability to launch a manned mission into orbit is practically nonexistent after recent events."

"I have something in the works," Nosferatu said.

The other two waited. Nosferatu pressed a button. Vampyr's face disappeared from the computer screen and was replaced by a picture of a stubby, delta wing craft on top of a large rocket. "The X-Craft," Nosferatu said. "A reusable, two-man, orbital vehicle. The launch platform is an Ariana 4 rocket. The X-Craft has thrusters for maneuvering in orbit, and it can land on any landing strip that can take a 747. One of my subsidiaries has been developing it for over twenty-five years. We've dropped it from altitude—manned—and successfully landed it. The only thing we haven't done yet is launch one into orbit."

Tian Dao Lin frowned. "The Americans only destroyed the mothership a month ago."

Nosferatu smiled. "My original plan—before recent events—was eventually to have a manned mission go to Mars. The X-Craft was the first step to a second generation of craft built in orbit capable of reaching Mars, landing, and getting to Aspasia and the other Airlia in deep sleep there at Cydonia." His eyes shifted to Tian Dao Lin. "Along with a simultaneous expedition into Qian-Ling to reach and destroy Artad and his followers. I estimated that both missions would be possible in twenty years and we might be able to defeat the Airlia while they slept. Recent events have caused me to adjust my plans and my timetable, with the follow-on objective becoming the number one priority."

Tian Dao Lin chuckled. "That is why you had me pull strings to get Professor Che Lu permission to enter Qian-Ling when it had been forbidden for so long. I knew you had something long-range in mind."

"I have been planning for thousands of years," Nosferatu said. "But the technology was never sufficient. However, in the past fifty years or so human technology has advanced greatly. And the fortuitous events of the past year now allow us unprecedented opportunity with much less risk much sooner than I had anticipated."

"The Airlia who died on the Talons inside the mothership's cargo bay would have bled out into space," Adrik argued.

"Most of their blood, yes," Nosferatu agreed. "However, I have had simulations and experiments done and they indicate there would be some residual blood left in the bodies. Not much, but if enough bodies were harvested, there would be a sufficient supply to make it worth gathering, especially as it would be pure."

"Even if we recover all this blood, pure and mixed," Adrik asked, "how will we be able to extract the Airlia virus, then purify our blood with it? How will we get rid of the human portion of our blood? And the human portion in the Ones Who Wait and the blood gathered by the SS and KGB?"

"The Americans have done us a favor in that regard," Nosferatu said. "They were delving into this very problem at the secret Majestic-12 lab in Dulce, New Mexico, where the former Nazi, General Hemstadt, was working after the war under the auspices of Operation Paperclip. One of his projects was perfecting a blood-purifying device, most likely on orders from Aspasia's Shadow and the Mission and under the cover of AIDS research.

"This machine removes all of a person's blood and replaces it with a freezing solution that cleanses the circulatory system completely. While this is happening, the body is chilled to keep it viable. Then the machine injects the new, already warmed blood and the body is brought back to normal temperature. The entire process lasts only about three minutes. The subject's blood is replaced one hundred percent."

"Dulce was destroyed," Adrik noted.

"Recovery of the device will be my task," Nosferatu said flatly.

"And if we agree to help you and recover all this Airlia blood virus?" Adrik asked. "What do we do with it?"

"I estimate that we will have enough to make four Un-dead immortals," Nosferatu said.

"You would give the fourth to Vampyr?" Adrik asked.

"No," Nosferatu said flatly.

"There are only four Undead still in existence," Adrik said.

"No," Nosferatu said, "there are five."

Adrik absorbed this startling bit of information with a sharp glance at Tian Dao Lin.

"There is another Undead here at the Haven now," Tian Dao Lin said.

"Who is this?" Adrik frowned. "Where is he?"

"*She* sleeps," Nosferatu said simply.

"Who is she?" Adrik demanded.

"That is not your business," Nosferatu replied.

"Why not make a deal with Vampyr with the blood for the fourth?" Adrik suggested.

"As I said, the fourth is accounted for," Nosferatu said.

Adrik folded his arms. "I will tell you what I believe. I think you knew you could only recover enough blood for four and you invited Vampyr here first and when he de-clined, then you invited me. If Vampyr had accepted, I would have been the unlucky fifth."

Nosferatu met the other's gaze and the two stared at each other for a long minute.

"What about the Watchers?" Tian Dao Lin asked, an abrupt change in subject.

"The Watchers are defunct," Nosferatu said, still staring at Adrik.

"All of them?" Tian Dao Lin pressed. "Including the Watcher-Hunters?"

Nosferatu shrugged. "There might be some of them left, but they are only a nuisance. They consider taking a quarter a great success, which is all they have ever achieved these many years. Any that ever came close to any of us perished."

"And Vampyr?" Adrik asked. "You said he will be pursuing these same things to get the blood?"

"Yes," Nosferatu said.

"That is why you really need us," Adrik said. "To fight Vampyr."

"Yes," Nosferatu admitted. "With my X-craft, I believe I can recover enough blood from the Airlia bodies on the mothership to make two of us immortal. So I could achieve this without the two of you. But I think it would be wise for us to band together.

"I can assure you that if Vampyr recovers the Airlia blood, he will not share it with you," Nosferatu said. "He cares for nothing other than his vengeance. Without the Airlia and their followers to hold him in check, I fear he will go after the blood and, in the process, destroy us." Nosferatu stood. "I believe we are headed for the final confrontation. Please reflect on the situation and let me know your decision when I return."

Nosferatu went out through the heavy wooden door, swinging it shut behind him. He walked down stone steps, deeper into his lair. Nosferatu came to a steel door. On one side was a retinal scanner and he pressed his eyes to it. When the computer recognized his pattern, the door's bolts withdrew and it slowly swung open.

The room he walked into was a crypt. In the center was a raised platform upon which rested a black metal tube. Surrounding the tube were dozens of plants and small trees, a veritable oasis of greenery underground.

Nosferatu went up to the tube, placing his hands gently on the lid. He leaned forward until his head was next to the front. Inside was the fourth Undead at Haven.

"Soon, my love," he whispered. "Soon we will finally be together forever."

Puget Sound, Washington

The girl had never been in a helicopter before. She was seventeen and had been working the streets for only a month. So far the experience had been quite terrible, but things looked like they were taking a change for the better, much better to judge by the luxurious interior of the aircraft. She had the entire back to herself, the pilots shielded from her by a dark glass partition. The windows were also blacked out and it didn't occur to her to wonder why. She was too interested in the leather captain's chairs, the state-of-the-art stereo system, and other accoutrements that adorned the passenger compartment.

The man in the limousine, claiming to represent someone very rich, had picked her up off the street over four hours earlier, just after dark. Instead of a hotel, he'd taken her to a clinic, where a silent doctor had examined her. Two thousand in cash up front had been enough for the girl to allow herself to be poked and prodded and two samples of her blood taken and tested. Along with the promise of another eight thousand for the rest of the night if she passed all the tests.

Apparently she had, as she was given a pair of expensive slacks, with matching top, along with low-heeled shoes to put on. Then she was hustled back into the limousine, driven to the airport, and loaded onto the helicopter. The man who had picked her up had told her nothing more than the amount she was being paid when he put her on board and shut the door behind her. She'd felt a moment of anxiety then, but the wad of cash in her cheap purse, the only thing of hers she still had, had put that feeling at bay. This was much safer, in her opinion, than the front seat of some of the cars she had climbed into during the past month.

The sound of the helicopter's engines picked up slightly and she felt her stomach flutter as the aircraft descended. It landed with a slight bump. The door slid open and one of the pilots stood before her, gesturing for her to get out. She climbed out and was surprised to step into knee-high grass. The pilot slid the door shut, then climbed back in the front.

The girl looked around. She was in the middle of a small field, barely big enough for the helicopter to land in, surrounded by tall trees and the blackness of the space underneath their branches.

"Hey!" she called out. She went to the pilot's door and banged on it with an open palm.

In response the engines whined and the blades picked up speed, blasting her with cool night wind. She backed away and held her hand in front of her eyes to protect them as the helicopter lifted straight up, then disappeared, the sound slowly fading away.

After a minute all she could hear was her own rapid breathing as she turned slowly in a circle, searching for any sign of civilization, a road, a building, anything. But there were only the trees.

"Hello?" she cried out. "Hello?"

Silence. Total, absolute silence, which truly frightened her. She'd grown up on a farm fifty miles outside of Seattle and been out camping with her friends several times. The girl knew there were always sounds in the forest. Birds. Insects. Animals. Something was always making some kind of sound. But here there was nothing, as if there was nothing

living within miles other than the vegetation. It was unnatural.

The girl took a step back, then spun about, fearing
someone sneaking up from behind. The trees were huge.
Old forest, hundreds, maybe thousands of years old, that
the environmentalists were always campaigning to save.
She had no clue where she was. They hadn't been in the
air that long. Fifteen minutes?

"Hello?" she cried out, her voice cracking halfway
through the word. "Please."

The girl took several deep breaths, trying to calm herself, but succeeded only in nearly hyperventilating. She
went down to her knees, not caring that the designer
slacks she had marveled over not so long ago were getting
stained by the grass. She clasped her hands over her
mouth, trying to bring her breathing under control. After
several minutes, somewhat back to normal, she got to her
feet and took a closer look at her surroundings, as much as
she could see given that the moon had not yet risen. She
looked up at the small patch of night sky above, then she
looked down.

The ground sloped, presenting her with a choice. Go
up or down? She looked at the dark wall of forest that
surrounded her. Or stay in the clearing until daylight?

She started as she realized there was someone standing
on the edge of the clearing to her right. How long had he
been there? she wondered as she took several steps away
from him. And why hadn't he answered her calls?

"Hello? Sir?"

She could make out little detail, but he appeared to be
dressed all in black. Pants, shirt, long, flowing coat. With
dark hair and white skin. Very white skin that almost
seemed to shine, as if lit from within. She took another
step away from him.

"Sir? Could you help me? Please?" Was this some sort of bizarre sex game? she wondered. Was she supposed to do something? The man in the limousine hadn't told her anything, and neither the doctor nor the pilot had spoken a word. "What do you want me to do?" she asked.

The man held up a hand, indicating for her to remain still. The man came forward until he was less than five feet from her, just out of arm's reach. She tried to smile and stood slightly straighter, thrusting her chest out. She would do anything to make it through this night, she told herself. And she silently promised to get the hell out of Seattle and go back to her hometown on the first thing moving as soon as she was back in civilization.

"What do you want me to do?" she asked once more.

"Run."

The voice as much as the word sent a chill up her spine. She had never heard such a cold voice.

"What?"

"Run or I will kill you here. You have a chance in the woods." Then he laughed.

She turned and sprinted for the forest, losing a shoe in the first five feet and not even noticing.

The man remained in the clearing, watching as she disappeared among the thick tree trunks. He gave her a few minutes, knowing the running would get her heart pounding and the blood coursing through her veins.

He cocked his head, listening to her crash through the undergrowth. She was easy enough to track by sound, even without the benefit of his exaggerated night vision. He started after her. He silently made his way through the forest, passing her without being noticed, then moving to a point where she would come shortly.

The shock on her face when she bumped into him was exquisite. She gasped, staggered back, then dashed off in another direction. As she ran off, he put a hand to his jacket and touched where her sweat and tears had made a small wet spot. He rubbed it with the tip of a finger, then brought that finger to his nose, inhaling. He smiled at the familiar scent of human fear.

He intercepted her five more times over the course of the next three hours. Sending her blindly off into the forest each time, redirecting her. She was moving more and more slowly, but still moving. He'd had some just quit. Drop to the ground and curl in a ball whimpering. Such were almost not worth taking. Almost.

An hour before dawn, the girl came out of the forest, emerging onto a perfectly cut lawn. She fell to her knees as she looked about. The moon was finally up, and she could see a magnificent house about fifty meters ahead. A mansion stretching almost a hundred meters left and right, sitting on a promontory overlooking Puget Sound. She could see the lights of Seattle beyond the house, on the other side of the water. The Space Needle. Her hometown was beyond the city, in the mountains. It was a beautiful night, a clear sky, and she could see the white-topped peaks.

She scrambled to her feet, crying out for help. She ran toward a wooden door set at ground level and pounded on it, screaming, looking over her shoulder, afraid he would appear at the last minute.

The door swung open and she threw herself into the arms of the figure in the darkened hallway.

Then screamed as she recognized her momentary savior as her pursuer.

He held her tight as she fought to break free with the little energy she had left. He leaned his head close to hers, his breath on her neck as he whispered to her, like a lover would.

"I was made Vampyr, in the First Age of Egypt, during the reign of the Gods, when they walked openly upon the Earth, the son of the God Amun and a human High Consort. I bring you honor by taking you."

And then he did just that.

Minutes later Vampyr looked down on her pale corpse.

With one arm he lifted her and carried her a short way down the tunnel to a two-foot-square iron door set at waist height. He opened the door and threw the body in, listening to it tumble as it fell down the old mine shaft for over three hundred feet before landing with a splash in a flooded cavern. He shut the door.

Then he made his way farther along the tunnel, stopping at a stainless-steel door. He placed his forehead against a rubber buffer, pressing his eyes against the scanners. His retinas were checked. Then he entered a code only he knew on a numeric keypad, his fingers flying over the keys faster than any human could ever hope to imitate, entering twenty-seven numbers in the appropriate sequence in less than four seconds. Last, but not least, he removed what appeared to be an old-fashioned key from a chain around his neck and inserted it in the keyhole. While the key looked old, it was state-of-the-art, sending the correct electrical impulse to the last hold on the door's locks.

With muted clicks, the fourteen two-inch-thick steel bolts holding the door in place retracted and the door slowly swung open on powerful hydraulic arms. The chamber beyond was surrounded by twelve-foot-thick mixed metal/concrete walls. The builder had assured Vampyr that there was no technology short of a direct nuclear hit that could get through these walls. It was similar to what lined the presidential bunker under Blue Mountain in West Virginia. Vampyr had thanked the builder, then had him killed.

Vampyr walked into the chamber and turned on the low-level lights. The contents of the chamber were a madman's—or a powerful country's—arsenal. Eight backpack tactical nuclear weapons rested on a long table. Each was small enough to fit inside a medium-sized piece of luggage. The American government had never acknowledged their theft, nor did it have a clue who had stolen them.

Along one wall was the control console from a missile launch site that he had appropriated from one that had been shut down in Montana. Scattered around the island were twelve Peacemaker ICBM rockets in working condition stored in silos, harvested from the drawdown in the Cold War. The silos were on an old Navy base that had once existed on the island, and it had cost Vampyr half a billion dollars to get them into working condition and almost as much to ensure secrecy.

On each Peacemaker was a strategic nuclear warhead, each powerful enough to take out a city. He had had them recovered from American nuclear submarines that had gone down in the oceans, using one of his subsidiary salvage companies. Such was the bureaucracy of the Pentagon that the twelve weren't even reported as missing. Located in Puget Sound, he could reach anywhere in the United States with the missiles. He had a similar compound, staffed with Russian warheads from their lost submarines, and Russian rockets from their disarming, located just south of Kiev, with the same capability for all of Russia and Europe. He could launch those from here.

Vampyr ran a hand along one of the tactical nuclear warhead's metal housing, almost the caress of a lover.

In the middle of the room, however, was the centerpiece of his arsenal. A triple-enclosed biohazard container. Inside were three different viruses. One developed by the Russians, one American, and one Japanese. Because of their lethality, each had scared their creators so much that immediate orders had been issued for their destruction. By the time the orders were implemented, Vampyr's far-flung organization had already gathered samples of each. The container was truly Pandora's box. If opened, it would spread three distinct viruses, each 99.9 percent lethal and highly contagious. One such virus might be contained. There was the remote possibility two could be. But three? The world would be dead within two months.

Money was power, and Vampyr had plenty of that. But this was power also, in a much different form. The most important power, though, was the ability to be ruthless, to be able to make the hard decisions. To be able to use these weapons if necessary. And that was something Vampyr had more of than any creature that had ever walked the face of the planet.

Vampyr had been made during the time of the Airlia Gods. He had lived through the rule of the Shadows, and the time when men thought they ruled but were actually still being manipulated by the minions of the Airlia. He had fought in many wars with many different weapons.

The humans now thought it was truly their time, given that they had defeated the Airlia. They were wrong. It was his time.

"It is time for the Fourth Age," Vampyr whispered to himself. "The Age of the Undead."

THE PAST

CHAPTER I

BEFORE THE THIRD AGE OF EGYPT, which was the rule of the Pharaohs, there was the Second Age, when the Shadows of the Gods made by the God Horus ruled, and before that, beyond the borders of what man knew as recorded history, there was the First Age, when those Gods, known as the Airlia, ruled the humans who lived along the lush banks of the Nile.

It was the time of the Gods who came to Egypt from the legendary land of Atlantis beyond the Middle Sea after the great Atlantean Civil War. It was fifty-five hundred years before the Great Pyramid would be built by the Pharaoh Khufu according to the plans handed down by the Gods. For now the Giza Plateau was graced only by the alien beauty of a magnificent Black Sphinx, over three hundred feet long with red eyes that glowed as if lit from within. The Black Sphinx, set deep in a depression carved into the plateau, guarded the main entrance to the Roads of Rostau. The warren of tunnels and chambers under the plateau was where the Gods lived, and from which they ruled through the human high priests, occasionally venturing forth to look out upon their subjects, an event that was becoming rarer and rarer. There were whispered rumors that the Gods were growing older, but how could that be, if they were indeed Gods?

Deep under the plateau, along one of the minor branches of the Roads, was a dead-end corridor with three cells along one side. In the first cell were what appeared to be a pair of black metal coffins over seven feet in length by three wide and high. They were not coffins, however, but special prisons, each holding a body. At the head of each tube was a small glowing panel with a series of hexagonal sections on which were etched markings in the High Rune language of the Gods.

Inside the tube closest to the cell door was a half-man, half-God, whose existence was one of unending exhaustion and pain. His name was Nosferatu. He had memories of sunlight and playing in the sand while a woman—his human mother—stood nearby, keeping a watchful eye on him. He'd even played with true humans, children of the high priests, who could look forward to serving the Gods as their parents did. Nosferatu's fate was to be one of service also, but in a much different way. His memories were of a time so long ago that he often wondered if the vague memories were not memories at all but instead a dream. Yet he held on to the concept that he could not dream something he had never seen. He must have been above ground in the sunlight sometime. He remembered palm trees and the sun reflecting off a sand dune and even the blue water of the mighty Nile flowing by. He remembered the stories the high priests told to their children, tales of Atlantis, the Gods called Airlia, and the great civil war among the Gods that had destroyed Atlantis. He'd listened to the other children being taught the language of the Gods and learned as much as he could along with the High Rune writing.

It was all for naught, though, because when he'd reached manhood, he'd been taken from the sunlight and brought below to serve. Three hundred years he'd been trapped in this tube in this underground cell. Not as a punishment, for he had done nothing to deserve this fate other than to be born who and what he was, but to serve the purpose for which he had been conceived: to provide pleasure in a most strange and twisted way for the Gods.

And although he had been the first, Nosferatu was no longer alone. There were four others in tubes in the two adjoining cells whom he could reach with hoarse whispers. And in the tube across from him in this cell was Nekhbet. His love. She was the bastard spawn of the God Osiris and a human High Concubine, brought there over a hundred years before, when Nosferatu was beginning to believe the world was comprised only of the mute priests who opened the lid and brought him human blood every new moon and the Gods who came every so often to in turn drain his blood. Now, once every month he got to sit up when the lid was opened, chains around his waist keeping him in the tube, and see his love while the mute priest held the silver flask containing blood just collected from supplicants to his lips. Even in the dim light and the grave circumstances, every time during that brief interlude Nosferatu always marveled at her beauty. Alabaster skin, high cheekbones, black-red eyes, she was tall and willowy, with blazing red hair flowing over her shoulders like a fiery waterfall. He always believed she represented the best of human and God.

Nosferatu's skin was also pale white, his hair bright red. His eyes had a reddish tint to them and the suggestion of an elongation of the pupil. He was tall, well over six feet in height, and slender. His skin was stretched tight over his bones, giving him a skeletal appearance. He was indeed half-man, half-God, as were his prisoner comrades. Although he had been alive over three hundred years, he appeared to be in his midthirties, the mixed human/God blood in his veins and the sustenance of human blood allowing him a vastly longer life span. How long that life span would be he had no idea and he feared either possibility.

In the beginning he had tried to count days, a most difficult task since no sunlight penetrated so far under the Giza Plateau, along the Roads of Rostau into the realm of the Gods. He'd worked off the opening of the tube and the blood he was fed once a month, keeping track. But after the number went into the hundreds, he gave up. What did it matter? Even with the half blood of the Gods and the constant feeding, he knew he was very slowly getting older and that he would spend all of his however-long life there.

He heard the latch securing the lid slide open and closed his eyes, prepared for the invasion of torchlight that came with each feeding. He felt the shift in the air as the lid was swung up.

"The Gods must die or you will never escape this. You will die a miserable death after a long and worthless life."

The words echoed off the stone walls of the chamber and the shocked face of Nosferatu as he opened his eyes and blinked. Leaning over him was a woman. Only men whose tongues had been cut out and ears punctured had come to feed him all these long years, never a woman. She was a human, not a God, dressed in a long black cloak with silver fringes. She did not wear the signs of the priests. She had short black hair, dark eyes, and pale skin. She was the first human other than the priests that Nosferatu had seen in over two hundred years. Looking past her, he could see a man, wearing leather armor and holding a sword, standing in the corridor, keeping watch. He too had dark hair, but his skin was tanned. He was peering down the corridor, on guard.

She looked deep into Nosferatu's eyes, then reached up and placed a finger on his throat, feeling his pulse. She then looked at the shunt in his neck from which he was drained to feed the Gods and lightly touched it. "You've been used for a very long time, haven't you?"

Nosferatu slowly sat up, the belt around his waist chained to the bottom of the tube keeping the lower half of his body in place. Around each arm and leg were straps with leads going into the side of the tube. Each time before he went to sleep, sharp pain came through those leads, causing his muscles to quiver and work themselves in tiny movements. And each time he came awake to the same pain. He had little idea how long he slept but he had no doubt it was longer than a normal night's sleep. There was also a headpiece, shaped like a crown, in the tube, set in a small recess near the top, but Nosferatu had never had it put on his head by the priests, so he didn't know its purpose.

He looked over at the other tube in his cell. The woman caught his gaze and went to it, opening the top and waking the occupant by tapping the appropriate hexagon on the panel. Nekhbet sat up, blinking. He could see that Nekhbet was also wondering who this stranger was and what she knew of their situation. The woman came back over to him, waiting for an answer. He didn't reply, waiting to see if she would tell him more. He had patience—if there was one thing three hundred years of imprisonment taught, it was that trait.

"You won't last much longer," the woman finally continued. "You have no choice. If you do not act, you will eventually die. Each time they drain you, the percentage of their blood in you is reduced and the human percentage grows. Soon you will no longer be effective for their needs. Then they will take another human female and make your replacement. They may already have a child, like you were once, growing up, guarded closely on the surface, ready to come here and be placed in this tube and drained as needed. They are very good at planning for their own needs and pleasures."

Nosferatu finally spoke. "How do you know this?"

"It is their way. They are not Gods, but creatures from"—the woman pointed up. "From among the stars. They use us—humans—and they use you, half of their blood, half human. It is hard for me to determine which is the worse of their sins. At least what they are doing to you is obvious. Their rule of the humans is more devious, pretending to be that which they aren't." The woman shrugged. "There is also the possibility that the Gods may decide to go into the long sleep as their brethren have done in other places, in which case they will kill you and the others they keep down here, as you will longer be needed."

Nosferatu tried to grasp the concept, but it had been so long since he'd been on the surface he could barely remember the sun, never mind the stars. And how could one be from them? If the Airlia weren't Gods, then what exactly were they? And what did that make him? And what was this long sleep she spoke of?

"Why do you want to help us?" Nekhbet asked. "You are human. We aren't. We're half like them."

"Because you must hate them as much as I do and more than those above," the woman replied. "Most humans"—she shook her head—"they are like sheep. Simply happy their harvest comes in and the Gods make all the decisions for them."

Nekhbet's lovely voice floated from across the chamber. "You cannot kill the Gods. They are immortal."

Donnchadh pulled aside her robe, revealing six daggers

tucked into her belt. "With these you can. They were made by the Gods themselves for use against each other."

Nekhbet still wasn't convinced. "Even if we kill the Gods, the priests will then slay us, won't they?"

The woman glanced over her shoulder at Nekhbet. "Not if you are immortal."

Nosferatu was the first to grasp the significance. "The Grail?"

The woman nodded. "You kill the Gods. You go into the Black Sphinx and recover the Grail, which is hidden there, then partake as has been promised by the Gods since before the beginning of time. You become immortal."

"Who are you?" Nosferatu demanded, trying to process all that she had said.

"My name is Donnchadh. My partner"—she looked into the corridor at the warrior—"and I have fought the Gods in other places. That should be enough for you. Your enemy is our enemy."

"Your enemies are our parents," Nosferatu noted.

"One of your parents," Donnchadh corrected, looking him in the eyes. "Your other parent was human, taken by an Airlia—the Gods—for their pleasure and to produce you so they can use you for their pleasure also. The Gods deserve neither your homage nor your respect. They will drain you and kill you without a second thought once they have a replacement ready or if they no longer desire the pleasure your blood brings them."

"How can we do this which you propose?" Nosferatu demanded, rattling the chains that held the belt at his waist.

Donnchadh pulled out a three-foot-long piece of black metal. "Tonight. After the Ceremony of the Solstice. You can follow the Gods who oversee it from the ceremony to their hidden places along the Roads." She pulled the metal rod out of her belt and placed the tip inside one of the links of chain that bound him. She raised an eyebrow. "Do you want your freedom?"

Nosferatu looked across the way at Nekhbet. Even if this woman lied, even if this was a trap, he didn't care. If he could simply hold Nekhbet in his arms after more than a hundred years of yearning, it would be worth it. "Yes."

Donnchadh twisted the rod and the link slowly gave, then popped open. She went to work on the other chains and within five minutes Nosferatu was free. He removed the straps around his arms and a red light flickered on the console but he ignored it. Grabbing the lid, he pulled himself out of the tube.

When his feet reached the ground, he took a tentative step and his legs buckled, tumbling him to the floor. Donnchadh was already at work on Nekhbet's chains as Nosferatu struggled to his feet. The tube had worked his muscles, but his body was so unused to moving that he had to put a hand against the wall to steady himself. Driven by a force stronger than gravity he took a step. And then another. By this time, Nekhbet was free and the woman was helping her out of the tube. Nosferatu staggered across to Nekhbet and took her in his arms.

With the touch of her flesh against his, Nosferatu was transported from the stone chamber that had been his prison for centuries. He wrapped his arms tight around her slight frame as if their flesh and bones and blood would meld together and they would become one.

"Are you tired?" Nekhbet whispered.

"Not anymore."

"You are weak, though."

Nosferatu blinked as she offered her neck to him, the blood pulsing in the vein, the short tip of the shunt drawing him in. He knew he needed the energy, but from Nekhbet?

Her voice was a seductive whisper. "Take as they take, my love. You are the Eldest and must lead. You need the strength. I am younger. I can afford to give it to you. I want to give it to you. It will make us one as nothing else can. And you must lead us."

He couldn't stop. His lips curled around the shunt, the one-way valve opening at the touch of moist flesh on the outside. The first taste of blood was electrifying, a charge throughout his body that brought every nerve screaming alive as it coursed through his veins. Decades of exhaustion faded. Her blood, with its alien component, was so much more than the human blood he was fed each month.

The strange woman's voice was an irritating buzz, trying to bring Nosferatu back to reality. "The ceremony has started above. You do not have much time to free the others and be ready."

Nosferatu did not let go of Nekhbet. Minutes of touch could not compare to the centuries of longing from across the prison chamber. And the blood, the power he felt pouring into his body from Nekhbet, the pleasure. Is this what he gave to the Gods? He could almost understand why they kept him there. He forced his eyes open. He could see her neck so close, the skin white, the beat of the artery so slow now, her eyes closed. Startled, he released his lips and stepped back. Nekhbet staggered and would have fallen, but he caught her.

"I am sorry," he whispered. "I took too much."

Nekhbet shook her head, slowly opening her eyes, but the dark pupils had difficulty focusing. "It is all right. You need the strength."

"If you do not act now, you will die," Donnchadh pressed.

Nekhbet let go first, running a hand across Nosferatu's face. "My love, we must do as she says. It is our only chance. We must free the others."

Reluctantly, Nosferatu let go of Nekhbet. He followed Donnchadh out into the corridor, where her partner had already opened the door to the next cell.

"And who are you?" Nosferatu asked him.

The warrior glanced at him. "My name means nothing to you. Gwalcmai I was called long ago. I have had other names and will have others in the future."

Nosferatu and Nekhbet followed Donnchadh into the cell while her partner remained outside. The twins Vampyr and Lilith were held here. Male and female, they had been brought into the darkness nearly seventy years before, as best Nosferatu had been able to determine. Nosferatu watched as the woman opened their tubes, noting which of the hexagonals she pressed. He shushed the twins' questions, working swiftly to free them from their chains, and they moved to the third cell and released Mosegi and Chatha, the youngest of the six, another male-female pair, chained up and entombed for only about twenty years. There were six half-breeds in total, one for each of the six Gods who desired the pleasure of drinking their blood.

As soon as the last were free of their tubes, the strange woman, Donnchadh, turned toward the exit to the last cell. "I will leave you to do what you must."

Nosferatu put a hand out, stopping her. "Tell me more of the Gods. Why do they need to do this?" He lightly touched the shunt in his neck.

"As I have said. They do it for pleasure. It is an elixir for them. They prefer it over pure human blood."

"That is all?" Nosferatu had always held on to the belief that at least he served the purpose of keeping the Gods alive.

"Do you not relish the feeding you receive?" Donnchadh asked.

Nosferatu nodded.

"And was not her"—Donnchadh pointed at Nekhbet—"blood so much more?"

"Yes."

"Then you should understand."

"We exist only for their pleasure?" Vampyr was holding his twin's arm, keeping Lilith upright while she learned to use her legs once more.

"Yes." It was obvious Donnchadh was not interested in talking.

"It is said the Gods are immortal," Nosferatu pressed.

Gwalcmai was restless in the corridor. "We must hurry."

"In a sense," Donnchadh said, "they are."

"Then am I immortal?" Nosferatu had shied away from that possibility, knowing it would mean an eternity chained to the wall.

Donnchadh shook her head. "No. But if you continue to drink human blood to feed the alien part of your blood—and don't get drained of any more of the blood you have—you can live a very, very long time. You can also go into the tube and use the deep sleep to let time pass without aging." Her eyes grew distant. "I have seen it before. Where I came from. They did the same to my people."

"Where are you from?" Nosferatu asked.

Donnchadh shook her head. "You would not understand." She pointed to the end of the short corridor. "You can go to the right and get out a secret door near the Nile. The ceremony will start shortly in the Sphinx pit. Wait until the Gods who will oversee the ceremony appear, then follow them down the main Road of Rostau."

"But—" Nosferatu wanted to know more but Donnchadh was moving away, then was gone to the left, her companion with her.

The other five looked at him, waiting.

"Follow me."

PROSTRATED BEFORE the massive paws of the Black Sphinx were fifty priests, chanting in an alien tongue the same prayers their ancestors on Atlantis had sung: *"We serve for the promise of eternal life from the Grail. We serve for the promise of the great truth. We serve as our fathers have served, our father's fathers, and through the ages from the first days of the rule of the God who brought us up out of the darkness. We serve because in serving there is the greater good for all."*

The chanting echoed and looped, reverberating off smooth stone walls surrounding the Black Sphinx. The Sphinx was over two hundred feet below the surface of the plateau, reachable only by a set of stairs cut in the stone wall. Just below the chest of the beast, a dark opening was cut into the rock beneath the paws, forming one of the entranceways to the sacred Roads, where only the select high priests were allowed to go.

Hidden in the shadows along the edge of the depression, amid a pile of discarded building stone, watching the chanting priests, were a half dozen figures—Nosferatu and the other five half-breeds. They clutched the sharp daggers the strange human woman had given them in sweaty hands. It was the Ceremony of the Summer Solstice, and the priests were thanking the Gods for a bountiful crop produced by the rich soil along the banks of the Nile and for keeping away the floods that occasionally ravaged the land.

It had occurred to Nosferatu during his long time underground that humans had never thought to question the power of the Gods when the floods did come. They would blame themselves, believing they had transgressed against the Gods in some manner, and pray even harder. The entire concept of worship and religion was something he found strange and most convenient for the Airlia. Behind it all was the tantalizing promise the Airlia had made so long ago on Atlantis—that the true believers would one day be granted immortality via the Grail. It had not happened yet, but again, the high priests told the people that was because they had not believed hard enough and been faithful enough.

Now the six waited, hunched over among the stones, for the ceremony to be finished. They were patient because their goal was the ultimate prize, that which generations of priests such as these had prayed for but which the six of them had decided to seize this night: eternal life. They had escaped from the Roads via an entrance on the bank of the Nile and made their way back here under the cover of darkness. For Nosferatu every breath of the fresh night air was a revelation, the canopy of stars overhead a wonderment to his eyes. The gifts of his Airlia genes combined with years of living in the pitch-black of his tube allowed him to see in the starlight as if it were daylight. He wondered what else he had gained from the Airlia that made him different from humans.

"Will the Gods be here?" Nosferatu asked.

"Isis and Osiris have come to give the final blessing every year as long as any can remember," Vampyr whispered in reply. "I saw them myself at this ceremony before I was taken below with my sister."

Isis and Osiris were the two principal Gods. There were four other Airlia—Horus, Amun, Khons, and Seb—but they appeared even more rarely. It had been many years since all six had been seen together on the surface. For many years Nosferatu had only been visited by one of the Gods. When others showed up, perhaps coming out of the deep sleep that Donnchadh had mentioned, the others like him were made and imprisoned. Nosferatu's mother had told him that his father was Horus and Nosferatu believed it to be true because that was the only one of the five that did not take blood from him during the feedings. In the same manner, Nekhbet's father had never taken from her.

The chanting paused as two figures appeared in the dark entryway. They were tall, thin, and unnaturally proportioned. From the forms it was obvious they were male and female but as they pulled back their hoods it was also obvious they were not human. Catlike red eyes peered down at the priests. White alabaster skin glistened in the glow of the torches. Elongated ears drooped on either side of their narrow heads. And when the male of the pair raised his right hand in acknowledgment of the priests' prayers, six long fingers, festooned with jewels, waved their blessings.

Nosferatu recognized them from the thousands of times they had come to his cell and fed from Nekhbet and him. They were Isis and Osiris, the Goddess and the High Protector of Egypt, who had ruled from beneath the ground for over two thousand years. Egypt had prospered under their reign, the borders expanding down the green belt of the Nile and west and east to the edges of the desert. It was the cradle of civilization, the place where the majority of the survivors of the fall of Atlantis had been brought by the Gods. Beyond the borders of the Gods' reign, there were humans, but they lived like animals according to what the high priests said.

Unseen by Nosferatu's group, the priests, or the Gods, there was a fourth party in the depression, not far from them. A man named Kajilil, covered with a gray cloak that blended with the stone, tucked into a slight crack in the rock wall. He saw the priests, the Gods Isis and Osiris, and the group of six hiding on the opposite side. He was as still as the rock that surrounded him and as patient. He was one of the *Wedjat*, a Watcher, the fifty-second of his line, sworn to observe the Giza Plateau and the Gods. His line had watched from the very beginning, when the Gods had first arrived with the survivors of Atlantis.

When the priests got stiffly to their feet and shuffled away from the Black Sphinx toward their stone temple near the Nile, the Watcher remained still, eyes on the small group of half-breeds across the way. Only one man remained in the open, the high priest, standing in the entranceway to the Roads of Rostau between the Black Sphinx's paws, waiting for the last of the supplicants to clear the area. As the high priest turned to follow Isis and Osiris into the depths, the group sprang into action, Nosferatu in the lead.

The high priest was reaching for an emblem around his neck to shut the stone door to the entranceway when Nosferatu leapt at him, dagger point in the lead. The tip of the blade punctured the side of the high priest's throat, and Nosferatu pulled the handle hard to the side, severing the man's jugular and preventing him from crying out a warning to the two Gods who were ahead of him.

The blood from the high priest's still-beating heart sprayed over Nosferatu, drenching his face and chest. Nosferatu's tongue snaked out, tasting the blood. He blinked, staggered, and felt a new surge of power. He leaned forward, mouth open wide, and drank in the weakening surges of arterial blood until the high priest died and there was no more. The blood coming from a living human was much more exhilarating than what he had always been fed secondhand from a flask, but not quite the same as what Nekhbet had shared with him.

With his free hand Nosferatu removed the emblem from the high priest's neck. Etched on it was an image of an eye within a triangle. Nosferatu moved into the tunnel, Nekhbet right behind him, the other four carefully stepping over the body of the high priest.

And behind them, like a shadow, the Watcher followed, keeping low to the ground and moving silently.

Nosferatu ran on the balls of his feet, his bare feet making no sound on the smooth stone. He felt powerful, stronger than he could ever remember feeling. He caught a glimpse of the tall figures of Isis and Osiris as he came around a bend in the tunnel and skidded to a halt, trying to control his breathing, sure the Gods would hear him in pursuit, but they continued around another bend, out of sight. He glanced over his shoulder. Nekhbet was right behind, and at his glance, she reached up and touched his shoulder lightly. He felt a wave of confidence from her touch. If they succeeded tonight, she would be at his side for eternity.

When the other four caught up, Nosferatu continued the pursuit, blood-soaked dagger at the ready. He heard the rumble of a large stone moving and picked up the pace, knowing the Gods had secret passageways that even the high priests knew nothing of. Doors that appeared out of solid rock and disappeared just as quickly.

He dashed around the bend in the tunnel. A stone was beginning to slide down at the end of the corridor twenty feet away. Nosferatu was prepared for this. He dived forward, sliding along the smooth stone, the piece of black metal the strange woman had carried now in his off-dagger hand. He stuck it in the way of the descending door, one end on the floor, the other up. The bottom edge hit the metal and the door shuddered for a moment, pressing hard on the metal, then halted, leaving a gap.

Nosferatu let out a sigh of relief. Looking under the door he could see the two flickering shadows of Osiris and Isis on the left side of the wall. And then they disappeared. He glanced back. Nekhbet was near his feet, the others crowded behind her, daggers grasped tight in their hands.

He knew that it was not the time to hesitate. He slid forward, underneath the door, into the lair of the Gods. Nosferatu got to his feet, peering about. There was light ahead, around a curve to the right, which explained the shadows he had seen. The only sound was the scrape of cloth on stone as Nekhbet slid through, then the others. He waited a minute, letting his eyes adjust as much as possible; but the light hurt, and he kept his eyelids closed to slits to protect his sensitive pupils.

Nosferatu began moving down the corridor, dagger held out in front. He pressed his back against the left-side wall and edged along the corridor, trying to peer around the bend. The stone walls were cut perfectly smooth, the work of the Gods, not human hands.

The priests said the Gods had built the Roads of Rostau in the very beginning after arriving from beyond the Middle Sea. And that there were six duats (chambers) where the Gods lived and kept their secret sources of power. Wondrous things were said to be hidden in the duats of which there were only whispers and vague memories of an earlier time when the Gods walked the Earth openly and flew about in the sky in golden round chariots. Now the Gods hid down here, ruling through the priests, rarely seen, as if they were hiding from something, but what could Gods be hiding from? Nosferatu often wondered. There was only one answer—other, more powerful Gods. As a child, he had heard the stories of the Great Civil War, when God had battled God and Atlantis had been destroyed. To him that meant one thing—they were vulnerable.

None of the six noticed the figure that silently followed them. The Watcher slid under the door, then halted as a hatch on the top of the tunnel slid open. Kajilil froze, covering himself with the gray cloak, and watched with wide eyes what came out of the small space and headed down the corridor in pursuit of the intruders.

Nosferatu came around a corner and bumped into Osiris, Isis being ahead of her partner. It was hard to say who was more startled, but Nosferatu was the quicker to react. He jabbed with the knife, the point puncturing Osiris's chest. Nosferatu continued his momentum, throwing all his weight behind the shaft of metal.

Osiris grabbed Nosferatu's throat with his six-fingered hands, squeezing, lifting him off the floor with inhuman strength. Nosferatu twisted the blade in the God's chest, ripping through flesh, piercing the heart. Red eyes went wide in shock, then life faded from them and Nosferatu was released. Isis finally reacted, jumping to her partner's defense but she was swarmed by the other five half-breeds, their daggers rising and falling with the deadly blows they rained down on her body. Decades, centuries of imprisonment, spewed forth, and over fifty blows punctured her skin. Blood spattered over all and tongues snaked out, tasting the God's blood.

They couldn't help themselves. Their plan disintegrated into a feast of blood as all six lay atop of the two bodies, licking, tasting, and tearing at exposed flesh to get to veins. They even suckled at Osiris's corpse, drawing the still blood from him as best they could.

And that was when the strange beast Kajilil had seen appear came upon them from behind.

Only Nosferatu had enough awareness. He spun about from Osiris's body in time to see the thing come around the curve. A glowing gold orb, two feet in diameter with black, pointed legs all around, scuttling along the floor. Mosegi was the last in the party and the first to die as the strange creature reached him. Two metal legs, razor-sharp at the tip, struck, punched into Mosegi's chest, and came out the back. They scissored together and Mosegi's body was sliced in half, falling to the ground.

Blood upon blood. Death upon death. Nosferatu sprang to his feet, dagger at the ready, knowing instinctively it would not stop the beast.

But something did. The thing poised, two arms up, the sharp ends dripping Mosegi's blood pointed at Nekhbet, but not striking. Suddenly a bolt of gold hit Chatha in the chest, knocking her back unconscious. The other four Gods appeared in the corridor behind the beast, three holding long spears in their hands. The fourth held a small black sphere with which it controlled the beast. Another bolt came from the tip of Horus's spear and hit Lilith with the same result. Vampyr reached for his sister but a bolt of gold struck just in front of him, causing him to pull back.

"Come." Nosferatu reached for Nekhbet. Too late, as she was struck and knocked into him. He and Vampyr pulled her body back along the corridor, away from the site of the murders. Two of the Gods halted there, checking the bodies, while the other two pursued. A door rumbled open in the floor in front of Nosferatu and he almost fell into the black hole that had suddenly appeared. A human hand beckoned. Vampyr slithered into the hole without a moment's hesitation.

"Come," a man's voice called as Nosferatu paused, something he would regret for thousands of years. Horus and Amun arrived, spears ready. Nosferatu dived into the hole, pulling Nekhbet with him as Horus struck. The spear blade sliced cleanly through Nekhbet's wrist.

Nosferatu fell with her severed hand clutched in his, slamming into the sidewall of the tunnel, tumbling, sliding, the reality of what had just happened not sinking in until he hit the bottom of a cross tunnel.

"Come." The same figure was urging him to move. Vampyr was next to the human, gesturing for Nosferatu to follow.

Nosferatu remained still, feeling the rapidly cooling flesh clutched in his hand, his mind replaying what had happened. He scrambled to his feet, looking up the passageway down which he had slid, reaching up with his free hand to grab hold of the lip and pull himself in.

"No," the voice hissed. Vampyr reached up and grabbed Nosferatu around the waist, stopping him.

Then Nosferatu heard the clatter of metal on stone and knew the beast was coming down after them.

"This way," the man urged, pulling at his arm along with Vampyr. Nosferatu followed them into a corridor half-filled with water.

DAWN FOUND NOSFERATU and Vampyr hidden on the Giza Plateau along with the strange man who had so far only identified himself as a *Wedjat*, whatever that was. The word meant "eye" in the ancient tongue. They were located to the south of the Black Sphinx depression, amid a pile of large granite blocks, each marked for placement in the construction of a temple dedicated to the worship of Isis. By climbing on top of several blocks and sliding into the hidden place between two of them, they were able to observe the depression in which the Black Sphinx sat. Throughout the night, criers had gone through the surrounding villages, ordering all to be present around the Sphinx at first light.

Nosferatu had Nekhbet's severed hand, swathed in linen, in a small leather pouch tied off at his waist. In order to protect his eyes from the morning light, he had wrapped a length of cloth around his head, leaving only the slightest of slits through which to peer. He and Vampyr had spent the night with the *Wedjat*, huddled in a small hut along the banks of the river, near where they had exited from the Roads. The man had offered no reason for saving them and Nosferatu had not asked, his thoughts on Nekhbet and what the morning would bring.

As dawn approached, both Nosferatu and Vampyr found themselves forced to tear strips from their cloaks and wrap them around their faces, covering their sensitive skin and eyes to protect them from the rays of the sun.

The sun slowly rose over the horizon, revealing two six-foot-high X's of wood that had been rigged by the priests on top of the head of the Black Sphinx. Behind them stood one of the black tubes, its front open. Surrounding the Black Sphinx along the top edge of the depression were thousands of Egyptians, all within hailing distance. The nearest were less than fifty feet in front of their concealed location, all staring in the same direction, into the depression.

Looking at the arrangement, Nosferatu didn't want to make the effort to deduce what the setup on top of the Black Sphinx might mean. He'd experienced three hundred years of imprisonment and abuse by the Gods. He knew that day would bring worse.

Vampyr turned to the *Wedjat.* "You have told us you are a *Wedjat,* but little else. What is your name?"

"I am called Kajilil." The *Wedjat* was a small man, with skin burned brown and leathery by the sun. He wore a gray cloak pulled tight around his body. Lines radiated in the skin around his eyes as if they had been shot like marbles into his head.

"What is a *Wedjat?*" Vampyr asked.

"A Watcher."

"And what is a Watcher?" Vampyr pressed.

Kajilil stroked his short beard as he considered the question. "We are an ancient order. Formed after the destruction of Atlantis. The first Watchers were ex–high priests of the Airlia who realized they had been betrayed. They vowed to monitor the two sides of the Airlia civil war."

"Why did you save us?" Nosferatu asked.

"Because Donnchadh—the woman—interfered. I am trying to set things right, but I fear regardless of what we do, there will be change."

"Who is she?"

"I do not know for sure. I have heard rumors. She, and her partner, the warrior, Gwalcmai, hate the Gods. Some say the two of them have walked the Earth since the time of Atlantis, subverting the Gods. That is difficult for me to believe, as they are human, or at least appear human, as do you. But some say they helped start the Great Civil War among the Gods that destroyed Atlantis." Kajilil smiled wryly. "Some say anything. That is why it is best just to watch and record."

"But you saved us," Nosferatu pressed. Vampyr was watching the Black Sphinx, searching for any sign of his sister, but also listening closely.

"To try to restore the balance, as I said," Kajilil said. "She interfered and I have tried to set things right. Although"—he shrugged once more—"who knows what right is? I have often thought about that. What if her actions are what was supposed to happen? It has occurred to me at times that doing nothing, as my Watcher creed decrees, affects things as much as doing something. That is why I acted when I saw you enter the Roads."

Nosferatu understood little of what the man was saying and he could tell that Vampyr didn't either. The burning issue remained: What did the Airlia Gods have planned for those they had captured?

Kajilil reached into his robe and pulled out a short metal tube, which he raised to one eye and peered through.

"What is that?" Nosferatu asked.

"It is something that was taken from Atlantis," Kajilil said. "Ship captains who sailed for the Airlia used them to see far over the water." He offered the device to Nosferatu, who brought it up and peered through the layer of cloth covering his eye into the end of the tube. He was stunned suddenly to see everything much closer and pulled it away from his eye, blinking, reassured to find he was still at the same distance and had not been magically transported to the Black Sphinx. He tentatively raised the tube and looked through it once more. He could see the lips of the priests move as they prayed.

"Men used this?" he asked Kajilil.

The Watcher nodded. "A gift from the Gods. In the old days when the Gods ruled openly."

Nosferatu had more questions to ask but the stone door between the paws of the Black Sphinx slid open and a phalanx of priests appeared, the three bound prisoners in their midst. In the front were Chatha and Lilith chained together. And behind them was Nekhbet, wrapped in loops of metal. All three were being held up by priests, and through Kajilil's device Nosferatu could see that they had been drained of their blood just short of death. Nekhbet's severed wrist was bound in dirty linen.

Nosferatu began to rise, but Kajilil's hand was on his arm, holding him down. "It is futile," Kajilil said. "You would be cut down before you even got close."

"What are they going to do?" Nosferatu demanded, as the priests and prisoners made their way up a hastily constructed wooden ramp to the top of the Black Sphinx.

"We must watch and see," Kajilil said.

Vampyr demanded the looking device and Nosferatu reluctantly gave it to him, wincing at Vampyr's curse when he saw his twin, Lilith, bound in chains and drained.

A hush rolled over the crowd as the four remaining Gods appeared. All the humans except the high priests and prisoners dropped to their knees, heads bowed. The Gods were wrapped in black robes with hoods drawn close around their faces. Nosferatu realized their garb was not to hide themselves, but as he and Vampyr had done, to protect the Gods' eyes and skin from the sunlight. The Airlia slowly walked up the ramp to the top of the Sphinx, towering over the surrounding priests and guards.

One of the four stepped forward, turned to the high priest and nodded. The priest began to chant out in a loud voice that carried clearly to all in view.

"Behold the price of rebellion. Behold the price of betrayal. Behold the price of disobedience."

The high priest paused as Chatha and Lilith were brought forward to the two wooden X's. Their robes were ripped off, leaving their pale skin exposed. They were pressed spread-eagle to the wooden beams, blinking rapidly and painfully in the bright morning light, heads turning to and fro as if in search of their immediate future. Priests went to work, dipping leather straps in buckets of water and wrapping them around the limbs, working from the hands and feet inward. Each strap was an inch wide and spaced about two inches apart, leaving pale white flesh exposed between. The priests slowly continued until the arms and legs were encased up to the armpits and groin in strips of wet leather.

When they were done, once more the high priest chanted. "Behold the price of rebellion. Behold the price of betrayal. Behold the price of disobedience."

Then there was silence.

"What are they doing?" Vampyr demanded.

"I do not know," Kajilil said. He had taken the looking device back and was peering through it. "I have never seen this before."

The sun was rising behind them and had just struck the top of the Sphinx and the captives. Nosferatu narrowed the open strip in the cloth around his head. He shifted his gaze from Chatha and Lilith to Nekhbet. He could see how close she was to death. They had drained her even after he had taken his fill the previous night. And she had lost much blood from her wrist.

A moan escaped Chatha's lips, carrying through the dry air. At first Nosferatu could not tell what caused her to cry out in pain. He assumed it was the sun striking skin and eyes that had not known daylight in many, many years. He took the looking device from Kajilil and peered through it. He noticed that the fingers on Chatha's right hand were twitching uncontrollably. She cried out once more. The other hand was also twitching. Then Nosferatu saw the devilment the Gods had concocted and he cursed them. The leather was drying, and in doing so, contracting, pressing into the flesh. The straps were drying in the order they had been put on, from the outer ends of the limbs inward. Cutting off circulation, and pressing into the skin.

Nosferatu realized it was also the most devious and terrible torture that could have been devised for the state the two half-breeds were in, the bands forcing what little blood they had left into the centers of their bodies and keeping them alive, stopping the flow to the limbs bit by bit, while cutting into the flesh with inexorable pain.

Both were crying out by then, the screams forced from them by the waves of pain reverberating through their bodies.

"We must do something," Vampyr hissed.

Nosferatu agreed with the emotion but he knew Kajilil was right. "There is nothing we can do."

"My sister," Vampyr whispered in despair. "They will pay. The Gods and the humans. They will pay for this."

Vampyr rose and began to run forward toward the Black Sphinx. Nosferatu leapt up and chased him down, covering the distance between them in an instant. He wrapped his arms around the younger Undead, dragging him to the ground. Vampyr thrashed to and fro in his grasp. The fight was over when Kajilil rapped a stone on the side of Vampyr's head, knocking him unconscious. They dragged Vampyr back to their observation post. Nosferatu tied Vampyr's hands behind his back and bound his legs tightly together, then returned his attention to the top of the Black Sphinx.

The high priest stepped between the two crosses, spreading his arms to encompass both. "Behold the price of rebellion. Behold the price of betrayal. Behold the price of disobedience."

The torture went on to the point where even watching was practically unbearable. Both women's bodies were vi-

brating so violently that the sound of their backs hitting
the wood as they spasmed in pain was clearly audible despite the screams. The bones in their legs and arms
snapped, the sounds echoing across the gathered crowd.
The humans gathered round looked on with perverted
fascination.

Chatha died first, at least an hour after the last bands
cut off all blood flow to her crushed limbs. The sun was
nearly vertical overhead indicating she had lived for almost five hours under the torture. And Lilith was still
alive, although her screams were more muted, her throat
parched and worn from the effort.

What would they do to Nekhbet? Nosferatu wondered. There was not a third cross on the Sphinx's head,
only the empty black tube.

Lilith finally raised her head and blindly looked to the
sky as she cried out, "My brother. Avenge me." Then at last
she died with a whimper.

At her voice Vampyr rose out of his unconscious stu-
por, eyes blinking, great pain etched on his face. "My sister." Vampyr hunched over in pain for his twin, bound
fists clenched as he felt her death to the core of his being.

One of the Gods gestured and the high priest went
over and leaned close to the God, listening. Then the high
priest went between the two bodies. "There are two others like these out there. Two who have betrayed the Gods.
If they do not make themselves known, a worse fate will
be their last companion's fate throughout the ages." At
that, the high priest pointed at Nekhbet.

Two priests grabbed her arms and pulled her back,
placing her inside the open black sarcophagus. A belt was
placed around her waist and she was chained to the interior. One of the Gods went over to her, placing the bands
with leads around her arms and legs. The God reached in

and took the crown out of its slot, settling it on top of Nekhbet's head. Peering through the cylinder, Nosferatu could see that there were also wires running from the crown back to the tube. Done, the God stepped away.

Over a hundred years. That was how long Nekhbet and Nosferatu had shared the same cell and fate. They had talked at every opportunity. At first of reality, but then they had begun inventing new worlds, imaginary places to which they could disappear together.

"She will suffer the living sleep," the high priest called out. "Trapped in this, unable to die, unable to sleep, unable to move. Aware all the time. Unless you show yourself."

Kajilil placed a hand on Nosferatu's shoulder. "If you show yourself, both of you will suffer the same fate as your two comrades. And they will kill her too. She is only alive because you and your comrade are free."

Nosferatu stared through the looking tube, focusing on Nekhbet's face. He had been alone for a hundred years before they brought her in. What they were condemning her to was even more cruel than the past had been. They were keeping her alive to draw him in. He knew that and he knew it would work. But not then. And not on their terms.

Patience. It was the one thing that Gods had forced upon him.

Nekhbet turned her head slightly so that her eyes were dead on with his, as if she could know where he was and could see him. She smiled and shook her head ever so slightly.

The top of the tube was swung shut, enclosing Nekhbet. Nosferatu stared through the looking tube as the God went to the panel and long fingers tapped on it. Through his despair, Nosferatu tried to memorize the pattern.

Before returning to his place at the front, the high priest again went to one of the Gods and listened. "Hear this, traitors and murderers. You will be tracked down. And you will suffer an even more horrible fate."

A phalanx of guards surrounded the tube, which remained on top of the Black Sphinx, a beacon to draw Nosferatu in. The high priests followed by the Gods, slowly walked down the ramp and into the darkness of the Roads of Rostau.

Vampyr twisted his head toward Nosferatu. "I will never forgive you for today."

"You would be dead if you had gone down there," Nosferatu argued.

"I would rather have died trying to save her," Vampyr said.

To that Nosferatu had no answer. For a long time they sat in the dark shadows, stunned and overwhelmed by what they had witnessed.

Kajilil's voice broke the silence. "Perhaps, when things have changed, as they will with time, you may return. But for now, I think it is best that you both leave Egypt and go as far away as possible." He took two large leather pouches that jingled slightly and handed one each to Nosferatu and Vampyr. "Take this gold. Go across the sands to the east until you reach the Red Sea. There you will be able to hire a boat to take you far away."

"There is no 'perhaps,'" Nosferatu said. "I will be back."

"But not soon," Kajilil said, the words both a statement and a warning.

Nosferatu knew Kajilil's words were true. It would be a long time before he could come back to claim Nekhbet.

"Can you get me into the Roads this evening?"

"You cannot rescue her," Kajilil said. "She will be

guarded. You saw one of the creatures the Gods use to guard the Roads. There are others."

"I know that," Nosferatu said. "Can you get me back to the chamber in which I was held? It is empty now. The Gods will not expect me to return."

Kajilil frowned. "Why?"

"If I am to wait a long time, I need to do to myself as they have done to her. I will need my own black tube so I can use the deep sleep."

"Mine too," Vampyr said. "I will bide my time. But I swear revenge for my sister." Vampyr stared at Nosferatu with half-lidded eyes, his lips still covered with the dried blood they had tasted on the Roads of Rostau.

Kajilil considered their request and nodded. "Tonight. Then you both must leave. They will be looking for you."

Nosferatu's eyes were on the Black Sphinx. "There will come a day when they will no longer rule." He tapped his chest. "Then I will be back for my love."

Vampyr glared down at the site of his sister's death. "This is the Third Age. The Age of Man." He tapped his chest. "Someday it will be *our* age. The Fourth Age. The time of the Undead."

CHAPTER 2

THE REED SHIP WAS AT THE MERCY of the winds and Nosferatu could not help but give a cold smile as the sailors prayed out loud each morning to the Gods of Egypt to help them in their travels. He did not think the Airlia Gods would help, even if it were in their power to do so. However, most days the prayers seemed to work, as a steady wind blew from the north, pushing the forty-foot boat southward, the coast always visible to the right. In two days' time they made it out of the Red Sea and into the Gulf of Aden. Another three days saw them round the horn of Somalia and sail into the Indian Ocean, still staying close to the coast of Africa.

Nosferatu spent his days inside the black tube that Kajilil had helped him steal from the Roads of Rostau. It was covered by a small thatch hut he had had the sailors construct in the middle of the boat. He had examined the crown but made no use of it. The same with the glowing panel of hexagonals. He had no clue what powered it, but there was writing in the Runic language of the Gods on each hex. When they had gone down into the tunnels, they'd found the three cells empty except for the tubes. Lifting one, they found the metal surprisingly light. Kajilil had given them gray cloaks that he said would hide them from the metal spider, but the creature had not appeared.

As Nosferatu had speculated, no one would have expected them to return to the scene of their imprisonment.

Vampyr and he wordlessly parted near the Watcher's hut, on the edge of the Nile. Vampyr slipped off into the dark, moving north along the west bank of the Nile, while Nosferatu climbed on board a raft provided by Kajilil and forded the river. Nosferatu knew that the other Undead was full of rage at both the Airlia and their human subjects and he feared for what Vampyr might do. He thought it highly possible that Vampyr would be captured by the Airlia in his quest for vengeance and be killed as horribly as his sister had been.

Once across the Nile Nosferatu had to wrap the tube in heavy cloths and have it dragged behind a pair of camels to cross the desert from the Nile to the Red Sea. The desert people—the *Bedu*—who had done this for him had asked no questions and made no protest about traveling only at night. They'd taken the gold payment Nosferatu had offered and disappeared into the desert as soon as he reached the coast. When he reached the Red Sea, Nosferatu had hired his boat. The crew worshiped the Egyptian Gods for lack of anything else, but they were from a tribe that lived along the coast of the Red Sea and knew nothing of the Airlia or the high priests along the Nile.

Nosferatu's thoughts swirled around Nekhbet and his last sight of her as the lid of the tube had closed. She had smiled and shaken her head. The high priest had said she would stay awake and alive forever in her metal prison. He knew that as long as the Gods ruled in Egypt he would not be able to save her. His last vision of the Black Sphinx confirmed that her tube was still resting on top of the large lion head, the bait for the Airlia trap for him. He wondered how long they would keep her there before taking her back underground. He would have to wait. Even the Watcher Kajilil had said change would come. When it did, Nosferatu knew he would return and rescue her. Until then he had to stay alive.

On the third day on board they all saw a golden disk flying low over the sands to the west. The crew threw themselves to the deck and prayed loudly. Nosferatu knew the Airlia were searching for him and Vampyr. He stayed inside the tube, hidden from sight as the disk flew overhead, hovering for a few moments before moving on.

Twice more in the following week they saw the disk in the distance, and each time Nosferatu crawled into the tube.

At night he paced along the deck, stepping over the sleeping forms of the half dozen men he had paid to take him away from Egypt. They tied up to shore every evening and occasionally Nosferatu ventured inland. The hunger grew in him and he knew that he would have to feed in order to maintain his age and strength.

He took his first kill after almost a month and a half at sea when he could hold the hunger at bay no longer and feared he would lose control and attack one of the crew. As they went south the shoreline had changed from desert to lush jungle. They had tied up to a tree near the mouth of a small river. The crew had refilled the water caskets by traveling up the river just before darkness fell, hurrying back, frightened of the strange noises that roared and bellowed out of the lush greenness. Nosferatu found the sounds intriguing—a siren's song of violence and death beckoning him to its darkness.

Nosferatu left the boat and waded ashore. He entered the dark jungle, and was immediately swallowed up into its blackness. He could see well in the darkness, having inherited the Airlia predisposition for lower levels of light. Indeed, he had found that the sun greatly hurt his eyes and he also had to protect his skin from the burning rays during the day as his flesh had no tolerance of its touch.

Nosferatu moved through the jungle, at one with the other creatures. In the limited light his eyes perceived the spectrum of colors and he marveled at the lush greenness all around him. Even the arable land next to the Nile had never produced color as vivid as this. And the bounty of life in the jungle—he could hear it everywhere.

Nosferatu also began to discover that he had other abilities beyond that of his superb night vision, thanks to his Airlia genes and blood. He could run swiftly, as fast as a deer—something he discovered while crossing a small clearing where he came across several of the creatures. He ran one down, startling himself as much as his prey.

Realizing he didn't know the extent of his capabilities, he spent a little time testing his body.

He discovered he could jump almost twenty feet straight up and land upright on a branch. With his bare hands he could break an eight-inch-thick piece of wood. When the feat left a scratch in his palm, he watched with amazement as it healed within the hour.

He became so caught up in exploring his newfound abilities, he almost forgot his hunger—almost, but not quite. After an hour following the bank of the stream inland, he came upon a clearing in which there were a dozen huts surrounded by a thorn thicket through which there was but a single opening blocked by a crude wooden gate. Nosferatu stood still, waiting and watching, until he saw movement. A young boy with skin as dark as the night and a spear in his hand was slowly walking in a circle just inside the wall of thorns, peering out at the surrounding jungle with wide eyes at the sudden silence that had descended at Nosferatu's approach. Nosferatu felt the blood fever come over him, remembering what it had felt like to taste of the priest at the base of the Black Sphinx. The blood he'd been fed by the high priests had always been cold and thick, an hour or two removed from the draining. Fresh blood, pumping straight out of the vein, that was a very different thing.

Nosferatu waited until the boy was on the far side, then he moved forward. He lightly jumped over the thorn fence. He crouched down, hidden in the shadows as the boy came round once more. Nosferatu leapt up, jumping straight for the boy, clamping one hand over his mouth and shoving the spear away with the other while his mouth fastened on the thin neck, teeth tearing into the flesh. He was rewarded with a spray of blood, which strengthened him. The boy's struggles were futile as Nosferatu drained him.

Distantly Nosferatu could hear a dog barking in alarm but he kept his mouth tight to the torn vein, allowing the blood to pulse in, the boy's wildly beating heart aiding in the feeding. When he heard voices crying out, only then did Nosferatu look up from his victim. A half dozen warriors, spears in their hands surrounded him. They stepped back in shock as he lifted his blood-soaked, pale white face from the body. His glittering eyes and alien white skin made him appear a demon. Nosferatu laughed, lifting the body over his head and throwing it at the men. They jumped out of the way and he leapt back over the thorn barricade and sprinted off into the jungle before they could attack him.

Before dawn Nosferatu had cleaned up and was back on the boat.

The kill lasted him well over a month before he felt

the urge again. By that time they had made their way farther down the coast of Africa than any of the crew had
ever been. They had passed a place where two tall white-
capped mountains beckoned in the distance and the land
changed from jungle to open plains reaching the shoreline. Nosferatu heard the men muttering about turning
around, about going back; but he pressed them to continue on, giving them more gold, a fortune that would
mean none would ever have to work again.

Unable to find anything on land as they passed an arid
stretch of coastline, three weeks later, Nosferatu's second
kill was one of the sailors. He took the poor man in the
night, silencing him, pulling him off the ship and onto
land, where he drained the man's blood and hid the body.
In the morning there was panic and consternation among
the survivors about the sudden and silent disappearance
of their comrade. Nosferatu said nothing, only pointing to
the south before retiring with his gold to the tube, making
sure he locked it from the inside as he knew they were
considering killing him and taking the gold. The man had
been the one who had been the most insistent that they
turn back, so the consensus among the others was that he
had jumped ship and was trying to make his way back by
land.

After two more weeks they rounded a storm-lashed
cape and began moving north. Nosferatu realized they
must be on the other side of the continent in which Egypt
rested. Was he far enough away from the Airlia to be safe
for a while?

He killed a second crewmember not long after they
began moving north. The remaining four were panic-
stricken and superstitious. They spent that entire day in
the rear, muttering among themselves as the boat made
its way north. The shoreline had also turned forbidding.

The land was edged with cliffs, rocky and barren. The men were running low on food and water but they pressed forward for another week. Nosferatu knew he had gone as far as he could without feeding again. He took a third that night, draining him, then sliding the body overboard, where sharks immediately took it into the depths.

Sated with blood, he climbed into his tube just before dawn, and sealed the lid against intrusion. As always he fell into an uneasy slumber, dreams of Nekhbet mixed with nightmares of darkness and confinement.

He woke when his forehead slammed against the top of the lid. Disoriented for a moment, he pressed against the metal sides of the tube to steady himself. The tube rolled one way, paused, then the other. The action didn't stop.

They'd thrown him overboard, Nosferatu realized with a rush of panic. He cursed at this unexpected turn of events. He'd counted on their fear to keep them in place and knew now that he had miscalculated. He held steady against the sway of the tube to the waves. He knew if he opened the lid, water would pour in and the tube would be lost, leaving him adrift in the shark-infested water.

He waited.

It was unlike his previous time in the tube underneath the Giza Plateau. Worse, much worse, as the days and nights went by. Then he had had the monthly feedings and the presence of Nekhbet. Here he suffered in darkness, enclosed, growing weaker as the strength of the feeding from the last sailor faded. And his strength was worn down further as he fought against the external motion of the tube to avoid being injured.

Several times he spent hours fighting severe motion, the tube sometimes rolling over completely. He had to assume that those were periods when he rode out storms. At times he would sleep, more a lapse into exhausted unconsciousness, always broken by a slam to one side or the other of the tube.

Never did he despair. Never was he tempted to unlatch the lid and let the ocean in to finish his agony.

Foremost in his mind was Nekhbet, his last vision of her. He could endure a thousand storms before he would let go of that vision, before he would abandon her to an eternity of empty life in her tube.

Nosferatu woke with a start as he was once more slammed against the right side of the tube. He braced himself, ready for the inevitable roll to the other side, but there was only stillness. He waited, not even daring to breathe. Total, complete stillness. He had almost forgotten what it was like.

Nosferatu took a deep breath, ignoring the overwhelming stench from inside the tube. He reached to the inner latch and pressed on it. The lid cracked open and a surge of water poured in, causing him to panic for a second before the inflow suddenly ceased. Then another splash of water, a wave. He almost slammed the lid shut, but the tube wasn't moving. Of that he was certain. And it was night outside. Through the slight opening he could see stars on the horizon.

Nosferatu swung the lid wide open and sat up.

The tube was on the surf line along a rocky coast. Cliffs towered over a thin sliver of pebble shore. Gingerly, Nosferatu climbed out of the tube, his feet touching solid ground for the first time in over a month. He pulled the tube inland, making sure it was above the surf line. Then he looked about. There was not a single hint of vegetation, just bare, forbidding rock. And no sign of animal life, not even birds overhead.

Nosferatu glanced up at the cliffs. There was a tinge of light—dawn was coming. He summoned up what little energy he had left. First, he cleaned out the interior of the tube with seawater. Then he pulled the tube across the narrow beach and wedged it in a crack in the cliff face. He piled up smaller rocks in front, hiding it from the sight of anyone passing on the ocean. He placed his hands over the control panel, reading what he could make out and remembering as best he could the sequence the God had set on Nekhbet's. With shaking hands he tapped out a code. The panel flashed and he crawled inside, putting the bands on his legs and arms before setting the crown on his head.

He had just completed this when he felt darkness overwhelm him.

THE GIZA PLATEAU: 8000 B.C.

Vampyr cut the soldier's throat with one smooth slice of the dagger. He grabbed the stunned man, pulling the open wound to his mouth, and drank as much blood as his engorged body would take. The soldier was the third he had taken in as many nights. He did not need the blood. They were Egyptian, serving the Gods, and this was vengeance, though he was sure none but the dead would know who was wreaking it.

Vampyr had demurred when Nosferatu had said they should travel south, into the unknown lands. He knew the Eldest was going to hide and bide his time. Vampyr did not want to hide. He wanted blood and vengeance and he planned to stay close to Egypt.

The men he took were those who wandered out of the fort in the evening into the local village, seeking wine and women. He slid the body of the most recent victim off the edge of the dock, into the dark water of the Nile. He knew there was already a level of unease in the fort from the two missing men and a third's disappearing would bring some sort of reaction.

Three soldiers from the army of an empire. Poor vengeance indeed, Vampyr thought bitterly to himself as he strode along the wooden dock toward the small boat that held his tube.

Once on deck, he paused and stood still, feeling the cool breeze blow over his skin. It was as if there were a hole in his chest, and all the blood he took could never be enough to fill it. Lilith had always been there, for over a hundred years. They had been together in the womb. Played together along the banks of the Nile as children, not knowing the fate that awaited them.

Shortly after the twins reached adulthood, the high priests had taken them and dragged them into the Roads, entombing them in adjacent tubes. Even in their imprisonment, they had still had each other. When Lilith died on the cross he had felt the connection with her inside his mind give way. It was as if together they had been one complete person and balanced each other—Lilith the light, and he the darkness.

A horn call rang out plaintively from the fort. When Vampyr looked landward, he could see a group of soldiers carrying torches issue forth from the gates of the fort into the village. Too many for him to fight.

He heard the slap of oars in the water and Vampyr looked upriver to see a boat floating with the current, about thirty feet away. A man wearing a black robe stood in the prow, staring at him. Eight men with drawn bows stood along the center of the boat, their weapons aimed at

Vampyr. Four other men rowed, bringing the boat closer to his.

Vampyr took a step backward as the prow of the other boat touched his and two of the men reached out to secure the two together. The man in the cloak climbed on board Vampyr's boat. Vampyr drew his dagger. The stranger drew a sword that glittered in the starlight, but he did not immediately attack, nor did the bowmen fire.

"Who are you?" Vampyr demanded.

"I am a Shadow of those you hate. Aspasia's Shadow."

Vampyr tightened the grip on his dagger. "What is a Shadow?"

The man drew back his hood, revealing a thin, pale face and dark eyes. With his free hand he pointed at his head. "I carry the memories of Aspasia, Lord of the Gods." He laughed. "At least one side of the so-called Gods. I am his Shadow. I have received a message from the Guardian that there has been trouble in the Roads of Rostau and I believe I have just found the source of that trouble. I have been looking for you for a while now."

Aspasia's Shadow glanced past Nosferatu at the Giza Plateau. "But." He let that word hang in the air for a few moments. "You killed Isis and Osiris?"

Vampyr stood taller. "Yes." He expected the other man to attack, but Aspasia's Shadow seemed to be thinking.

"Interesting," Aspasia's Shadow said. "Two of the six who hide in the Roads dead. They were supposed to be caretakers only, not set themselves up once more as Gods. Perhaps they will have learned their lesson."

"And what is your task?" Vampyr asked.

"A caretaker also, in my own way. To maintain the truce while the Gods sleep. To win for my side if the opportunity presents itself." Aspasia's Shadow shrugged.

"I'm a backup, an afterthought. I must say, though, that's better than what you are."

Aspasia's Shadow put the point of his sword into the wood and leaned on the pommel as he considered Vampyr. The bowmen, however, did not relax the tension on their strings and the barbed points of their arrows were aimed directly at Vampyr's chest.

Vampyr could hear the soldiers searching along the riverbank, growing closer; but Aspasia's Shadow did not seem concerned.

"You're just another piece on the board," Aspasia's Shadow said. He cocked his head, staring at Vampyr. "You burn with hatred. I can feel it. This should be interesting." He pointed downriver, toward the Middle Sea. "Go. Take your hatred and leave this place. Nurse it. The time of the Gods will be over here someday." He leaned over and looked under the thin wooden deck and saw the black tube. "As you know, you can sleep without dreaming or thinking for a long time using that. I would recommend you go far away and go into the deep sleep for a long time. Then awaken and see what has changed in the world."

"How do I do that?" Vampyr asked.

Aspasia's Shadow climbed down belowdecks and tapped something into the command panel.

Vampyr watched his movements carefully. "How do I know you aren't setting that to kill me? Or put me to sleep forever?"

"You don't," Aspasia's Shadow said. "But the Airlia move very slowly. If you want to scavenge about this world for millennia, waiting for things to change, be my guest. Things will change over time, but slowly. The deep sleep, which I use myself, is a way to 'speed' the process. And it keeps you from aging during the time you sleep."

"Why should you care about what I do?" Vampyr demanded, still holding the bloodstained dagger tightly in his hand.

"It is a game," Aspasia's Shadow said. "As I said, you're just another piece on the board, making things interesting. I may have Aspasia's memories, but I have lived a long time since they were imprinted on me. I do not necessarily have the same motivations or goals anymore."

"What is your goal?"

"That is none of your business." Aspasia's Shadow waved his hands wide. "There is an entire world out there. Take your hatred and lust into it. Make the world a more interesting place to watch. We will meet again."

With that, Aspasia's Shadow sheathed his sword and walked onto the dock, heading toward the soldiers. Vampyr watched him for a few seconds, then looked at the other boat. The bowmen still had their weapons aimed at him. Vampyr untied the rope holding his boat to the dock. The Nile's current grabbed hold and took him and the boat with it, heading toward the Middle Sea.

CHAPTER 3

THE SKELETON COAST: 1450 B.C.

NEKHBET WAS DEAD. NOSFERATU
screamed, the cry echoed back to him by the metal lid
just in front of his face. She was just a skeleton lying inside
of her tube, her flesh long since consumed by the ages.
Her red hair crowned a skull, empty eye sockets leading
into an empty cranium. Completely panic-stricken in the
confinement and absolute darkness, he flailed his arms,
smacking into the sides of the tube.

A dream. A nightmare.

Nosferatu fought to bring his mind and heart under
control. He reached for the inner latch and pressed on it.
He screamed, this time from pain, as a searing bolt of sunlight poured into the opening. Blindly he reached up and
slammed the lid shut, the pain in his eyes unbearable.

Nosferatu waited for darkness, the ache in his eyes
slowly fading. While he waited he inventoried his body.
He was weak, very weak. It was an effort to lift his hand.
Running his fingers over his body, he realized he was little
more than skin stretched over bone. He needed to feed.
Desperately.

He removed the crown from his head and the leads
from his arms and legs. He reached up and pressed the
latch, carefully pushing up the lid so only the tiniest of
cracks appeared. Blessed darkness. He didn't have the

strength to throw the lid all the way open. He pushed it up enough to slither out of the tube, onto the pebble beach, letting the lid slam shut behind him. He lay there for a few minutes, gathering his strength. It was warm on the pebbles as the heat from the day dissipated upward.

The desolation of the area he had hidden in had kept him safe for all the years he had been in the tube, but it worked against him now. Nosferatu looked about. He saw a bird fly by high overhead, but other than that no sign of life along the shore. He knew he didn't have the energy to climb the cliff and search farther inland, and given the desolation of the shore, he didn't suspect farther inland would yield much.

Nosferatu lay on his back listening to the surf and staring up at the stars. Is this how it would end? He cursed himself for not thinking things through when he entered the tube. But how could he have changed anything? How long had he slept? He'd set the tube for 650 years as best he could read the High Rune figures on the hexagonals— an amount of time he felt was sufficient to check to see if the Airlia still ruled in Egypt.

Nosferatu's nostrils flared as they caught a whiff of something. He sniffed. Blood. Not human. Not anything he had ever smelled before. But close in some way to human. He turned his head from side to side, trying to determine from which direction the scent came.

The sea.

Nosferatu frowned. Blood in the water. He crawled to the water's edge. A wave splashed cold water into his face, but he continued until he floated in the ocean. He lifted his head and sniffed. The blood was ahead. Again, not human, but close. Similar.

He kicked weakly, pushing himself forward. A swell sprayed water into his mouth and he tasted the faintest trace of blood. Indeed not human but mammal. Close enough in his desperate situation. He pressed on.

Nosferatu cried out as something brushed along underneath him. He looked down and saw a long gray form. A dorsal fin passed by his left side. Shark. Yes, they would be drawn to blood too, he realized, remembering dumping the bodies off the boat on the way there. Or had they caused the blood? he wondered. He was closer to the blood. His entire body felt it.

Something bumped into him on the right and he instinctively pushed away before he realized whatever he had hit wasn't moving. He edged closer. A dolphin. Its belly ripped open. Then he heard it and saw it all around him. The feeding frenzy as sharks tore into a pod of dolphins. The ripping of flesh. The squeals of the dolphins as they fought back and tried to protect their young from the marauders.

Nosferatu didn't care about the sharks that surrounded him. He pressed forward, holding tight to the corpse. With trembling hands he ripped into the flesh above the water, exposing a vein. Blood seeped out and he fastened his mouth onto it, drinking the trickle.

Something hit his legs but he ignored it, his entire being focused on drawing the blood in. He felt strength slowly spread through his body but the flow came to a halt. Nosferatu let go of the body and turned seaward, toward the worst of the savagery. He saw another corpse and swam to it, repeating the process. A shark took a chunk out of the body he was feeding on and he ignored it. He repeated this four times, growing stronger with each feeding.

The sharks also ignored him, perhaps satisfied with their meal of dolphin, or perhaps knowing on some primordial level that Nosferatu was kin, a hunter like them, drawn to the blood. Or, perhaps, sensing that he was something that they had never encountered and avoiding the unknown.

Nosferatu turned for shore, full of dolphin blood and feeling stronger but ill. He swam to the beach, staggering to his feet. The current along the shore had pressed him northward from where he had launched. He turned south and walked, heading back toward his tube.

Suddenly, he fell to his knees and vomited a mixture of dolphin blood and seawater. He felt woozy, both from the gorging after so long a fast and the difference in blood type. He knew he needed human blood. He was stronger, but could not survive for long like this.

He reached his tube and crawled into it, his stomach protesting, his head pounding. He'd drunk so much to gain so little.

Nosferatu spent the next day in his tube, planning. That evening he exited the tube and climbed the cliff to the top. Looking inland all he saw was rocky desert extending to the horizon. He doubted that anyone lived within hundreds of miles. Could he cross the desert to inhabited land before running out of energy? Nosferatu stood for a long time, peering inland. Then he turned to the sea. He could see for miles along the barren coast in either direction.

At the very least he knew there was life in the water. Enough to keep him alive.

He turned back toward the land, looking to the northeast, his focus drawn that way as if there were a beacon over the horizon. He knew that was where Egypt lay. And Nekhbet waited. Staying alive wasn't good enough. He had to get stronger so he could travel. He stayed on top of the cliff the entire night and when the first sign of dawn appeared in the east, he climbed down and entered his tube.

The next evening he did the same, but now he simply sat on the cliff, peering first one way, then the other along the coast, waiting. That went on for three complete cycles of the moon.

His patience was rewarded in the fourth month. Right after dark, as soon as he reached the top of the cliff, far to the north he spotted a small glowing spot on the shoreline. He knew immediately what it was—a lantern aboard a ship beached for the night. Nosferatu made his way in that direction along the top of the high cliff.

It took over four hours before he was above the light. A wooden ship was drawn up on the shore, the flickering lantern hung on a short mast. The ship was about fifteen feet long, open-topped, with one bench across the center and a long oar extending to each side. At the rear, the handle for the rudder swept inboard. Nosferatu counted three people—two sleeping in the front of the ship and one standing guard next to the mast.

Nosferatu moved south about two hundred yards until he reached a cleft in the rock face. He climbed down to the shore and considered his options. His heart was racing, not so much from the descent, but from the nearness of human blood. He could literally smell the people nearby. He crept closer but paused as the guard woke one of the sleeping figures.

The two switched places, the guard wrapping himself in a blanket and lying under the bench. The newly woken man leaned the sword against the mast and climbed off the boat and walked stiffly toward the cliff. Nosferatu began moving again, closing the gap. The new guard was urinating onto the pebbles when Nosferatu came upon him from behind. His hand clamped over the man's mouth, stifling any cry, and he wrapped his other arm around the man's body, pinning his arms to his sides. Nosferatu's head darted forward, mouth open, and he sank his teeth into the man's neck, tearing at the flesh.

Blood. Human blood. As the man's struggles grew weaker, Nosferatu grew stronger from the blood surging into his mouth. He completely drained the man in less than a minute.

Nosferatu slowly let go of the body, lowering it to the ground. He turned toward the boat and considered the two sleeping men. His lust for blood was strong and the urge to take another victim almost made him go forward, but he held back. He needed them. As they would need him.

Nosferatu took the body and threw it over one shoulder. He made his way south. He crammed the body into a split in the cliff wall, covering it with rocks so it couldn't be seen. Then he went to his tube and covered it completely. He took a piece of cloth and wrapped it around his head, covering his eyes with a double layer. Then he waited for dawn.

When the sun came up, light penetrated the cloth, but it was filtered enough for him to be able to see shapes and forms without pain. The boat did not appear until almost noon. Nosferatu assumed the two survivors had spent the morning searching in vain for their missing comrade. He waved as the boat grew closer and he could see the two sailors arguing, already jittery from the unexplained disappearance of one of their own and having difficulty handling the boat lacking one man. Nosferatu reached into his pocket and pulled out a piece of gold coin and waved it, the sun reflecting off the precious metal.

Greed overcame fear and the men drew the boat in closer, calling out in a strange tongue. Nosferatu simply shook the gold, then pointed at himself and the tube, then at their boat, then to the south. There was no mistaking his desire. He pantomimed rowing, and that really got their attention as the boat needed three men to move if the wind failed them, as it often would along this coast—two men on the oars and one on the rudder.

The two sailors brought the boat to a halt about fifty feet from shore, still arguing. Nosferatu waited. Greed and reality won as he suspected it would. The boat came closer to shore and he waded out to it. The sailors were obviously asking him questions but he ignored them, waving a hand in front of where his mouth was and shaking his head. He also pointed at his eyes, then at the sun, shaking his head more vigorously.

Then they pushed the boat back out into the swell, raised the short sail, and began heading south, one of them manning the rudder, the other sitting on the bench next to the left oar. Nosferatu sat next to the right oar, but for now no rowing was needed. Nosferatu's eyes ached even though the turban wrapped around his head blocked most of the sunlight. He wanted to hide under one of the benches and sleep, but he knew it was too soon, the sailors too jittery, to do this now.

He pretended to sleep that night and the next day spent the time on the middle bench, suffering the sunlight that forced its way through the cloth. Not long after dawn they were becalmed and Nosferatu joined the other sailor in rowing. It was agony but he continued in this way for eight days as they made their way south. During that time he listened to the two sailors talk, picking up words and phrases. He learned they were from a land far to the north, above the opening to the Inner Sea along which Egypt lay, a country which they had never heard of.

They'd been blown far out to sea during a storm. It had taken them over a week to make it back into sight of land and when they tried to make their way north along the west coast of Africa both the current and wind defeated them. They'd then made the difficult decision to go with the flow and head south.

Sketching with a piece of charcoal on the deck, Nosferatu drew for them a rough representation of the continent as he remembered it. He drew a line around the southern tip and up to the north. Lying, he indicated there was a way to sail up the Red Sea and into the Middle Sea on which they had come, not that they needed convincing as they had already given up on going back up the west coast even before they met him.

Two cycles of the moon after getting on board the boat, they passed the southern tip of Africa and began making their way northward. Nosferatu pretended to eat the scant food they offered him, but slipped it overboard when they weren't watching. Nosferatu's eyes had adjusted slightly to the sun, but he still kept them covered with the cloth. He felt the hunger inside growing. The land grew more lush as they made their way up the coast and one day the sailors proposed stopping to hunt. Nosferatu begged off, letting them go inland with their bows and knives. Once they were out of sight, he also left the boat, taking a different direction.

He had to travel far to find a village, arriving just before dark. He waited until the middle of the night before striking, taking down a warrior who came out to investigate when the dogs barked at Nosferatu's approach.

Nosferatu came back to the boat just before dawn to find his two comrades with fresh kill and full of fear over his disappearance. He explained nothing, keeping to his silence, even though he understood their language well now.

Thus they continued. He killed and fed on humans five more times before they rounded the horn of Somalia and entered the Red Sea. After such a long sleep and a long journey, even Nosferatu began to become anxious. He was nearing Nekhbet. When he saw the sands of the Arabian Desert to his left, he knew it was time to leave the boat.

He departed one night, leaving the two sailors alive, even though he had the hunger. As he crossed the desert between the Red Sea and the Nile he slept during the day, covering himself with sand to protect his eyes and skin from the sun and moving at night. The third night he fed on a lone Bedouin. The next night he spotted a camp of Bedouins, probably the group from which his earlier victim had wandered.

Nosferatu was stopped by a guard as he approached the cluster of tents. He greeted the guard in the same manner he had all he met that he did not feed on—with a hand raised, holding gold.

The negotiations with the Bedouin chief were fast and simple. Nosferatu hired a half dozen of the desert warriors for a full moon of service. No questions were asked about what tasks were to be fulfilled or destinations. Along with the six desert dwellers and their mounts, he also hired four extra camels. The next evening, right after nightfall, they left the camp and headed west.

On the fifth day the lead Bedouin in his group indicated they were near the Nile.

The moon was three-quarters full as Nosferatu climbed up the steep slope of a large dune and caught his first glimpse of the heart of Egypt since he'd left. He was staggered by what he saw. A massive pyramid built of stone and almost five hundred feet high capped the Giza Plateau. It was flanked by two other pyramids almost as large. In front of the Great Pyramid, where the Black Sphinx had once lain in a depression, the ground had been covered and there was a similar sphinx made of stone with a painted face. Between the paws of the stone sphinx was a statue that Nosferatu recognized: It was of Horus. A temple had been built in front of the large pyramid, with a long causeway connecting the two. To the north, along the river, there was the glow of a huge city.

The six Bedouins stood behind him, swords in hand, awaiting his commands.

Nosferatu stood still, taking in the changes, particularly the pyramids. There were piles of stone at the base of the Great Pyramid, as if it were not complete, or perhaps, Nosferatu mused, there had once been a facing on it that had been stripped off for some reason. So much change in 650 years. It was quite incredible considering how little change had occurred during his time imprisoned along the Roads of Rostau.

The real issue, though, was who ruled now? The sailors had been able to tell him nothing of Egypt, their home being far to the west along the Inner Sea. They had talked of an island kingdom ruled by a fearsome lord in the Middle Sea but it had meant nothing to Nosferatu.

Even in the deep desert, what happened in Egypt mattered nothing to the Bedouins, who stayed away from the Nile and the rule of law there. To them it was a place to avoid.

Nosferatu could see people on the plateau, even though it was the middle of the night. Soldiers on guard. Priests scurrying about. There were ships moving on the Nile, carrying grain and other cargo.

Nosferatu rode down the far side of the dune and to the Nile, where he spurred his camel into water and crossed over, followed by his small party. On the east bank, Nosferatu skirted the large temple, where armored guards stood watch. He moved to the place he remembered, the secret riverbank entry to the Roads of Rostau.

He was surprised to find that the entryway was submerged, the level of the river obviously having risen over the years. Nosferatu considered the change for a few moments, then made a decision. He needed information before he took precipitous action. He left four of the warriors with the camels, hidden among some massive building blocks. He took the remaining two Bedouins with him farther along the riverbank.

The small stone hut was still there, huddled among dozens of others. The mark was still in place above the entryway, faded with time, but visible to those who knew to look for it. Nosferatu didn't bother knocking. He pushed aside the cloth hanging in the doorway and entered without knocking, the two Bedouins right behind.

There were four people inside. A man and a woman sharing a pallet to his left; a young girl sleeping on another slightly raised platform to the right, and a young boy sleeping on the floor directly ahead. Nosferatu was across the room in three steps. He snatched up the boy, hooking an arm around his neck and pressing a blade against the flesh.

The other three in the room were awakened by the noise. The man held his wife back as she lunged for the boy whom Nosferatu held.

"You are the Watcher?" Nosferatu asked. "The *Wedjat?*"

The man was blinking sleep out of his eyes, fear slowly taking its place. "I am Kajihi."

"The Watcher?"

"How do you know—"

"Tell me what you have seen," Nosferatu said.

"What? Who are you?"

Nosferatu tightened his grip on the boy's neck, eliciting a yelp of pain. "I ask the questions."

"May they leave?" Kajihi asked, indicating his wife and daughter. "They will go to a friend's. We cannot go to the Pharaoh's guards, as you may know, if you know I am a Watcher."

" 'Pharaoh'? " The word was unfamiliar to Nosferatu.

"He who rules here."

Interesting, Nosferatu thought. That was not the name of one of the four remaining Gods. Of course, that might be what one of them was called now. "A man? Or a God?"

Kajihi shrugged, relaxing slightly as he realized his intruder was interested in information. "He appears to be the former. Although there are some who claim he is a God. But each Pharaoh has died after a normal life span, so if they are Gods, they only enjoy the benefits in the afterlife. The Pharaoh before this one caught the water fever just like a man and died shortly afterward, just like a man."

"How many Pharaohs have there been?"

"The Great Pharaoh Tuthmosis, son of Amenophis, is the seventy-fourth Pharaoh to rule and the fourth of the Eighteenth Dynasty."

Seventy-four, Nosferatu thought with a shock as he did the math. Thousands of years of human rule given their life span. Nosferatu felt a chill of unease. "And the Gods? Where have they gone?"

"Who are you?"

Nosferatu nodded, indicating for the two females to leave. Then he let go of the boy. "Go with them," he ordered. He took a seat, indicating that Kajihi should do the same. The Bedouins flanked Kajihi, their swords at the ready, their faces unreadable. "My name is Nosferatu."

Kajihi's eyes widened. "You are the Undead. I was told of you by my father who was told in turn by his father and down the line for many, many years. I thought you were just a myth."

"I have been away for a while," Nosferatu said. "Many years as you note. When I last saw the plateau, there was only the Black Sphinx."

"The Black Sphinx!" Kajihi was astounded. "The Black Sphinx is only spoken of in whispers. Some say it never was. Some say perhaps the Great Sphinx that is on the plateau was once painted black and gave rise to the legend."

"There was a Black Sphinx and it was not made of stone but of some metal," Nosferatu confirmed, remembering Lilith's and Chatha's horrible deaths atop the structure. "Most noble and imposing, much more than the stone image that sits on top of it now."

"You are indeed from the First Age then."

Nosferatu spread his hands, indicating he had no clue. "What age is this?"

"The Eighteenth Dynasty of the Third Age of Egypt. The Age of the Rule of the Pharaohs. The First Age is spoken of as legend. The Age when the Airlia Gods themselves ruled."

Nosferatu nodded. "Yes, they ruled. I saw them myself. I killed one of them with these hands. So much for Gods. Who ruled in the Second Age?"

"The Shadows of the Gods made in the image of Horus."

Nosferatu knew Horus well, one of the six Airlia Gods, and his father. "And what are Shadows?"

"Men who have minds of the Gods and are constantly

reborn. They are long gone although I have heard there is one who still wanders the world, the Shadow of the God Aspasia, made to do his bidding while the God himself sleeps."

That made little sense to Nosferatu. "And now a man rules here?"

"Yes."

"What happened to the Gods?"

"Some say they are still in the Roads of Rostau. Others say they've gone far away. No one really knows. Not even the high priests, although they pretend to know. Often they will point up to the sky, as if that is where the Gods have gone."

Or where they came from, Nosferatu thought, remembering what the strange woman, Donnchadh, had told him when she freed him. "And the Shadows?"

"Gone also, although, as I said, there is rumor that the Shadow of the great god Aspasia is across the Red Sea in the wasteland of the Sinai. That he has been there since the beginning of time. Waiting."

Nosferatu understood waiting. "Waiting for what?"

"No one knows."

Gods, then Shadows, and now men. Nosferatu felt a surge of fear and hope. Time had worked in his favor, but how much time? More than 650 years, that was certain. "How long has it been since the First Age?" He had an idea how long the humans had ruled here, but none about the Shadows of Horus.

Kajihi spread his hands. "Over six thousand years according to the records kept here by my family."

Six thousand. Nosferatu felt as if he'd been hit in the chest. He'd been off by about a factor of ten when he'd set the tube to wake him. A slight miscalculation in terms of pressing the hexes, a massive one in terms of time. Was

Nekhbet still alive? Was the influence of the Airlia Gods now little more than a representation in a human called a Pharaoh?

Nosferatu pointed at Kajihi. "You will take me to the Roads of Rostau. There is something I must get."

"The Roads are guarded. The Gods may be gone, but there are others about who do their bidding. The Ones Who Wait. Guides. They keep the Atlantean truce. They will not allow any disturbance of the truce."

The world had indeed changed, Nosferatu thought. Six thousand years. If Nekhbet was still living, was she sane? Could anyone survive that long in the state they had put her with their mind intact? "Who are the Ones Who Wait? And these Guides?"

"The Ones Who Wait are like you, if what I was told about you is true. Half-human, half-God. They serve the God Artad. I have never seen one, but my order reports they are active. The Guides serve the God Aspasia. They are human but they obey with more vigor and blind obedience than even the high priests. And as I said, there is a belief that Aspasia's Shadow is nearby and can also control the Guides. It is said he is a fearsome creature with little love for any other living thing."

Nosferatu rubbed his head. Even when hidden, the long hand of the Airlia Gods still reached out and affected things. "Can you get me into the Roads?"

"It is dangerous. And it is against my charter as a Watcher."

"Your ancestor took me into the Roads a very long time ago," Nosferatu said. "He thought it was part of doing his duty." He waited as Kajihi wrestled with the problem. "Let me be more blunt. If you do not take me, I will kill you and your family, then there will be no more Watcher here. How will that fulfill your charter?"

"What is it you need from the Roads?"

"My love."

Kajihi frowned. "I do not understand."

"My betrothed. She is buried there. I promised her I would return and I have. And I am late. Very late. Taking me to the Roads will not upset the balance of anything." Nosferatu rose to his feet, towering over the Watcher. "I have had great patience, suffered much, and traveled far, but my patience is wearing thin. Take me where I want to go. Now."

Kajihi had jumped to his feet and he stepped back in fear as Nosferatu came forward. The two Bedouin warriors closed in on either side of the Watcher.

"The Roads are dangerous," Kajihi sputtered. "I have only been down there a few times. I do not know if I can find—"

"I'll find her. You just get me in there. One entry I knew of is now underwater. The one along the Nile. The other was at the base of the Black Sphinx. Is there another way in?"

Kajihi nodded. "Yes. There are several. There is an entry at the base of the stone sphinx behind the statue of Horus, but I cannot enter there. Also one through the Great Pyramid."

"Can you get in that entrance?"

Kajihi nodded.

"Take me. Now. No more words, Watcher. I have no more patience. If you do not take me, I will kill you. And your family."

Kajihi stood still for several moments, then seemed to diminish in size as his shoulders slumped. He grabbed a gray cloak and tossed it to Nosferatu before throwing one over his own shoulders. Then he got one for each of the Bedouins. "Put these on and follow me."

They left the hut and made their way to the large temple built along the shore of the Nile. Just before the temple, Kajihi turned to the left and moved toward the Great Pyramid, creeping in the shadow of a long stone causeway that connected the two. They reached the large pile of limestone rubble at the base of the massive pyramid.

Briefly Nosferatu wondered what had become of Vampyr. Was he still alive after so many years? And if so, where had he made his lair? Did his anger and hatred still burn so brightly?

"What happened here?" Nosferatu asked, as Kajihi paused.

"According to Watcher records, shortly after the Great Pharaoh Khufu had the pyramid built, he had the smooth limestone facing that had been put on it ripped off. He also killed everyone who had ever been inside, sacrificing them to the Gods."

"That makes no sense—to destroy what you have just built."

Kajihi shrugged. "Such is the way of Gods and Pharaohs. It is not for men to understand." He pointed toward a dark opening about fifty feet up the pyramid. "There."

"Are there no guards?"

"Not outside. There is no need. Fear keeps people out. There are guards of a sort on the inside, though, for those who would be foolish enough to overcome their fear. Do as I do and we may survive."

Nosferatu remembered the strange metal spider that had killed Mosegi. His hand strayed to the knife at his belt although he knew it would do little good against the creature. When he had entered so many years ago for his tube, Kajilil had told him the gray cloak would help hide him from the creature so he had to assume that was still true.

Kajihi clambered up the large stone blocks toward the opening, Nosferatu and the two Bedouins following. He could see clearly in the darkness, but his senses were picking up something beyond what was visible.

Nekhbet.

He felt her nearby presence as something palpable, emanating from the ground. She was alive. Of that at least, he had no doubt. They entered the tunnel and the presence grew stronger. The air was still and dry as they descended into the Great Pyramid.

He could hear Kajihi counting to himself. After perhaps a quarter mile the Watcher abruptly halted. He placed his ring on a spot on the smooth rock wall and a door appeared. "Hurry," Kajihi hissed.

They passed through the door and Kajihi shut it behind them. "You are now in the Roads," he informed them.

Nosferatu slowly turned, facing one way in the stone corridor, then the other. He had no doubt about which way to go. "This way."

The other three followed as Nosferatu led them deeper along the Roads. They came to a juncture and Nosferatu unhesitatingly turned to the right. Nekhbet was close, very close. Nosferatu felt as if his chest would explode his heart was beating so wildly.

They turned another corner and he recognized the hallway through which he and his five companions had escaped so many years ago. He broke into a run, the others hustling to keep up when Kajihi suddenly halted and hissed a warning.

Nosferatu almost ignored the Watcher, but he forced himself to halt. Kajihi tapped his ear, indicating for him to listen. Nosferatu cocked his head. Metal on stone. Coming closer. Kajihi lay down, pressing against one side of the wall and throwing his cloak over his body, indicating that they should do the same. Nosferatu forced himself to the stone floor, draping the gray cloak over his body.

The sound grew closer, moving more slowly. Nosferatu could visualize the golden orb and black metal legs. His body tightened as the sound grew much closer. It was next to them, then passing. The sound faded slowly and Nosferatu twitched, anxious to move. He pulled aside the cloak and started to get to his feet, but Kajihi reached out and grabbed him, shaking his head.

Reluctantly Nosferatu once more buried himself under the cloak and waited. Minutes of silence passed. Then he heard it once more. Metal legs on stone walls. Coming their way. The creature came back down the corridor and passed once more.

As soon as the sound faded, Nosferatu was on his feet. There was no holding him back. He ran down the tunnel and skidded to a halt outside the metal bars of the cell. The gate was open and he pushed it aside, stepping in. One black tube rested on a slab in his old cell, covered with millennia of dust. Sometime in the past seven thousand years they'd moved Nekhbet back here.

Nosferatu ran his hands lightly over the lid as if he could feel her flesh instead of cold metal. Kajihi and the two Bedouins came into the cell and watched him quietly, sensing the emotion pouring off of him. Nosferatu went to the top of the tube and delicately wiped the dust from the glowing control panel.

"We must hurry," Kajihi whispered.

Much as he desired to open the tube and see his love, Nosferatu knew the Watcher was right. Plus, dawn was not far off. He gestured and the two Bedouins grabbed hold of the ends. They lifted the tube off the platform. Kajihi was back in the corridor, leading the way out. Nosferatu brought up the rear, his eyes on the tube.

They exited the Great Pyramid just as the first reddish hint of dawn was showing in the east. Nosferatu lent a hand getting the tube down the giant blocks of the pyramid to the surface of the plateau. They scurried along in the concealment of the stone causeway until they reached the large pile of stone blocks where the other four Bedouins waited.

Nosferatu had them lash the tube to the two spare camels, protecting the end still on the ground with a piece of heavy cloth. He turned to Kajihi, anxious to be into the desert before the sun cleared the horizon. "Go back to your Watching."

K☉SS☉S, CRETE: 145☉ B.C.

Seven girls and seven boys. Virgins all.

The ship from Athens delivered the yearly tribute to the long stone dock that extended from the port city of Iraklion into the harbor. Soldiers flanked the chained youths and escorted them along the dock to the waiting wagons. They were loaded on board and the small convoy made its way through the town, flickering torches in the lead soldiers' hands lighting the way. Even though it was early evening, not a person was about and store windows were shuttered. No one wanted to gaze upon the doomed youths, for it was said the very sight of them brought ill fortune.

The wagons rolled into the hills, approaching the capital palace of Knossos. It was a sign of the king's power that the palace was not surrounded by defensive walls. The

Minoan Navy ruled the waves for many miles about Crete and any enemy would have to get through that powerful force before it could even approach the island.

On top of the tallest tower in the palace, a dark figure stood, gazing down at the slowly approaching lights. To all he ruled, he was known as King Minos, who held sway over Crete, and many of the surrounding Cycladic Islands. There were those who said he was the son of Zeus and the Princess Europa. There were none alive on the island who remembered when he had taken power, and the whispers passed down said he had been in the palace for over 350 years. Some said even longer. Thus the rumors of a God as his father.

Of course, it was true to an extent.

Vampyr pulled back the hood covering his head and looked up at the stars. He felt the lust for blood rising as the caravan carrying the tribute from Athens came closer. He had learned to be careful over the years, to hide his feeding from people. He took only one victim a month, in the secrecy of the Labyrinth he had had built underneath the palace, away from the prying eyes of others. The extra two he took on special occasions—one was the anniversary of Lilith's death. The other was the anniversary of the date he had become king of Crete over 350 years earlier.

He had come there over five hundred years ago. After leaving Egypt with his tube and Aspasia's Shadow's admonition, he had traveled about the edge of the Mediterranean for two hundred years. He'd even gone inland, traveling into the Black Sea and northward into Russia, spending many years exploring. He'd seen much and learned much, but his hatred had not abated in the slightest.

Finally, growing weary, he'd taken Aspasia's Shadow's advice and hidden his tube in a cave along the coast of

Greece and climbed inside, going into the deep sleep. He'd awoken five hundred years earlier. He'd traveled back to Egypt, where he learned that the Airlia had disappeared and that Shadows had ruled. Then even the Shadows had given way to men. He made plans to enter the Roads of Rostau and search out the four surviving Airlia to slay them—if that was indeed where they slept—but Aspasia's Shadow had appeared and Vampyr had been forced to leave his ancient land and go back to wandering.

He'd killed many humans over those years, many for sustenance and many more for vengeance.

He'd eventually realized that he needed power and leverage in the world of men if he was ever going to strike back at the Gods and destroy Aspasia's Shadow. He'd traveled to this island, where he slowly began taking command. First one village, then another. Banding together disparate groups until finally the island was one kingdom.

He ruled through fear, which he had found to be the strongest of human emotions. The slightest transgression against his reign was punished with torture, then death. He had had every man who worked on the Labyrinth underneath the palace executed after its completion so that none knew its secret ways but he. The fate of the youths who were sent into its depths every year was the subject of much conjecture among the populace. Some said a monster, half-man, half-beast, lived under the palace and fed on the flesh of the youths. Close, Vampyr mused as he watched the convoy approach. It was a rumor he did nothing to contradict. A king who held sway over monsters was a powerful king indeed.

Vampyr estimated that he needed forty more years of conquest and expansion before his kingdom would be powerful enough to challenge Egypt. While a long time for a human, it was but a moment for Vampyr.

The convoy had entered the palace and passed from sight below. Vampyr left the turret and made his way down the stairs that wound around the interior of the tower. He passed through ground level and continued to the roads he'd had built underneath. Vampyr moved through rough, rock-hewn corridors, the workmanship shoddy compared to that of the Roads of Rostau.

The hunger grew in Vampyr as he got closer to the Labyrinth. He knew his soldiers had already pushed the youths into the antechamber, which opened onto four doorways. Each doorway led into the Labyrinth, but the youths didn't know that. And each doorway opened inward but there was no handle on the other side. For the first fifty years or so, Vampyr had watched the antechamber through a peephole, interested to see how the youths would react. They always ended up taking the doors. Sometimes all fourteen would go through the same one; sometimes the group would splinter. But they all ended up in the Labyrinth.

There were places in the Labyrinth where food would be lowered daily, allowing the youths to feed. There were also two wells. And once a month Vampyr would hunt, taking a tender, young neck and the fresh blood. One by one they would fall to him while those that survived grew ever more frantic.

None had ever escaped.

Tonight he would take the first.

Vampyr moved to a large stone inset in at the end of the corridor. Putting his hand in the right spot, he pushed and the balanced rock turned, opening up a slight space on the left. Vampyr slid through, closing the rock behind him. He was in the Labyrinth.

Vampyr stood perfectly still, listening.

There was a strange noise, one he had not heard before. From beneath him. From the earth itself.

Vampyr staggered as the stone floor shifted under his
feet. A tremendous roar filled the air. Vampyr looked up
in time to see a large stone come crashing down on him.

CHAPTER 4

NEKHBET. NOSFERATU SENSED HER presence in the tube being dragged behind the two camels as strongly as he felt the sun beating down on the cloth wrapped around his body to protect his skin and eyes. They pushed on, into the Great Desert, leaving Giza behind. The Bedouins were keeping a southerly course, the Nile far off to their left, the Great Desert extending in all other directions. One Bedouin followed behind the party with a palm branch, sweeping away their tracks.

KAJIHI HAD SAID nothing as Nosferatu and his Bedouins headed to the southwest, into the desert. As soon as they were out of sight he hurried back to his hut. His wife and children were still gone and would stay away until he sent for them. He pulled out a piece of thick papyrus paper. He wrote, telling of Nosferatu's visit. He rolled the papyrus and stuffed it into a piece of bamboo, sealing each end with wax that he imprinted with the Watcher crest from his ring. He then placed the tube on top of four others, his reports of activity in Egypt for the past fifteen years. Soon it would be time to forward them to England, to Watcher headquarters.

As he tied the tubes together he sensed a presence. He

looked up to see a man—no, not a man—a creature in human form standing over him. He knew who it was even though they had never met before.

Kajihi bowed his head, refusing to meet the stare of the other.

"Kajihi, the Watcher, the *Wedjat*."

Kajihi nodded. "Aspasia's Shadow."

"You have had a visitor." Aspasia's Shadow sat down cross-legged on the dirt floor. He looked very much like Nosferatu, tall, thin, with an evil grin. The major difference was that Aspasia's Shadow had jet-black hair instead of red.

"How did you know?"

"Someone has been in the Roads of Rostau with you."

Kajihi nodded.

"Who?"

"Nosferatu."

"Ah, so the legend is true. I remember when Isis and Osiris were killed. Two of the brood who committed the crime escaped. I've met one several times. Vampyr. But that was a very long time ago," he added, almost to himself. "What did Nosferatu want?"

"He took a black tube. He said his love was in it."

Aspasia's Shadow nodded. "Nekhbet. Where did he go?"

"Into the desert to the south and west."

"Interesting."

Kajihi kept his eyes downcast, hoping the creature would leave, also knowing it was just as likely that Aspasia's Shadow would kill him.

"What did you write?" Aspasia's Shadow indicated the tubes.

"A report of recent events."

"That will be so useful," Aspasia's Shadow said with a

laugh. The smile disappeared and Aspasia's Shadow leaned over Kajihi. "Watcher."

Kajihi reluctantly looked up. "Yes?"

"The Roads of Rostau are not for you or the Undead. Do you understand?"

"Yes." But Aspasia's Shadow was gone.

T⊕ +HE S⊕U+HWES+, the last things on Nosferatu's mind were Watchers, reports, or Aspasia's Shadow. The sun was well over the horizon, shooting beams of light across the desert. He wrapped another turban around his face, further protecting his skin and eyes. They rode through the day, putting distance between them and Giza. By noon, Nosferatu had triple-wrapped his head, practically cutting out all light, allowing himself to be led by the Bedouins deeper into the desert known as the Great Sand Sea. When he questioned them about how far it was to the other side, they always shook their heads and indicated the next destination was an oasis they knew of. Beyond that, they didn't say anything. He realized their concept of travel was much different than his and he didn't know enough of their language to make himself understood.

As the day wore on, Nosferatu rode in a daze, directly behind Nekhbet's tube. He had no doubt she was in there and that she was alive, although he had little clue as to what condition he would find her in when he opened the tube.

At his urging they rode straight through the night and finally halted just before the next dawn at the small oasis. Nosferatu felt the hunger, but he knew he needed the aid of the Bedouins more than he needed to feed. The desert people were a strange race, having nothing to do with

Egypt or the Gods, or, now, the Pharaohs, preferring to live in a land where survival was an everyday struggle. To them, distance and time all related to water holes like this.

As the sun rose, Nosferatu lay next to Nekhbet's tube, covering himself with blankets despite the heat. He placed both hands against the side of the tube. Surprisingly, the metal was cool. He slowly fell into unconsciousness, the effort of the last few days and the growing hunger forcing his mind and body to retreat into itself.

He woke at dusk. He pushed aside the blankets and unwrapped the turbans from his head. It was cool, the sand giving up the day's heat, a light breeze blowing in from the deep desert. The Bedouins were cooking a meal on the other side of the small water hole, ignoring Nosferatu and the tube. When complete darkness fell, Nosferatu went to the head of the tube. The control panel was alive with a glow that grew brighter as the sky grew darker.

Nosferatu's hands trembled. From hunger, from anticipation. He tried to control the shake, but couldn't. He knew he should wait. Opening the tube there and then would do no good. They must get across the desert. But she was there, so close, only the lid between the two of them after so many years apart, after so many years so close.

He tapped on the hexes. With a hiss, the lid cracked open and slowly swung up.

She was as beautiful as the first time he had seen her brought into the cell under the Giza Plateau. Long flowing red hair splayed about her head. Smooth white skin stretched over high cheekbones. Red eyebrows cut across her lower forehead above her closed eyes. She was swathed in the same white robe he had seen her entombed in. Her pale lips were slightly parted, revealing perfect white teeth.

Nosferatu placed his hand on her forehead, just below the metal band. Her skin was cool to his touch. He moved his hand to just over her mouth. He felt nothing. There was no rise or fall to her chest, but he knew she was alive. The metal crown was still set on her head and he carefully reached in and removed it.

He knew how to bring her to full life. In the same way she had given him power so long ago.

But he was weak. He had the hunger. He looked up, across the water hole at the half dozen Bedouins. A muscle on the side of his face twitched. His heart was racing. He ran his fingers over Nekhbet's face, marveling at the smoothness, the coolness, longing for the heat he had imagined for so long, that they had discussed for centuries.

He knew better. Patience had been chained into him. To act just then would be a mistake.

Nosferatu stepped away from the tube. He began walking around the water hole. All six of the Bedouins stopped what they were doing and looked at him. Despite his weakened state, the presence of Nekhbet gave him power unlike any he had ever known, even when he had drunk from Osiris himself. The six blades, the blades with which they had killed Osiris, were strung about his belt.

One of the Bedouins, the leader, was the first to realize the danger, drawing his scimitar. The blade didn't even clear the scabbard as Nosferatu drew and threw the first dagger, the blade hitting the leader's neck square on. The man staggered back, hands grasping at the handle. Nosferatu threw the second blade with his other hand as he pulled the third. Four of the Bedouins were down before they could mount a defense. The last two had their swords out as he threw the fifth dagger.

The man blocked the oncoming missile and charged Nosferatu.

The sixth ran away.

Nosferatu dodged the man's wild strike, stepped in close, and wrapped the Bedouin in his arms. He clamped down on the man's neck, tearing through flesh to blood. As it had always been, the struggle was one-sided as Nosferatu gained strength and his victim lost it. Out of the corner of his eye, even as he drank, Nosferatu watched the sixth man running—keeping track. The Bedouin tried to leap onto one of the camels, but his fear made the animal skittish and he was unable to mount it.

Nosferatu drank, knowing he needed to break free and capture the last man. Love won out against hunger and he threw the victim from him and ran toward the sixth man, who was by then running up the side of a dune. With the energy from drinking, Nosferatu easily caught him and dragged him down. The man fought, but a blow to the side of his head rendered him unconscious.

Nosferatu dragged the man back to the side of Nekhbet's tube. He lifted the Bedouin and slid him into the tube next to his love. With a dagger, he punctured the man's neck, quickly sliding a finger in to keep the blood from spurting out. He dropped the dagger and turned Nekhbet's head toward the man.

He waited, letting a little blood seep out. The first sign of life was a slight flare of her nostrils. The head moved ever so slightly, the mouth opening. Her eyes were still closed but she could scent the blood, feel its proximity. As her open mouth closed on the wound, Nosferatu removed his hand, letting the life force flow forth.

Nekhbet drained the man in less than a minute. Nosferatu marveled to see the glow come to her cheeks, her chest begin to rise and fall with steady breaths. Her eyes flashed open, fixing on his. She smiled, red-stained lips parting to reveal crimson-covered teeth. He leaned over and kissed her, blood on blood.

EIGHT DAYS. And still no end in sight to the desert. Nosferatu looked over the moonlit sand, the same view they'd had every night since he'd brought Nekhbet back. She was at his side on one of the camels, another two animals behind them, dragging her tube. He knew she was weakening. He cursed himself for not keeping more of the Bedouins alive so they could feed again. He had anticipated being out of the desert in a day or two and able to hunt. But there was nothing out to hunt. The only living thing he'd seen since leaving the site of the massacre was a lone bird far off in the distance one evening.

His mind was feverish with hunger. He had to fight to convince himself that they were actually moving forward and not simply marching in the same spot night after night. He kept them oriented by the position of the stars, steadily moving to the south. How long could such desolation go on? He knew the Nile was to the east. Where there was water there would be people to feed on. But Egypt's reign extended far down that strip of water and the long hand of the Airlia Gods reached down the blue waterway also.

The days, though, were bliss. Lying next to Nekhbet in her tube, talking, touching, and feeling each other's closeness. Even the intense heat blazing into the tube was tolerable to be close to his love.

But if they did not feed soon, he knew they would run out of energy and be consumed by the desert.

"Feed from me and go on."

Nosferatu was startled by Nekhbet's words. They

didn't just intrude on his dark thoughts, the words assaulted his mind. "Never again."

Nekhbet brought her breast next to his and reached out, touching his arm. "You freed me from the living sleep. That is love enough."

Nosferatu had not wanted to know about the years she had been in the tube and she had said nothing yet. "Was it bad?"

"I could only lie there and think. I could not move even though twice every twenty-four hours the wraps on my body did as they had done when we were imprisoned together, working my muscles—it was the only way I knew the passage of time.

"At first I thought I would go mad. But then I started remembering all we had talked of. And I thought of those conversations." She smiled. "And then I kept them going. I would try to think of what you would say. And then I would reply. We had the most wonderful talks. I would also invent places. That we would visit together. Beautiful places."

Nosferatu was silent. His time in the tube before his escape had been horrible indeed, but at least he had been able to sleep almost half the time. And he could always look forward to the daily feeding when he would see Nekhbet. She had had nothing to look forward to and been unable to sleep for over six thousand years. A time he had spent in darkness and ignorance. He spurred the camel.

"We will make it out of this desert together. I promise you that."

Nekhbet smiled sadly once more, but her head was shaking ever so slightly. "You do not believe me. You saved me from something worse than death. I would welcome becoming part of the desert. And I have had the last seven nights and days with you. That is worth a lifetime."

"We will go forward together or perish together," Nosferatu said simply.

But on the next night he knew it would be their last. They were expending too much energy with nothing to replenish their stores. Perhaps they could go into Nekhbet's tube and set the device to put them to sleep for a millennium or two and hope the land had changed by then. But there was only one crown in there and one set of wraps.

"Feed on me, then put me into the deep sleep in my tube," Nekhbet said. "It is the only way we will manage it."

Just before dawn he draped cloths over the tube to protect it from the direct rays of the sun and climbed inside with Nekhbet. They passed the day holding each other and whispering of a future in a land that was green and full of life, one where they did not have to worry about the Airlia Gods swooping down out of the sky and destroying them.

As the temperature went down in the tube, they knew darkness was not far off. And that Nekhbet did not have the strength to ride on. He sensed she would not even have the energy to lift herself out of the tube.

"We must have a plan for the future," Nekhbet finally said.

"We have been talking—" Nosferatu began, but she hushed him with a light touch of her finger on his lips.

"We have been fantasizing. The real world is much harsher. You have told me there are those out there who would kill us. The Ones Who Wait. Guides. Even the Gods who made us and hate us lurk somewhere, I am sure. I've waited long enough. I want to sleep. To truly rest. To wait for the time when we can be free. And there is this also—" She halted.

"What?" Nosferatu prompted.

"I have been drained far too many times," Nekhbet said. "Without the blood of the Gods, like we took from Osiris, I have aged. Not as fast as a human, but faster than you, my love."

"I do not know where the Gods are," Nosferatu said, understanding what she was saying.

"I know. That will be your task. If you love me, you will take responsibility. You will be the one who watches and waits to bring me back when we can have a life together and when I can drink from a God."

Nosferatu knew she was right. His plan had been shortsighted. If they were to have a life together, he would have to envision time much differently. He held her tightly, wasting precious hours of darkness.

She gingerly unwrapped his arms from around her body and whispered, "Now. Drink from me one last time."

"You said—"

"One last time," she said, leaning her head on his shoulder. "It will not matter since I will go into deep sleep, but it will give you the strength you need, and it is the closest we can be."

He pulled aside the cloth from around her neck and touched the shunt with his lips. The first trickle of blood sent a surge of energy into his body. He only took a little, enough to keep him going for another couple of days, then he stopped. He climbed out of the tube and looked down on Nekhbet. Her eyes were half-closed and unfocused, her skin pale. He prepared her, putting the wraps on her legs and arms.

With the stars shining down on him, Nosferatu stood over the tube. "Good-bye, my love. I will awaken you when we can freely walk the world together."

Nekhbet's lips twitched in a weak smile. She didn't even have the energy to speak. Nosferatu slowly closed the lid. Then he went to the control panel. He touched the hexes, directing the alien technology of the tube to put her into the deep sleep he'd been in.

He attached the tube to the ropes connected to the camels' saddles. Then he mounted his own camel and continued the trek south. He felt the isolation of the desert, the utter loneliness. Nekhbet's aura was so muted he could hardly sense her.

By dawn, nothing had changed. Nosferatu slept next to the tube, covered in robes. As soon as the sun began to set, he rose and resumed the journey. Just after midnight he rode to the top of a high dune and paused as he peered to the south. There appeared to be a silver mist on the horizon. He didn't know what it was, but it wasn't the same view he'd had for the past ten nights. Any change had to be for the better.

He pushed the mounts forward, the two camels dragging the tube struggling to keep up with him. After an hour the mist seemed no closer, and Nosferatu began to fear it was an illusion. Even after several more hours the silver apparition still hovered over the horizon, but lower and closer, he saw a dark line on the ground. Just before dawn the line was close and he knew it indicated vegetation—the edge of the desert. And where there was plant life there would be people. And where there were people, there would be blood.

KNOSSOS, CRETE: 1450 B.C.

It was completely dark. As black as the inside of his tube. Vampyr turned his head to and fro, trying to find any light, while his hands explored the large stone that lay across his thighs, pinning him in place. How long had he been unconscious? He had no idea, but the hunger was gnawing at him.

He tried with all his superhuman might to move the stone off his legs but to no avail. His legs didn't feel injured, but he couldn't move them. After several more attempts to free himself, he laid his head back on the stone floor and closed his eyes.

Vampyr had no idea how long he stayed like that, trapped in his own Labyrinth. Days at least. Perhaps a week. The hunger grew stronger with each hour that passed. He tried several times to free himself, each attempt draining him of energy.

Sometimes he thought he heard voices, but in his weakened state he wasn't sure if they were real or delusions. His soldiers didn't know where he was and, even if they did, he knew they would not come for him. Ruling by fear had its disadvantages.

There was a noise and Vampyr turned his head, straining to hear. Something was moving in the dark, coming slowly closer. He heard voices and now he was sure they were real. Young voices, speaking Greek.

"Help me," Vampyr cried out in the same language.

There was total silence in response.

"I know the way out," Vampyr yelled. *"If you help me, I will get you out of here."*

Vampyr couldn't make out the whispered words the youths exchanged. He knew they had to be hungry and scared. He sniffed, picking up their scent. He felt the hunger surge, but he fought to control it.

"Who are you?" a fearful voice queried.

"A caretaker of the tunnels," Vampyr lied. *"I know the passages. I will help you escape."*

There was more whispering and Vampyr reined in his impatience. What choice did they think they had even to be discussing it? One of the youths was crying, a girl, and someone hushed her angrily.

A decision apparently made, he could hear the youths making their way toward him in the darkness. He called out several times so they could find him. He directed them to the stone across his thighs. With their help, he was able to push it off. He staggered to his feet. He knew the exit from the Labyrinth was right behind him.

The blood scent of the fourteen youths all around him was overpowering.

Vampyr reached out and grabbed the closest, a young girl. He wrapped one hand over her mouth while he tore into her neck with his teeth. He savored the blood flowing into his mouth even as he heard the leader of the youths just a few feet away demand he show them the way out. Vampyr slowly backed up, the girl in his arms, unseen in the darkness. His back hit the swinging stone and he passed through into the tunnel beyond.

He pressed the stone shut while he finished draining the girl. He lowered her body to the floor and turned, making his way back the way he had come so many days before. The torches that lined the corridor had burned out and he picked his way carefully, several times having to step over stones knocked loose by the earthquake.

After several minutes he saw a glimmer of light ahead and knew he was approaching ground level. The light grew stronger and he reached the wooden door leading to the palace. The frame around the door had buckled and he could see starlight through the cracks. With a mighty shove, he yanked it open and walked into the courtyard.

The palace was destroyed. What had taken over seventy-five years to build had been destroyed.

Vampyr slowly turned, taking in the ruins. He sniffed the air and his nose confirmed what he had suspected—

not only was the palace destroyed, it was abandoned. Centuries of work building an empire undone in one moment.

Vampyr wandered through the remnants of his once magnificent palace. There were bodies here and there, some killed by the earthquake, others in the fighting afterward. The palace had been looted and stripped bare—even his throne had been stolen.

Vampyr went behind the throne room, to a secret passageway hidden by a rotating stone similar to the one leading to the Labyrinth. He passed through, then down a set of stone stairs to a thick wooden door, which he unlocked with a key hanging from a chain around his neck. He entered, locking the door behind him. Inside the chamber, set on a stone pedestal, was his black tube. He crawled into it, pulling the lid shut.

Vampyr slept for fourteen straight days, recovering.

On the fifteenth night, he arose. He left his lair and went back to the Labyrinth to feed. Catching another of the youths was easy, as they were slowly starving to death. Sated from the two feedings in two weeks, Vampyr went back to the surface to ponder his future, leaving the twelve surviving Greek youths trapped in the Labyrinth without a thought.

The tall tower had been destroyed in the earthquake. He sat on the pile of rubble that was all that was left of it and looked about. He could see smoke from fires slowly rising into the air. He had kept a tight leash on the people of Crete for over a century. He was enough of a realist to understand that leash could not be put back on.

He went below the palace to his hidden tube chamber. He barred the door and climbed inside. He set the control panel as he had watched Aspasia's Shadow do, except adjusting the time for a shorter amount. Then he shut the lid on his ruined empire.

AFRICA: 1450 B.C.

Nosferatu had been forced to leave Nekhbet's tube for three days while he ranged the edge of the jungle in search of blood. On the third night he came upon a small hunting party and turned the tables on them over the course of the next two nights, taking down four of their number, a pair each night, to feed on.

Gorged, he returned to where he'd left Nekhbet's tube. He knew he could wake her and feed her human blood, but then they would be back where they were before. She would still age more rapidly than Nosferatu because she'd been more completely drained of her original half-Airlia blood more than he. He needed the blood of the Gods, and that was not possible just then.

The camels had refused to go forward shortly after entering the jungle. Nosferatu had been forced to release them so they could go back to their beloved desert. He slept next to the tube that day, robes and blankets covering him, the noise of the daytime jungle all around. When darkness fell he packed up all he had, tying everything to the top of the tube. Then he grabbed hold of the harness, looping the straps over his shoulders, and leaned into it.

Nosferatu made it a half mile into the jungle that first night.

The second night he did slightly better, covering almost a mile.

The third night he quickly fed, got back in harness, and pushed forward into deepest, darkest Africa for another mile.

And so he moved south, pulling his love behind him, blazing a narrow trail through the thick jungle.

After a month he passed along a ridgeline and an opening in the jungle gave him a view of the land to the south.

Nosferatu came to a halt, staring at the vista. Mountains with their peaks covered in white clouds filled the southern horizon. He realized they were what he had seen from the desert so long ago.

Nosferatu looked left and right. The mountains stretched in both directions. He assumed there was a way around, and his inclination was to the right, to the west, as he needed to get to that coast eventually. But how far would it be to get around the range? Would there be more desert? Nosferatu stepped back, releasing the pressure from the harness. He had calluses on his shoulder where the leather bands had rubbed for so long. His body was hard, all muscle.

It had been four days since he'd fed, and he was burning energy at a high rate. He realized he would never be able to pull Nekhbet's tube across another desert, even a small one. The mountains ahead promised to be an extremely difficult endeavor.

And what did it matter, he realized, if he did get her to the Skeleton Coast? So they could sleep next to each other every day, while he waited for the time to bring her back?

Nosferatu looked at the peaks. He focused on the center one, a mountain slightly apart from the others. Leaning into the straps, he headed toward it.

He reached the base in a week, surprised to find himself in the midst of swamp and marshes. He splashed his way through, the going actually easier where he could partially float the tube. Then he reached a place where the watery landscape gave way as the ground sloped up. He began the arduous task of pulling the tube upslope. He wondered if the peaks were the source of the Nile as streams splashed down the rocky terrain around him. It was certainly the strangest place he'd ever been. At one point he passed through a bizarre level on the slopes where monstrous plants grew among the rocks, some over ten or twenty times the normal size. Nosferatu picked up a sense of the primeval about the place, as if it had been forgotten in some hole in time, while the world around it had progressed.

After ten days, most of the vegetation fell behind as he passed above the tree line. The terrain now was the exact opposite of what it had been. A few bushes struggled to grow, clinging to wind-scoured rocks. He was in the mist now, able to see only a short distance ahead. Several times he had to retreat and try to find a different way as he ran into slopes that were too steep to pull the tube up.

Twice he had to abandon Nekhbet's tube and make the climb down to the more temperate zone to hunt the villagers who lived at the base of the mountains. Each feeding cost him a four-day round-trip and almost wasn't worth the effort by the time he climbed back up.

Soon he was in snow, the whiteness blinding as he pulled the tube upward. Finally, he could go no farther. There was no trail and he would have to climb hand over hand to go higher. Nosferatu rested the next day, then spent the evening searching the mountainside.

On the third night, he found a small cave, more a crack in the side of the mighty mountain that extended about twelve feet in, but was only waist high. The fourth night he moved Nekhbet's tube into the cave, shoving it ahead of him until it touched the end.

He spent the next day sitting cross-legged at the foot of the tube, swathed in robes and cloaks taken from victims to protect him from both the cold and the white mist light. He was tired and the hunger was strong. But he did not want to leave. Though he had slept for thousands of years and some things had changed, the world still was not a safe place for Nekhbet and him. How many more years would have to pass before he came back and recovered and revived her so they could walk the world together?

Nosferatu felt the cold hand of loneliness begin to grip his heart.

He spent another day and night and the following day at the foot of her tube until finally he knew the time had come. He leaned over and placed his hands on the cold metal. His lips lightly touched the smooth surface with a last kiss, then he slid out of the hole and began piling rocks in it, covering the tube. When he was done, there was no sign of the hole, just a small clutter of rocks along the side of the mountain.

"I will return," he whispered. Then Nosferatu turned and headed downslope, leaving his love behind on the mountainside.

CHAPTER 5

VAMPYR WATCHED THE PLUMES of gray smoke rise in the night air. The horizon in the direction of the Giza Plateau glowed blood-red from the hundreds of fires the invaders had set. Even at this distance he could hear the cries of the wounded and the pleas of prisoners prior to summary execution by the invading Assyrians.

The Third Age of Egypt was over.

Vampyr knew there were battles raging in other places throughout the kingdom. The third Pharaoh of the Twenty-fifth Dynasty, Taharqa, still had forces under his command and was slowly giving way to the south, continuing a war that had been going on for fifty years and ranged in scope from Palestine to Ethiopia. Chaos was rampant, and the opportunity for which Vampyr had waited so long finally presented itself.

He moved quickly, running across the desert sands toward the east and the plateau. He'd followed the western flank of the Assyrian Army, staying far out in the desert, as it closed on Giza. He hoped in all the turmoil to steer clear of Aspasia's Shadow if he was about.

As he crested a dune, Vampyr saw the plateau. The three pyramids were silhouetted by flames from the wooden temples and other structures that dotted the area. Vampyr headed directly for the river area, but the Watcher's hut was empty. Hiding, Vampyr had no doubt. He grabbed a gray cloak from a peg near the door and left the hut, throwing the Watcher's cloak over his shoulders.

Vampyr ran to the edge of the Nile, moving along until he saw an old weather- and waterworn stone pillar. Vampyr looked around and spotted a large rock. He picked it up and grasped to it his chest. Then he jumped into the river.

The weight of the stone quickly pulled him under. Even in the dark water he could see relatively well and he spotted the opening for the Roads of Rostau. He let go of the stone and pulled himself toward the opening, only to find that the water of the Nile was streaming into the opening with such force, that he was immediately sucked in. He was pushed along with the current, tumbling against the smooth stone walls.

Vampyr spread his arms and legs wide, pressing against the walls of the tunnel. His left hand slipped into a side opening and his fingers clawed at the edge, grabbing hold and bringing him to a halt. It took all of his strength to pull himself into the side opening against the force of the current. He was in another tunnel, one where the water was still. Lungs bursting, Vampyr swam forward, not sure at all what direction he was going in.

He popped to the surface, gasping for air, looking about. There was a ledge about two feet above his head where the tunnel he was in opened up. He realized he had diverted into a shaft that went upward and he must have achieved the surface level of the Nile. He reached up and pulled himself into the chamber. There was a minute bit of light given off by a thin strip that ran around the top edge of the chamber, not enough for a human to pick up, but enough for Vampyr's half-alien eyes to see his surroundings. The chamber was twenty feet square with a door in one wall. Dripping, Vampyr went to the door and walked into a corridor. He sniffed and picked up the faint scent of humans. He turned in their direction.

He found the Watcher and his family camped inside the Great Pyramid entrance to the roads, a stone guarding the outside opening. They were huddled in the darkness and did not see or hear him approaching. He saw an old man, an old woman, and two grown sons. He had no desire to negotiate. He walked right up to the family, grabbed the old man, and tore his throat out.

Screams echoed in the darkness as one of the sons tried to light a torch and the mother and other son yelled for the father. When the torch came alive, it revealed Vampyr holding the eldest male in his arms, drained of blood and life. Vampyr threw the body to the floor and glared at the three survivors.

"I will kill all of you unless you take me where I want to go."

The son with the torch had a dagger in his other hand and charged Vampyr with a yell. Moving faster than the young man could have anticipated, Vampyr snatched the dagger from his attacker's hand. Vampyr hit the young man in the chest with an open palm, sending him tumbling back, the torch flying from his hand. In the flickering light, Vampyr took a threatening step forward. He pointed at the one who had held the torch.

The young man got to his feet. "You are one of the creatures. The Undead." He looked at his father's body. "He warned me about you." He turned to his mother and brother. "Stay here. I will be back."

The old woman took no notice, throwing herself on

the body of her slain husband and letting loose with an ululating wail that echoed down the tunnel. The younger brother went to console his mother.

"Your name?" Vampyr asked as he nudged the older brother away from the spectacle and into the Roads.

"Kajin of the line of Kaji the Watcher."

"You people are like rats," Vampyr said, as they continued, the mother's cries chasing them.

"And what do you consider yourself?" Kajin demanded.

Vampyr did not answer. "I want to know where the Gods sleep. And where the Grail is kept."

"You cannot get to the Grail," Kajin said. "The key was taken away from here a long time ago. And where the Gods sleep is guarded by a terrible creature. You cannot enter."

"Take me to the Grail first anyway."

Kajin shrugged. They wove their way deeper into the rock, Kajin counting steps and intersections to himself. Finally, he halted and turned to what appeared to be a blank wall. He placed a medallion that hung around his neck against a point on the wall. The outline of a doorway appeared and the door slid open.

Kajin and Vampyr walked in. Vampyr halted on a narrow ledge overlooking a huge cavern. Light that hurt Vampyr's eyes reflected down from a five-meter orb overhead. The far end of the cavern was a half mile away and the walls, which Vampyr recognized, were curved. When last he had seen them, they had been open to the light of the sun and stars. A hundred feet below was something else Vampyr had last seen under an open sky: the Black Sphinx.

"The Hall of Records," Kajin said. "The Grail is within. The Ark and sword, though, are gone."

"The Ark? What sword? Who took them?"

"When the Israelites rebelled, a woman and man came here. They knew the tunnels. They were able to get into the Black Sphinx, as they had their own key with them. They took the Ark and the Grail, and the great sword Excalibur, and left, joining the Israelites in their Exodus. Forty years later, one of my order came here with the Grail and put it back inside. Then he left with the key and went far away. I do not know any more than that."

Vampyr had never heard of this Ark or the sword Excalibur. He suspected the man and woman who had come here were the same that had freed him so many years ago—Donnchadh and Gwalcmai. Troublemakers. Trying to upset the order of things, something Vampyr could understand quite well. The woman had said she hated the Airlia Gods, and that was also something Vampyr felt a kinship to.

Stairs cut out of the rock itself led down to the floor on which the Sphinx rested. Its paws extended almost sixty feet in front of the head, which rose seventy feet above the floor. The body stretched one hundred and eighty feet back from the head, making the whole thing almost three hundred feet long. Between the paws was a statue about three yards tall, which Vampyr recognized—a statue of Horus, one of the six original Airlia.

"You have no idea where your order hid the key?" To have the Grail so close yet be unable to get to it grated on him.

"None. He who took it never returned."

Vampyr cursed. He believed the Watcher, as it was what he would have done. "Take me to where *they* sleep."

"It is guarded."

"Take me there."

"You will not—"

"Now."

Kajin's shoulders slumped in resignation. He led the way, moving through the tunnels. Three times he opened hidden doors. They were going deeper into the Roads than Vampyr had ever been.

Kajin paused. "The way beyond is guarded by the golden spider. We can use the cloaks to hide from it, but if we move, it will come to us."

"How far is it to where they sleep?" Vampyr asked.

"The corridor beyond goes straight for twenty feet, then splits into two branches. The Gods sleep to the right. To the left is another duat, directly underneath the Great Pyramid."

"What is in that duat?"

"A horrible weapon that my father said could destroy the entire plateau."

"Is there another door to the chamber where the Gods sleep?"

"No. This is the last door."

"You will open this door, then you will go to the left, toward the weapon," Vampyr said. "If you do that, I will let your brother and mother live."

Comprehension came over Kajin's face in a cascade of emotion. Fear, anger, then resignation. "Why should I trust you?"

"Because you have no choice."

Kajin put the medallion to the wall and another hidden door appeared and slid open.

"Go," Vampyr ordered.

Kajin took a deep breath, pulled his gray cloak tight about his body, then entered. Vampyr watched him as he went straight, then turned left. Vampyr remained perfectly still, and his patience was rewarded as the strange glowing gold creature with black metal legs appeared, scuttling across the intersection from right to left.

Vampyr then sprinted into the lowest level. He turned right and the tunnel descended. He saw a red glow ahead and skidded to a halt when he came into a large chamber. There were six platforms on which rested black tubes. Vampyr ran to the closest. The lights on the control panel were dark. He realized this tube had been either Isis's or Osiris's and was empty. He moved to the next. Also dark.

The third was lit. Vampyr tapped in the commands shutting the tube down. The screen went dark. He moved to the next three, doing the same thing.

A scream echoed into the chamber from the corridor outside.

Vampyr saw a rack of six spears, the ones the Gods had used against him and the others so long ago. He grabbed one on his way out of the chamber. He ran up the tunnel but just before he reached the intersection the golden spider appeared, blood dripping from two of its metal legs. Vampyr leveled the spear and slid his finger into an indentation on the grip. He pressed it and a golden bolt came out of the end of the spear and hit the orb. The creature was knocked back several feet and Vampyr fired again, smashing it against the walls. The legs gave way and it fell to the ground, inert.

Vampyr stepped over it to the intersection. He paused. Kajin had said there was a powerful weapon in the other duat. Vampyr knew there were other Gods, sleeping in other places. The high priests had been certain of that and Aspasia's Shadow had confirmed it. A powerful weapon could be useful.

It could also be dangerous.

Time was pressing. Vampyr headed for the surface, arriving at the place where he had left the Watcher family, not surprised to find they had fled and left the outer door open. He exited onto the side of the Great Pyramid. Dawn was not far off and he had a feeling Aspasia's Shadow wasn't either.

Turning to the west, Vampyr fled into the desert, heading for the spot where he had left his tube.

M✪UNT SINAI, ARABIAN PENINSULA: 671 B.C.

It wasn't the tallest peak in the region, a mountain to the southeast being a few hundred feet taller, but it dominated the terrain all around. The locals called it *Jabal Mosa* for the Hebrew leader who had brought his people here on their Exodus from captivity in Egypt on the way to Israel. Of course, if one drew a straight line from Egypt to Israel, *Jabal Mosa* was not anywhere close to being on that line.

Even before the Israelites came to the foot of the mountain, the place was one of reverence for the people of the desert. They worshipped the moon God, *Sin*, for whom the entire peninsula was named, but the mountain was one they feared and avoided. There was always a cloud around the top of the peak, even on the clearest day, a most unnatural thing.

There was rumor of a creature, who might be a god but looked like a man, named Al-Iblis, who haunted the mountain and the surrounding area and who traveled to Egypt and other distant lands on occasion. This legend stretched so far back in time, that none had heard of a time when the shadow of Al-Iblis did not stretch over the desert.

Deep inside *Jabal Mosa*, which the Christians would not rename Mount Sinai for several centuries, Aspasia's Shadow had cultivated his persona as Al-Iblis among the people of the desert for centuries. He had no Airlia blood running through his veins and thus was required every normal life span to return to Mount Sinai to have a new body regenerated and his memories and personality implanted into the new clone, much as he had been "born" with Aspasia's memory and personality so many years before.

He carried these memories in a small device that hung on a chain around his neck in the form of two hands outstretched in prayer. It was called a *ka* and he kept it as updated as possible. Against the unlikely event he died while away from Mount Sinai, a fresh body was always ready in the regeneration tube and the memories through his last visit were in the Guardian computer. If he did not return by a specified year, the memories would be implanted, the body brought up to speed, and Aspasia's Shadow would live once more, lacking only the most recent memories since the last update.

As alarms sounded and the Guardian informed him of the trouble in Egypt—that someone had penetrated the Roads of Rostau—Aspasia's Shadow had other matters on his mind. He had just returned from a foray into the Mediterranean to assess the burgeoning civilization in Greece. He was impressed with what the humans were accomplishing, but they were millennia away from being a threat to Aspasia, who was his charge. However, the journey had taken a toll on his body and a fall from a horse while traversing Anatolia, which would later become Turkey, had wrenched his back, leaving him in agonizing pain.

Aspasia's Shadow walked up to the Guardian computer—a golden pyramid buried deep in a chamber inside the mountain—and sat in a chair just in front of the ten-foot-high object. A golden glow came out of the

Guardian and encompassed him. His body hurt, not only from the bad back but also from the arthritis that often plagued a human body beginning to succumb to age. He was immediately updated on the situation in Egypt from the various surveillance devices hidden there by the Airlia.

Great changes had occurred while he had been away and Aspasia's Shadow slowly reviewed them.

The Assyrians had overthrown the Pharaoh and held sway in the land. And Vampyr had infiltrated the Roads and shut down the tubes of the four remaining Airlia. Aspasia's Shadow was not surprised by that. He knew the power of vengeance and he had let Vampyr live this long, expecting such an outcome sooner or later. The six Airlia who had been left in Egypt had overstepped the mandate given them by Aspasia prior to his departure to Mars with the rest of his followers to go into the deep sleep. They were supposed to set up a civilization with instructions to get the Great Pyramid built as a signal into space, not set themselves up as Gods. The last four had finally gone into the deep sleep—following two thousand years of rule—after the Undead had rebelled and killed Isis and Osiris.

The pyramid plan had failed. It had been built by one of the Pharaohs according to the plans passed down, but rather than signaling more Airlia, it had drawn in the Ancient Enemy of the Airlia, a spacefaring race known as the Swarm. The Airlia had immediately ordered the smooth limestone facing of the massive pyramid—which sent a massive radar signature out into space—to be torn off and the plan abandoned. Thus there was no longer a need for the four Airlia who slept beneath Giza and Aspasia's Shadow felt no great loss at their deaths.

Aspasia's Shadow had been imprinted with Aspasia's memories and personalities, but layered on top of them were millennia of his own experience as a human on Earth. He was no longer that which he had been set up to be. He had awareness, a dangerous thing to give to something that is just supposed to be a tool. He knew that he existed simply to serve a purpose and that once that purpose was fulfilled and Aspasia came out of the deep sleep on Mars and returned—or Artad came out of his deep sleep under Qian-Ling in China—that the war would be renewed, one side would win, and he would no longer be needed regardless of which side won.

If Artad won, Aspasia's Shadow knew he was doomed. But in a strange way, he had enough of Aspasia's personality to know that even if his side won, he was also doomed. Aspasia would not allow a creature that held so much of his essence to live. Either way, the future was bleak if left to run its obvious course. That was one of the reasons he had not bothered to track down either of the surviving Undead. They were a wild card that not only made things more interesting, but added potential allies, depending on how the future developed. One thing he could count on was their hatred of the Airlia.

With a sigh of pain, Aspasia's Shadow left the Guardian chamber. He went down a stone passageway to another chamber. Inside, a body floated in a large vat of green fluid, a black tube pumping air into the mouth, thence to the lungs. The head was shaved and covered by a skullcap, with several dozens leads running from it to a main line connected to the command console. The body's eyes were open but showed no sign of intelligence. Next to the vat was a black tube, similar in size and shape to the sleep tubes used by the Undead.

It was time to pass on.

Aspasia's Shadow went to the control console and put his hands over the backlit hexagonal display. Quickly he tapped out a sequence, just as he had done hundreds of times in the past. The lid to the black tube swung up, revealing a contoured interior designed to fit his body.

Aspasia's Shadow removed the *ka* from around his neck and slid it, two arms forward, into the small holes on the right side of the console. It fit tightly and a small six-sided section next to it glowed orange, indicating it was in place.

Aspasia's Shadow went to the black tube. He stripped naked and lay down inside. The lid lowered onto him, trapping him in utter darkness. A few probes lightly touched his head, injecting painkillers. There were several minutes of stillness as the top of his head became numb. Then nanoprobes slid out of the lining of the tube into his brain, tapping into the needed sections for update.

His memories and experiences since the last download were transferred to the *ka* and the probes withdrew. Aspasia's Shadow took a shallow breath, never prepared for what came next, because he didn't know what it was going to be like. It was the one memory that was never transferred.

Out of small pockets in the lining of the tube, black particles, the size of grains of sand, were expelled onto his naked skin.

He screamed helplessly into the darkness of the tube as the particles dissolved flesh, muscle, and bone from the outside inward, triggering every pain response the body had. The only positive aspect was that it lasted for barely five seconds before the body was gone.

The console hummed as the data in the *ka* was integrated with the basic profile of Aspasia, then sent to the figure in the glass tube through the line, into the wires and thus to the brain. The imprinting took slightly over a minute. The probes were withdrawn from the figure's head.

The eyes blinked, awareness filling them as Aspasia's Shadow came to life once more. The green fluid drained, leaving Aspasia's Shadow lying on the tube's floor, trying to get oriented. The tube slid up and he tentatively stepped out. He wiped himself off with a towel, then pulled on the garments that had been left by his previous incarnation.

Dressed, he paused, staring at the black tube that had held his former self. A shiver passed through him, knowing that he would bring this body to that tube sometime in the future. Already, the green vat was humming, beginning work on the next clone to await his presence. Despite being in a body that was the equivalent of a very healthy twenty-year-old, Aspasia's Shadow felt weary.

With great effort, Aspasia's Shadow went back to the Guardian chamber and sat in his throne in front of the golden pyramid. He accessed the computer's database.

Egypt was a mess. He'd known that before he'd regenerated.

The Airlia base at Cydonia on Mars was secure and all was well, according to data relayed from the Guardian on the Red Planet.

And Artad? What of him? It had been a while since Aspasia's Shadow had checked on the other side's leader in the civil war. All seemed quiet and Aspasia's Shadow knew that it was very doubtful that Artad would break the truce without something dramatic changing and so far nothing like that had occurred.

Still. He would have to send a probe in that direction soon. Of course, for Aspasia's Shadow, who thought in terms of centuries and millennia, the term "soon" was relative. At that moment, all he wanted to do was sleep.

QIAN-LING, CHINA: 634 B.C.

A cold wind blew from the western desert, scouring the side of the three-thousand-foot-high hill. There was no doubt the formation was not natural, as the slopes in all directions were uniform and nothing grew on the wind-blasted dirt that covered the mound. It was a desolate place, normally empty of life and avoided by those who lived nearby.

There was one human currently in the area, though. A woman, heavy with child, staggered into the wind, holding a tattered cloak tight around her swollen body. She had one hand cradled underneath her belly, the other holding a small flask made of black metal that had not come from the Earth. Her teeth chattered in the chill and her exposed skin was growing numb.

She went downslope, following the power of gravity. She had no destination in mind even though her village was to the north, about fifteen miles away. She knew she would not be welcome if she showed up there and she doubted if she could make it that far in her condition.

She was cursed and had been sent out into the wilderness to die along with what she bore inside her. She reached the base of the mound and peered about in the dark. A black line ahead indicated trees lining a riverbank and she staggered forward, heading for the water. She tripped over something and fell hard, cutting her cheek. She blinked in the moonlight, not quite believing what her eyes showed her as the cause of both her fall and the cut. A pile of bones.

The woman realized then that this was the remains of another like her, another sent out into the desolate land to die.

She did not want to die. A cry of pain and anguish

escaped her lips as she got to her feet. She was only seventeen and had been a virgin nine months earlier when she had been chosen by her village to be their yearly sacrifice to the Gods of Qian-Ling. The choice had not upset her, as no one could remember a year when the Gods had taken the offering. Usually the chosen was taken to a spot a quarter of the way up the mound and tied loosely to a stake. Two days later, the priests would come back, and untie the girl, and take her back to the village—the duty done, the gesture made.

No one knew when the tradition had been started but it had seemed best to continue it. The girl had not been overly concerned when chosen; indeed she had felt she was being honored, as those girls who had been chosen in previous years had always returned to the village to acclaim. She'd walked in the middle of the processional to Qian-Ling and allowed the rope to be lightly tied around her waist and watched her people disappear to the north. Her greatest concern had been spending two nights alone on the mound.

That changed the first night when she heard a rumbling noise and the ground shook. She tried to untie the rope, but the knot was too complicated. Then a man had appeared in the darkness, holding a long spear. He'd cut the rope where it was attached to the stake and pulled her with him, taking her into an opening on the side of the mound, which sealed behind them.

The horrors that had happened after that she had blotted from her mind. One hand was still cradled under her swollen belly, while the other crept to her neck, to the shunt that had been put in place there.

She reached the line of trees and stopped, seeing in the starlight that the ground dropped off abruptly. With difficulty, she slid down the steep stream bank. There was a slight shoal consisting of small pebbles between the bank and the water. Ice framed both sides of the flowing water, leaving a free-flowing center channel. The stream was not deep, a few inches at best.

The girl slumped back against the dirt bank, exhausted. Looking up, she could see stars and remembered her grandfather pointing out the various animals formed by the twinkling lights.

She cried out as a place deep inside her mind remembered the touch of six-fingered hands on her body while red cat eyes peered at her. She stopped her mind from going further along that thread of thought.

Pain ran through her body, focusing her brain on the situation at hand. She whimpered as a contraction rippled through her. Despite the cold air, sweat began to run down her face and along her body.

The girl cried out for her mother. The only answer was the howl of the wind.

She had witnessed numerous births in the village, but there had always been a midwife present to supervise and assist. Pain consumed her and she pressed back against the bank of the stream, her sweat merging with the dirt into mud.

When the child came it was as if it were ripping its way out of her body with single-minded determination. Her screams echoed up out of the streambed and across the plain to the mound.

After ten minutes the baby was out and she used what little strength she had left to wrap it in the rag that had covered her body. Naked, she instinctively curled her body around the infant to keep it warm.

She gazed at the child her body protected. It was not crying, nor had it made any noise, but its chest rose and fell as it breathed, indicating it was alive. Its eyes met her gaze and she was startled to see a thin sheen of red covering the black pupils.

The child leaned into her body, taking her warmth.

She barely noticed when it opened its mouth and tiny teeth tore into her throat.

CHAPTER 6

NOSFERATU WAS BETTER PREPARED this time, having learned his lesson on the last awakening. Instead of leaving the tube and blundering forth, he left the lid to the tube slightly cracked each night and lay still, conserving energy, until he caught the scent of something alive. He slid out of the tube and found several birds resting on the cliff. He refreshed himself as best he could, experiencing again the nausea from imbibing nonhuman blood.

Strengthened, but hardly satisfied, he made his way north along the coast, knowing he could not attempt the interior of Africa in his present condition. He had barely made it back to the Skeleton Coast alive after leaving Nekhbet in her mountain crypt. Between the mountains and the west coast had been mile after mile of desert, then thick jungle, then, as he neared the coast, desolate, rock-strewn desert once more.

He'd set the tube for approximately one thousand years, yet he noted nothing had changed in the immediate area as he went along the coast. It was the perfect place for him to rest undisturbed, but because of its ruggedness, a hard one in which to find people to feed on.

He saw no ships sailing along the coast. Finally, the land began to turn green and he encountered his first village. He took two that night, a couple who had escaped into the jungle to copulate. Refreshed he moved more quickly and soon reached the point where an enormous river cut the coast, pouring a wide swath of brown, muddy water into the ocean. Nosferatu could barely see to the other side in the moonlight and wasn't certain whether what he saw was the riverbank or the shore of an island in the river's mouth.

The Congo made the Nile's flow look like a trickle. Still, Nosferatu felt a pang of longing for the blue water of the river in Egypt. He had a sudden vision of a dark-haired woman holding him, looking down at him, smiling. He was small, tiny, a baby. But he knew she loved him. But that, like so much of his life, was just a memory now.

Even animals had others like them. Nosferatu was perhaps the most isolated being on the planet. Nekhbet was in the deep sleep in the cave on the mountaintop. Vampyr might be out there somewhere, but Nosferatu didn't know where the other Undead was.

Nosferatu growled. A bird fluttered out of a nearby tree in fright. All had been stolen from him. His nostrils flared as he sniffed the air. Blood. Human blood. To his right, upriver. He turned in that direction, moving through the jungle like a ghost, able to see clearly even under the thickest canopy that blocked out all starlight and moonlight.

He came upon a village. A thicket of thorn bushes surrounded the perimeter; a single entrance with only one branch and a youth with a spear barred the way. Nosferatu ran forward, leapt the thicket, and was on the young warrior in a flash. His teeth ripped through the tender flesh, bringing forth a gush of blood. Even as the artery continued to spurt red sustenance, he lifted his face and glared about. Another warrior was coming, spear leveled. Nosferatu jumped up, knocked aside the warrior's thrust, and jumped on the man's back, teeth sinking into the throat, ripping and tearing. The warrior screamed, then the sound died as Nosferatu tore in farther, his teeth cutting through the man's windpipe.

He threw the warrior from him and bellowed out a challenge, his face and chest covered in blood. He could see faces appear in the doorways of huts. Men staring with wide eyes. Women fluttering behind them, yelling at their children to hide from the demon that had invaded their village.

"Come," he screamed, throwing his arms wide, exposing his chest. "Come and get me." He didn't even realize he was speaking in the language of the Gods and that none could understand his words, although his intent was clear.

None rose to the challenge. All remained indoors, weapons at the ready, watching Nosferatu's rage spill out in screams and curses.

Sanity slowly returned as his throat knotted up in pain from the yelling. Backing up, Nosferatu left the village and disappeared into the darkness. He found a small cave along the riverbank and slid into it, covering himself with leaves and bushes for the coming day.

He lay there as the sun made its way overhead, occasionally slipping into an uneasy sleep. Each time he woke, he was shaking and sweating. As darkness fell, he left the hasty lair and searched for a way to cross the river. When he approached the village he'd attacked the previous evening, he could see numerous warriors manning the perimeter and a large fire stoked up just inside the thorn barrier. He circumambulated the village and came upon several dugout canoes pulled up on the riverbank. He took one and shoved it into the dark brown water. Snatching up the paddle, he began to stroke, blinking sweat out of his eyes.

After several minutes he realized that while he was indeed making it across the river, the strong current was also carrying him from left to right. Nosferatu tried to pull harder but was seized by muscle spasms that almost caused him to drop the paddle. Every muscle and joint in his body ached and his forehead felt as if it were on fire. He feared that one of those he had fed upon had been ill and he had drawn in the sickness. He wiped a shaking hand across his face, trying to clear the sweat pouring into his eyes.

When he could see again, he realized the current would win. He would be swept into the ocean long before he reached the far bank. He looked over his shoulder and realized the bank he had left from was also out of reach. He was too sick to care. He put the paddle down and curled up in a tight ball on the rough wood bottom of the canoe.

NOSFERATU WOKE IN greater pain and discomfort than when he'd passed out. The first rays of the sun were slashing across the edge of the canoe just above him and he couldn't open his eyes to their brightness. He heard no sound of land—no winds in trees, no cries of bird or animal, just the sound of water against the outside of the canoe.

Nosferatu could feel the heat of the sun closing on him, edging down the inside of the canoe. He knew he had no choice. He grabbed one side of the canoe and rolled, bringing it down over him as he fell into the water.

He popped his head up under the security of the canoe and slowly treaded water.

It was a very long day. Several times, Nosferatu felt something brush by his legs and feet; but he kept his eyes shut, for even the sun reflected through the ocean water was too much for his delicate pupils. As soon as the sun set, he righted the canoe and collapsed inside it, his legs quivering from the day. Sitting up, he peered about but saw only ocean in all directions. He had no clue which way to head to try to get back to land.

NOSFERATU LAY ON his back and watched the stars wheel by overhead, conserving his energy. He realized it was the first time he had ever really looked at the stars—strange, given he was a creature of the night. But then he had spent the time of darkness either hunting or traveling, not contemplating the little points of light overhead. When he had been a child it was whispered the stars were where the Gods came from. And then Donnchadh had told him the same thing. How could that be? he wondered. How could they come from such small places? Of course, if the points of light were far away, then he imagined they might be very large.

Nosferatu cursed both the Gods and the stars as the sky above him began to brighten, indicating another day's beginning. He waited until the last moment before rolling the canoe over and entering the water.

As the day progressed, he contemplated simply letting go and sinking into the dark depths. All that kept his grip on the edge of the canoe and his legs slowly moving to keep his head above water was the image of Nekhbet.

By the eighth day even that image had faded. He was only aware of exhaustion, wetness, and despair. That night he sat in the canoe and looked about. Stars and sea were the only things visible.

The Gods had given him life for their own selfish purposes. For over three hundred years, they had consumed his life for their pleasure. Since then he had been hiding, running, like a frightened child, for thousands of years.

Why?

What was the overall purpose of life? The goal of the Gods? Why did they treat other living beings as they did?

Nosferatu blinked. There was a glow on the horizon behind him. He stared at it for almost a minute, then picked up the paddle and began to stroke. For a little while he thought his eyes were fooling him as the glow faded, but then it became brighter. Soon he could see flames shooting into the sky, then the shoreline. A fire was raging in the tall grass, coming closer to the shore. Nosferatu could see herds of animals running, trying to escape the flames. And on the shoreline, bands of humans waiting for the kill.

Nosferatu felt the pull of the hunger.

NOSFERATU HAD FED well the previous night. He strode north along the beach, miles flowing past in the darkness. It appeared that he had come back to land farther up the coast from where he'd been pushed out to sea. Instead of jungle, lush grassland stretched out to the interior of the continent. Several times he saw villages ahead and made slight detours to pass around them and their barking dogs unless he had to feed.

He continued up the coast like this for almost a full moon, feeding twice more. The grassland began to give way to rocks and desert, and early one evening, shortly after he set out, he saw a two-story stone tower on a finger of land enclosing a small natural harbor. Several boats were anchored in the cove. They were of a type he had never seen, with an upthrust, curved prow and a tall mast in its center. They were made of wood planks, not reeds, and as large as the barges that hauled stone on the Nile, but sleeker.

There was light in the windows in both levels of the tower and Nosferatu could see a pair of guards with bows on the top. As he got closer he could see that there were several stone-and-wood buildings at the base of the tower. Soon he could hear voices coming from one of the buildings. Nosferatu halted and contemplated the situation. He was hungry, but not desperate. And these men had ships. Pulling his cloak tight around his lean body, he walked forward.

One of the guards spotted him and called out a warning. Nosferatu halted and held up both hands, empty palms out. Several men scrambled out of the building and came up to him, swords drawn. They spoke in a strange tongue, but once again, the universal language worked as Nosferatu drew out several gold pieces from his purse and offered them.

The men took him into the building and offered him food and drink, which he made a pretense of consuming. What did catch his attention, however, was a piece of hide staked to one wall. A map was drawn on it. Seeing his interest, one of the men walked him toward it.

The man pointed at a spot near the bottom of the map, then pointed down at the ground, indicating that was where they were currently located. Nosferatu put his finger on the spot, then ran it up along the coast, around through a narrow strait and into the Middle Sea, along the coast until he reached what he knew was the Nile. Then he pointed at himself.

The man nodded. He pointed to a spot above Egypt along the eastern edge of the Mediterranean, then at himself. "Phoenicia."

Nosferatu had never heard of the country, but he knew much had changed while he slept. How much, he hoped to find out. Jingling his purse, he indicated himself once more, then Egypt.

The man frowned and called out to one of the others. The man who came over was weathered by the sea and old. He had a scar running down one side of his face, disappearing into the collar of his dirty shirt. The first man pointed at Egypt, then said something as he indicated Nosferatu.

The old man shook his head and spit. He pointed to a land on the north side of the sea, west of Egypt's location. Apparently that was where he was going, Nosferatu realized, as the two men argued some more. It was closer than he was now. Nosferatu opened his purse and paid the old man.

GREECE: 354 B.C.

While the legend was that the Three Hundred had died to the last man in the Gates of Fire at Thermopylae in 480 B.C., the real number was actually 299. Three hundred Spartans had indeed marched with King Leonidas against King Xerxes and met his massive Persian army of 150,000 men in battle in the narrow pass. The Spartans had held for four days, allowing the rest of the city-states of Greece to mobilize and eventually defeat the invaders. It was an event celebrated in song and onstage across Greece, no place more so than in Sparta.

There was one who knew the truth of the Three Hundred. One who still walked the face of the Earth over 125 years after the famous battle. He was the Three Hundredth, and he was not a man. He stood on the parade field of Sparta, just as he had so many years ago, and watched as the army mustered for battle, just as it had so many years ago, and so many times since.

Vampyr had fought at Thermopylae as long as possible, before slipping away into the night, leaving his comrades to be massacred to the last man. Even now, years later, he saw no point to the famous last stand. Yes, it eventually led to victory for the allied Greek cities, but not long after, those same city-states had fallen once more into battle among themselves in the First and then Second Peloponnesian War. Men who had fought side by side against the Persians were within a few years lining up against each other in mortal combat.

Such was the folly of humans, and such folly was fodder for one who lived on hatred and blood.

Vampyr remained in Sparta because it was the first place he felt at home among the humans. The rest of Greece viewed Sparta as a bizarre enigma. While the arts were celebrated elsewhere, only martial prowess was rewarded in Sparta. The entire city-state was set up to support the army. From 404–371 B.C. Sparta had ruled most of Greece, despite being heavily outnumbered and never being able to field more than ten thousand men. The strain of this rule, though, had taken its toll, and over the past fifteen years, the kingdom had relinquished much territory back to the locals.

Sparta was located in the southwest, connected to the rest of Greece by a narrow isthmus. Vampyr had wandered there after being able to stow away on a ship leaving Crete over a thousand years earlier. He'd hidden his tube in a cave on the southern shore of Peloponnese and gone into the deep sleep for over five hundred years, hoping to have enough time pass for his rule in Crete to be recalled only as legend.

When he awoke he traveled around Greece, taking in the burgeoning civilization, before settling in Sparta. At first he did so out of black humor, as the people there claimed to be descended from Lacedaemon, a son of the god Zeus. Also, he was able to feed with relative impunity because of the way the classes were stratified. There were the Spartiates, who could fight and vote; the Perioikoi, or freemen, who did not have the vote but were graciously allowed to fight and die for the state; and the helots, who—while technically not slaves—were only slighter better off than if they had been, and on whom Vampyr could feed relatively unnoticed.

Three lochoi of Spartan warriors were lined up in formation in front of the Hellenion—the temple—preparing to depart for war against Pylos on the western coast of Peloponnesia. It was just before dawn. Vampyr had fought in so many campaigns he actually had no clue what real or imagined cause was behind the upcoming battle. He had changed his identity six times over the centuries, earning his way each time into the ranks of the knights through feats of arms, rather than by family as most did.

The squires and battle train had departed before dawn, as they rated no fond farewell. The families of the knights who made up the ranks of the lochoi stood in the shadow of the temple, stoically keeping tears at bay. The boys of the agoge—training barracks—not old enough to come on the campaign, stood in their own formation watching their fathers, older brothers, and uncles prepare to leave.

The commander of the expedition, Acton, turned for the road leading west and the women began to sing a hymn to the god of battle. Row after row of Spartans stepped from the grass field onto the dirt road and headed to the west.

Battle. Vampyr had grown to love it over the years. He'd honed his skills until he was the most feared warrior in Sparta, and thus in all of Greece. That combined with his inherent abilities made him practically invincible and his leaders were inclined to grant him latitude regarding his strange behavior. He was never around during the day unless there was to be a battle, and then he was completely garbed in armor from head to toe, with a cloth wrapped across his eyes to guard them from the light. He'd explained that he had a defect which did not allow him to expose any part of his skin or his eyes to the light, and such was his prowess with arms that the other Spartans gladly allowed him this idiosyncrasy.

So as the sun began to rise in the east, Vampyr slipped away from the column and disappeared into the forest along the side of the road.

ATHENS: 354 B.C.

It was the easiest journey Nosferatu had made so far even though it took the better part of six months. The Phoenician's ship had a lower deck, where Nosferatu could sleep in darkness. The large sails and the skill with which the crew maneuvered the ship moved them up the coast at a faster pace than anything Nosferatu had experienced before. They even sailed at night, stopping only about every eight days at another outpost like the one at which Nosferatu had met them. They would refill their water casks, load fresh food, and spend a day resting. Then set out again.

Nosferatu realized the outposts were spaced that way for a reason, indicating a sophisticated trading system. He would feed just prior to departure, taking someone from the outpost and hiding the body so that it couldn't be found. Usually they left before the loss was even discovered, although twice a search was instigated before they set sail. The second time, Nosferatu knew the Phoenician captain was suspicious, but a few more pieces of gold ensured his continued presence on the ship.

Still Nosferatu slept lightly during the days, anxious that the crew might turn on him at any time. He found he could maintain a half-sleeping, half-waking posture during the day, so that the approach of anyone would bring him to full awareness. They passed from the Atlantic into the Mediterranean after a month's journey and he could sense the relief of the crew to be in more familiar waters. He also began to understand some of what they said and learned they were a people who sailed not only south along Africa, but north along Atlantic coast of Europe. Their ships had been crisscrossing the Mediterranean pursuing trade for hundreds of years and they had colonized both the northern shores of Africa and eastern Spain from their homeland in Palestine.

The most interesting news was that Egypt was now ruled by the Persians, the last Pharaoh having been defeated in battle just a few years earlier. Nosferatu had never heard of the Persians, but he had the ship's captain point out the Persian Empire on the map and show him where its capital was.

If foreigners ruled in Egypt, was it safe for him to venture there? Would he be able to get to the Grail and take it to Nekhbet? Where were the four remaining Airlia?

The Phoenicians had Gods they worshipped, with names Nosferatu did not recognize; but they were not the same as the Gods he had known in Egypt. Every morning the crew knelt in front of several small idols placed in the bow of the ship. They prayed for fair weather and a wind at their backs and for safety from the wiles of the sea. Nosferatu didn't understand praying to an object. What power could a piece of stone hold? At least the Gods who had ruled Egypt had been real.

After several days of sailing with no shore in sight—another advancement over Nosferatu's last voyage—they made landfall at a port city called Selinus on an island the locals called Sicily. Things had changed, he realized as he roamed the city at night, looking for a victim to sate his hunger, yet in many ways, they had remained the same. There were new empires and gods, but people and technology seemed to be basically unaltered. In fact, other than their having the sailing ships, Nosferatu judged the Phoenicians to be inferior to the Egyptian culture he had known. And they knew nothing of history. Their societal memory only went back a few generations. He had heard no mention of Atlantis or the Great Civil War among the Gods.

Nosferatu spent the week the ship stayed in Selinus feeding and listening. He heard nothing of the Airlia, the Ones Who Wait, the Guides, or anything else to do with the Gods from the stars and their minions. Perhaps the world was free of them? Nosferatu could wonder and hope.

They sailed from Selinus, around the foot of Italy, to the ship's final destination, Athens, one of the main city-states of the most powerful empire in the Mediterranean, according to what Nosferatu had picked up from the conversations he listened in on. From what he had learned he knew he could find another ship to take him from Athens to Egypt. He stayed belowdecks after they docked in

Piraeus, the port city of Athens, waiting for nightfall. By the time he departed the ship, the cargo had been unloaded and the crew was gone, off to the local taverns to celebrate the successful completion of their long journey and the surprising and pleasant addition of Nosferatu's gold.

Athens was very different from Selinus. Nosferatu wandered the streets of the city, impressed with the architecture, but even more so with the discourse in the various public meeting places sprinkled throughout the city. He spent several weeks simply soaking in the conversation, learning the language. There was a difference to the people here, something Nosferatu sensed even before he understood the words.

It took him a few evenings before it suddenly came to him what was different about these people from what he had known in Egypt. Here they had a sense of the future.

In Egypt, life had been cyclical. There was little sense of time because all things repeated themselves and there was no progress. Here life was linear. Ideas were discussed and argued about. People were asking *why*, something that had been frowned upon in Nosferatu's Egypt. He wondered if it were the absence of the Gods and the high priests that allowed this freedom of thought. The Greeks had Gods, many of them, but they appeared to be more a theory than a reality. Something people even argued about along with everything else. In Egypt the price for doubting the Airlia Gods or the high priests had been death.

Nosferatu fed well, taking those who also walked the night, usually thieves and prostitutes who worked near the docks of Piraeus, and who would not be missed. He was feeling stronger and more confident that he could return to Egypt and rescue Nekhbet when he heard a word as he was passing a group of men gathered on stone steps in front of a temple that froze him in his tracks.

Atlantis.

The sun had set only an hour previously, but Nosferatu had already fed, taking a young man who had tried to rob him as he walked a back alley after rising from his hiding place underneath a wharf. Nosferatu edged closer to the group. The man at the center had white hair and a long beard. He had a scroll in his hand.

"You speak of the Flood of Deukalion and Pyrrha, Solon," the old man read, "but I tell you they pale in comparison to that which destroyed Atlantis. There have been and will be many destroyers of mankind, the greatest two of which are fire and water."

The old man looked past the group at Nosferatu, who was now along the outer circle of men listening. Nosferatu was startled by the sharpness of the glance and almost stepped back, but held his ground, interested to hear what the old man had to read. This was also something that was new, the only other written language Nosferatu had seen before being the High Runes of the Airlia.

"Many are the truths and great are the achievement of the Greeks," the old man continued. "However, there is one accomplishment that is rarely spoken of, and that many think is a myth. A long time ago, before the time when the Dorians came to this land, our ancestors fought a great battle against a host that came from beyond the sea, from beyond the Pillars of Heracles, and were led by Gods themselves.

"Beyond the Pillars there was an island larger than Libya and Asia put together. On this island was a confederation of powerful kings who ruled not only that island but many other lands. The empire of Atlantis stretched through the Pillars of Heracles to Libya as far as Egypt, and Europe as far as Tyrrhenia, but in a noble battle we stopped them from extending their rule here to Greece.

"Not long after, there was a great earthquake which caused the sea to swallow the island of Atlantis up in its entirety so that it disappeared from the face of the Earth."

The last part agreed with what Nosferatu had learned as a child, but the bit about the Greeks defeating the Airlia and their Atlantean human forces, he thought, wasn't very likely. He checked that thought. If the battle had taken place during the Airlia civil war, then it was possible that the Greeks had had the assistance of Artad and his forces. Even the priests had known few details of the Great Civil War.

"You, stranger." The old man startled Nosferatu by pointing directly at him. "What do you know of these things?"

"Why do ask me?" Nosferatu replied.

"I have seen your kind before."

Nosferatu felt a chill pass through his body. "What do you mean my kind?"

"Tall. White skin like the finest marble. And most important your eyes, my friend, they speak of having seen much, as did he to whom I talked."

"Did this man, who you think is my kin, have a name?"

"He called himself a Shadow of Aspasia, whatever that might mean."

Nosferatu remembered Kajilil speaking of the creature, a creation of Aspasia, the Airlia commander. "When did you speak with him?"

"So you know him?" the old man asked in reply.

"I have heard of him, but I do not know him."

"He was here two days ago. I have met him several times. We have had the most interesting conversations."

Nosferatu felt the hope of the past few weeks collapse.

"So what do you know of Atlantis, my friend?" the old man pressed.

"Nothing," Nosferatu muttered as he turned and slipped away into the darkness. He wandered the streets of Athens, wondering what he should do next. If Aspasia's Shadow is here in Athens, who is in Egypt, in the Roads of Rostau? Where are the Gods?

He sensed more than saw the blade coming at him. Reacting, Nosferatu jumped to the side, the knife slicing the air where a split second ago his throat had been. The attacker followed through on the strike, wheeling, bringing the blade to bear once more. Nosferatu retreated, but his back hit the wall of a building and his attacker maneuvered to trap him.

"Who are you?" Nosferatu demanded, holding his hands up in front of himself in a defensive posture. He felt as if he were looking into a mirror—a tall man wrapped in a dark cloak with pale skin and red hair. The eyes, though, caught his attention. Red and elongated like a cat's. "Aspasia's Shadow?"

In reply the man thrust with the dagger. At the same moment there was a flash of metal coming down from the right, smoothly slicing through the man's arm, severing it at the elbow. The hand holding the dagger fell to the stone street. Nosferatu watched with wide eyes as the sword cut back, piercing his attacker's chest. The man collapsed to the ground as Nosferatu turned to face the wielder of the sword.

"*I* am Aspasia's Shadow," the man said. He wiped the blood off the sword, using the dead man's cloak. "This is a One Who Waits." Aspasia's Shadow reached inside the dead man's tunic and removed a small object from a chain around his neck. Nosferatu had seen such a shape before—the *ka*, two hands without a torso raised as in prayer. Aspasia's Shadow put it inside a pocket and in turn pulled out a small glass vial filled with what appeared to be black sand. He unscrewed the lid, then shook the black powder over the body. Immediately the flesh began to disappear as if the sand were eating it. Within ten seconds there was only the empty clothing lying in the street.

Aspasia's Shadow stood. "You are Nosferatu."

It was not a question, so Nosferatu remained silent as Aspasia's Shadow sheathed his sword.

"Come." Aspasia's Shadow did not bother to look over his shoulder as he headed down the alley. Nosferatu paused to retrieve the assassin's dagger, then followed.

After a little way around the base of the Acropolis, Aspasia's Shadow passed between two statues, literally into the base of the hill on which the Parthenon stood. Nosferatu followed him down worn stone steps. They paused at the bottom, where a wooden door made of scarred beams barred the way. Aspasia's Shadow did something that Nosferatu couldn't quite see and the door smoothly swung open.

The two entered and the door swung shut behind them. Nosferatu could see quite well in the dark, but he winced when Aspasia's Shadow lit a lantern. Shading his eyes, he followed the other along a tunnel cut through the stone of the Acropolis.

"This tunnel was made by some of the first people who lived here," Aspasia's Shadow said, his first words in a while. "They must have put a fort on the top of this hill, then cut this tunnel as an escape route, or perhaps a way to get water. Who knows? It must have taken them many years. I imagine it took generations of these people chipping away at the stone with their simple tools. Humans are a most strange species. Most of the time their attention span is that of any animal, short. But then they do something like this. Most strange."

They turned a corner and entered a chamber containing a table, some chairs, and a bed. Aspasia's Shadow put the lantern on the table. He glanced at Nosferatu. "Does this hurt your eyes?"

"Yes."

Aspasia's Shadow made no effort to turn the lamp down. He sat in a chair and leaned back, putting his boots up on the table. Nosferatu took the seat across from him, one hand on the dagger hidden under his cloak, the other shading his eyes.

"I should kill you for slaying Isis and Osiris," Aspasia's Shadow said. "If I were true to the persona that was implanted in me so many years ago when I was made by Aspasia. It was Aspasia who left Isis and Osiris, his lieutenants, in charge in Egypt." Aspasia's Shadow sighed. "But much has happened in the years since then. I have walked this planet longer than you. And I assume you have slept some of those years in the tube—something I have done also on occasion. I have been reborn many, many times. My memory and my experience grow even as I switch from one body to the next."

Nosferatu remained silent, his hand still on the dagger.

"I met Osiris and Isis and the other four several times. They always treated me with contempt because I was a Shadow, and human in form. When I heard Isis and Osiris had been killed I did not shed any tears."

"Where did they go?" Nosferatu asked. "The four who lived?"

"Why do you want to know?" Aspasia's Shadow did not wait for an answer. "Where is your love? Nekhbet, the one you stole from the Roads?"

Nosferatu remained silent. Aspasia's Shadow laced his fingers together on his lap and regarded Nosferatu for several moments, as if pondering a problem. "She sleeps, doesn't she? Or else you would be with her. And you seek something. Blood. Airlia blood. The human blood keeps you alive, allows you to maintain, but you need Airlia blood for her, don't you?"

Nosferatu realized he was dealing with the only other being on the planet, besides the Gods, who had lived longer than he and had more experience. Plus, Aspasia's Shadow had inherited Aspasia's knowledge along with his own experience.

"Or more likely, you desire the Grail," Aspasia's Shadow said. "Wouldn't we all?" He sighed. "But the key to the Hall of Records, where it is kept, had been hidden well by the Watchers. Even I don't know where it is now. Plus, I have had to put aside that temptation because activating the Grail would bring both Artad and Aspasia after me. It is the one thing that is forbidden even to me."

Still Nosferatu remained silent. It occurred to him that Aspasia's Shadow was bored. More than bored, Nosferatu realized. Aspasia's Shadow was lonely, a feeling that Nosferatu could certainly understand.

"I've met Vampyr, your brother in blood," Aspasia's Shadow continued. He seemed disappointed that Nosferatu still made no reply. "He, at least, makes the world an interesting place. He had a kingdom. On an island south of here. He was getting quite powerful and earning quite a fearsome reputation. I feared I might have to take action, but the planet itself brought his plans, quite literally, to ruin."

Nosferatu had no idea what Aspasia's Shadow was referring to.

"He did take his revenge though," Aspasia's Shadow

said. "You asked about the other four Airlia who dwelt in the Roads. Vampyr killed them. They are dead in their tubes."

His father was dead. Nosferatu felt neither elation nor sadness. He thought back to his proud boast to Kajilil about there being a time for the Undead to rule. He looked at the creature across from him and realized this war would never end. Power was a dangerous thing. The only reason Aspasia's Shadow did not kill him was because he posed little threat. Nosferatu shook his head, trying to clear the flurry of thoughts that Aspasia's Shadow's words crowded into his mind.

Aspasia's Shadow mistook the gesture. "You do not believe me?"

"I believe you," Nosferatu said. "Vampyr vowed vengeance many years ago. I am surprised it took him so long."

"It took him so long because I stopped him all the times before," Aspasia's Shadow said.

"And why not this time?"

"I was tired. And I cannot be everywhere. Vampyr chose a time when the kingdom in Egypt was in disarray."

"Where is Vampyr now?"

"Not far away."

"Where?"

"To the south. He has spent the last two centuries fighting. Spilling blood. And drinking it, of course. He revels in it. It keeps his mind from other things."

From the reality of being alone for centuries, Nosferatu thought. He realized that the three of them had that one thing very much in common.

"Why did you save me?" Nosferatu asked.

"I know where you can find Airlia blood. And you are free to take it if you can."

"Where?"

Aspasia's Shadow pointed to his left. "China."

Nosferatu had never heard of the place. "And where is that?"

"To the east. Very far to the east. Farther than any here have ever traveled." Aspasia's Shadow leaned back in his seat and regarded Nosferatu with hooded eyes. "I will do you a favor, my Undead friend, if you will do one for me."

"And that is?"

"Kill Artad and his Kortad. You can have their blood."

"By myself?"

"No, you would need an army to do this. They are asleep, in a mountain tomb called Qian-Ling in the land called China."

Nosferatu spread his hands. "I have no army."

"Not to worry," Aspasia's Shadow said. "I've prepared one. And I've prepared their leader. He is but a boy now, but eventually, with my help, he will go far. Perhaps he may even reach China."

"What is his name?"

"Alexander, son of Philip, from a small state north of here called Macedonia."

GREECE: 354 B.C.

Vampyr wrapped the cloth around his head, covering his skin and eyes. The material was blood-red and he could see through it in daylight, which was less than a half hour away. The effect was terrifying, but it did have its disadvantages. The warrior with the red face had become a legend in the area around Sparta, and sometimes Vampyr had a difficult time finding enemies to engage during battle.

It had been a long march to Pylos. Wandering the camp at night and listening, Vampyr had learned that this expedition had nothing to do with politics. It was purely for economic reasons. The three lochoi were being rented out to another city-state, Pirgos, in conflict with Pylos.

Fighting for money.

Vampyr looked to the right of the three Spartan units. The local militia from Pirgos was forming in uneven ranks to help support what they had paid the Spartans to lead. In reality, Vampyr knew they were there to loot the city once the Spartans defeated their enemy.

Dawn was not far off and with it death. Vampyr could smell the fear in the air. Even from some of the Spartans, as well trained as they were in the art of logophobia—the discipline of conquering fear and controlling one's body—were giving off a palpable aura.

They had reason, of course, to be scared. Every battle hinged on uncertainty. It was also not so much a matter of killing the enemy as breaking their spirit and these foes would be defending their homes and families, a circumstance that made for the most desperate fighting.

Overall, though, the Spartans were calm. Vampyr had gone through their training as an adult, a most unusual thing, as Spartan boys were sent from their homes to an agoge—training barracks—at age seven. He had been sponsored by one of the leading knights in the city after saving the man's life in battle and asking only this favor of him. On the first day some of the older boys had made fun of the man among them, but Vampyr had quelled that quickly and brutally by killing the leader of the bullies. In the strange way of the Spartans, he was not punished for doing so, but praised and accepted.

The training had been worth it. Despite his Airlia

blood, Vampyr was still predominantly human and he had realized long ago that that part of his being required discipline and training in order to survive over the years.

The focus of Spartan training was more than just martial prowess. It encompassed the body and mind, with a specific emphasis on the science of fear. Initially, the trainees were taught to control their muscles when every instinct they had screamed to do other than that which they were ordered to. They participated in exercises where they had to stand perfectly still and blindfolded while instructors walked among the ranks, unexpectedly striking out with a wooden stake. In this manner the muscles were disciplined against their natural fleeing instincts. A man thus trained held a great advantage in combat over one who did not possess this capability.

Looking out from the plain they were on, Vampyr could see the walled city of Pylos, which was their objective. The ground rose in a gentle slope up to the walls. Not favorable terrain for an assault.

Muffled orders were being issued and the lines were being formed. The Spartans would be out in front, the local Pirgosian militia sliding over to take a position behind them. Vampyr felt quite ready to spill some blood. He had not fed in over eight weeks while on the march. It was a deprivation he suffered deliberately to build his lust for the coming battle.

As the main line formed, a skirmish line of Rangers—Skiritai—began to move out on the flanks like the horns of a bull. Vampyr had seen this tactic used again and again, and it rarely failed to work. He knew the Spartan commander did not want to lay siege to the town. It would be time-consuming and difficult, requiring the construction of siege machines followed by a dangerous assault against a fortified position. Spartans fought best in the open ground.

Vampyr took his place in the center of the Spartan line, directly behind the commander, Acton. It was lighter now, and even the humans around Vampyr could see the city and the men manning the walls. The sun's light was amplified by a red glow as the Skiritai began to set fire to the homes and businesses that surrounded the walled part of the city. Crops also began to burn. The people might be safe inside, but their homes and livelihoods were mostly outside and being destroyed while they watched.

It only took fifteen minutes, before the gates of the city swung open and the Pylosian troops poured through. There was no hesitation on Acton's part. He immediately gave the order to advance and the Spartans moved out into the field toward the city at a quick pace as the Pylosians tried to get into formation.

The Spartans were in perfect alignment as they moved, their spears held upright. If one stood to the side and looked along the line, it would appear as if there were only one spear at the end in each rank, so perfect was their training. In contrast, the spears of the first rank of Pylosian troops to form trembled and shook as if in a storm.

Vampyr could hear the Pylosian officers screaming commands, trying to get their men into proper formation. He knew it was already too late. The front rank of enemy troops could see the Spartans coming and began to shift without even realizing it, each man moving slightly to his right, trying to get closer to the protection of the shield of the man on that side. To add to their disarray, the Skiritai began to fire their bows, sending arrows high into the air, coming down in the half-formed enemy ranks.

Just as intimidating as the sight of the red-cloaked lines approaching was the sound the Spartans made, their oxhide sandals hitting the ground in unison with each step, the ground practically trembling at their approach. The cadence was 120 paces per minute, beaten into each Spartan at the agoge and practiced constantly.

Less than a quarter mile from the Pylosian lines, Acton yelled the order to change from quick time to charge. Spears snapped in one precise movement from vertical to horizontal and shields jammed tighter together, presenting a solid wall as the Spartans broke into a controlled run at 180 steps per minute. Vampyr adjusted slightly as Acton fell back into position next to him on his right, a position of honor for Vampyr as his shield protected the commander.

The Pylosian lines had never completely formed, and what little order there was began to break in the face of the bristling juggernaut heading toward them. Some in the rear tried to run and were cut down by officers stationed there specifically for just that event.

Vampyr felt the bloodlust and had to use all the discipline he had learned in the agoge not to sprint ahead of the rank of Spartans. He gripped his spear shaft tighter as they closed on the enemy line. The Spartans smashed into the Pylosians with a thunderous sound of spearpoint on metal and flesh. This was immediately followed by the screams of dying and wounded.

With their eight-foot spears, the Spartans were able to use their first three ranks to attack the Pylosians. As soon as a spear became caught in the flesh or shield of an enemy warrior and could not be pulled back, each Spartan would draw his xithos—a short sword designed for jabbing rather than slashing.

The Pylosian line broke and the slaughter began. Vampyr had run his spear through not only the warrior directly in front of him, but also into the man behind him, spitting the two on its wooden haft, leaving them both writhing on the ground. He drew his sword and leapt forward, giving up his position in the Spartan line. The Pylosians were fleeing and thus making themselves more vulnerable to attack due to the lack of armor on their backs. Vampyr jabbed once, twice, then a third time and three men went down at his feet. He whirled, and even though the sword was a jabbing weapon, he put such power behind the stroke that his xithos beheaded a fourth Pylosian. For the first time Vampyr halted, watching the blood pulse up from the still-beating heart in the headless torso, which remained upright for several seconds, before slowly tumbling over.

That man's blood mixed with that of the other casualties along with urine from bladders emptied from fright and the spasms of death. The ground was turning into a horrible quagmire, but the Spartans relentlessly pressed forward, continuing to slay and advance.

The Pylosians began to surrender and beg for mercy. Vampyr gave no quarter, slaying those with weapons in their hands and those who held them empty in the air. Those who had hired the Spartans now surged forward, slaying those who surrendered. Vampyr continued his own murderous spree toward the gates of the city. He saw the enemy commander, tears streaming down his face, as he screamed futile orders at the warriors fleeing by him, trying to make a last stand before the open city gates, knowing there would be no safety inside.

Vampyr was soaked in blood, the cloth wrapped around his face tantalizing him with the taste as the red nectar he craved seeped through. He bounded up to the enemy commander. He parried the other's thrust, knocking the sword from the defeated leader's hands. Vampyr dropped his own sword and grabbed the man's throat with both hands, squeezing until the other passed out. Then he dragged him into the gates of the city and through the door of the nearest building, where he ripped the man's throat open and drank his fill.

He was not sated.

The screams of women and children now filled the air as the Pirgosians moved into the city, raping, killing, and stealing. The Spartans remained outside, content with the gold they had been paid and not wanting to lose any more men to desperate last stands inside the city.

Vampyr was the exception as he kicked open doors, searching. He found a woman huddled with two young children. He killed the mother quickly by breaking her neck, then drank from the children until their small hearts stopped beating. He emerged from the house, wrapping the cloth around his face. In his engorged pleasure he did not see a shadowy figure in armor watching him.

He could not wait for the next battle.

He walked out of the city. He could see that the Spartans had pulled back, tending to their few dead and wounded. He also saw that a man on a horse, a messenger from Sparta, was next to Acton, talking to him. Vampyr made his way over. There was indeed news.

A council had been held at Corinth. A treaty had been signed by representatives from practically every city-state, including Pylos and Pirgos, to unite under a young warrior-king from the north named Alexander. Sparta had also agreed to the pact and would send four lochoi to support the new king's proposed assault against the Persians.

Vampyr wanted to laugh at the folly of humans. Every man who had died that day was one less the Greeks could send against the Persians. And all three forces were now allies.

A campaign to the east. Vampyr nodded. Something to occupy the next decade or so. He needed to stay busy.

As Vampyr turned away from Acton and the messenger, he sensed movement behind and whirled, a split second too late, and the flat side of a xithos slammed into his temple, just below the brim of his helmet.

Vampyr crumpled to the ground unconscious.

I☉ WAS NIGH☉ when Vampyr awoke. He was on his back and when he tried to move, ropes around his chest, legs, and arms, kept him in place. There were torches flickering all about him and when he turned his head, he could see Acton and the other senior knights of the expedition staring at him. He was on one of the field tables used by the surgeons to work on the wounded.

"What are you doing?" Vampyr demanded. "I am a warrior of the first rank."

Acton stepped forward. "I do not know who—or what—you are. But I saw what you did with those two children in the town. And I—we all—have heard the stories about you. That you do not age. That you never expose yourself to the light of day. That you drink blood, something I now know to be true, having seen it with my own eyes."

"So?" Vampyr spit, the glob landing just in front of the Spartan commander. "I am the most feared warrior in all of Sparta, in all of Greece. What does it matter if I drink blood when we spill gallons every day?"

"There are the matters of honor and the code of a warrior," Acton said.

Vampyr laughed. "Honor? What honor is there in fighting against a city one day, then marching arm in arm with the same people you were just fighting against, to fight against some *other* city or empire? I have seen nothing of honor among you."

"There is the honor of following orders. Of being true to those who are your comrades. You can barely restrain yourself to stay in the shield wall and when we make contact with the enemy line you always break formation and battle on your own. I gave you the position at my side not out of honor, as it should be, but because I did not want to expose anyone else to your recklessness and disregard for your fellow warriors."

"I slay more enemy than any five of you combined," Vampyr boasted, glaring at the knights.

"If it was just about slaying," Acton said, "then butchers would reap many honors."

Vampyr snarled, trying with all his might to rise, but there were numerous ropes wrapped around his body, and all he could achieve was lifting his head. "You fools. What do you think you're doing? Are you going to kill me?"

"There would be no honor in that," Acton said. "And you have fought for Sparta for as long as any can remember."

"You have no idea what I have done for Sparta," Vampyr shouted. "I was one of the Three Hundred. I stood with Leonidas in the Gates of Fire."

Acton took a step back, startled by these words. "That cannot be. That was many lifetimes ago. No man can be alive from then."

Vampyr said nothing.

"You are not a man, are you?" Acton finally asked. He turned to his left and gestured. A man stepped out of the darkness into the torchlight. An old man with long white hair, leaning heavily on a cane, dressed in a long black robe that was worn and dirty. "It is as you said," Acton said to the newcomer. "He is not human."

"Who is this?" Vampyr demanded.

"My name is Tyrn," the old man said, speaking Greek with a strange accent. "I have traveled long and far to come here. I am of the *Wedjat*."

Vampyr was surprised for the first time in many centuries and it showed on his face.

The old man nodded. "You know the word from the ancient tongue and you know what it means."

Vampyr remained silent.

Tyrn looked at Acton. "He has walked the Earth much longer than Sparta has existed. He is one of the Undead. I have read of his kind in the records of my order. They are a blasphemy of mankind."

There was murmuring from the ranks of the knights at these words.

"He lies," Vampyr said.

"He does not lie," Acton said simply. "He said you drink blood and that has long been the rumor in the agoge. I followed you into the town and saw you do exactly that with my own eyes. He says you have lived a very long time. And you yourself said you were at the Battle of Thermopylae, something impossible for any man still alive."

"He must be killed," Tyrn said. "He is an affront to mankind."

"Easy, old man," Acton said, putting a hand on Tyrn's shoulder. "He is a Spartan. He earned that, regardless of where he came from or even what he is."

"Let me go and I will leave Sparta," Vampyr said. "I am done with people's petty squabbles anyway."

Acton held up his xithos. "As you learned in the agoge, a sword has two edges. Because you earned being a Spartan, I will not kill you. But, I cannot allow you to leave being what you are and having learned what we taught you. If you leave Sparta, you must leave behind what Sparta gave you."

"And how do you propose to do that?" Vampyr demanded.

Acton walked up to the field table. He slid his xithos into its scabbard, and then held a hand out to his rear. A knight came walking up with a bloodstained axe in his hands.

"What are you going to do?" Vampyr demanded, straining against the ropes with all his might.

"I am taking back what Sparta has given you as best as I can," Acton said. He raised the axe over his head. It came down in a straight and accurate blow, slicing into Vampyr's right arm midway between wrist and elbow, severing the end of the limb. Vampyr's right hand flopped off the table, the fingers still twitching.

Vampyr gritted his teeth and glared at Acton, holding back the scream of pain by virtue of the very training Acton was trying to undo. Blood spurted from the stump, pulsing onto the table and ground. The Spartan commander walked around the surgeon's table to the other side. Lifted the axe. And swung it down, severing the left hand at exactly the same point.

Vampyr screamed.

Two surgeons rushed forth, wearing leather gloves to hold red hot irons they had just pulled from a fire. They pressed the glowing metal against the forearm stumps. The smell of burning flesh filled the air, along with Vampyr's screams. He didn't even notice the Watcher Tyrn gingerly gathering his two severed hands and sprinkling them with black powder from a vial. Both appendages withered away at the touch of the mysterious powder.

The surgeons cauterized the wounds, then bound tight leather strips around the upper arms, further stemming the flow of blood to the severed limbs. All Vampyr knew was pain, radiating up both arms, into his core, then circling, mixing with his hatred into a black cauldron that would never know peace and solace.

CHAPTER 7

FOR NOSFERATU THE DECISION TO follow the course of action proposed by Aspasia's Shadow was not a difficult one to make. If he could somehow find more of the Gods, he might be able to get some of their blood and take it back to Nekhbet. That he was being played by Aspasia's Shadow he had no doubt, but one could always try to change the rules of the game.

Nosferatu had traversed Africa on foot and sailed around it by boat, both astounding feats. But China was a different matter. No one in Greece had ever heard of such a place and Aspasia's Shadow had laughed when Nosferatu had asked where the land lay. "To the east. Far to the east," had been his answer, before letting Nosferatu know it was time for him to leave.

While no one knew where China was, everyone now knew of Macedonia and the boy-king from that province; Nosferatu had a hard time getting anyone to talk of anything else. But the more he heard, the more interested he became in Alexander, son of Philip II, king of Macedonia, and Olympias, a princess of Epirus. Besides what Aspasia's Shadow had said, Nosferatu knew that to go east would be more than a matter of pointing his face in that direction and walking. The Persian Empire, the most recent conqueror of Egypt, lay that way and it was not fond of strangers passing through. He would need help and it made sense to seek out the most powerful ally available.

Nosferatu was impressed by what he heard. Tutored by Aristotle, who was held in great esteem among the intelligentsia in Athens, Alexander was now king of Macedonia to the north of Greece as a result of the assassination of his father the previous summer. In one short year, surrounded by enemies in his own kingdom and those surrounding him, Alexander had brutally exerted his will, executing any who stood in his way.

His power was so great that a Greek congress of states gathering at Corinth had elected him commander of their latest campaign against the Persians, during which he had attacked to the east as far as the Danube River, a fact that certainly intrigued Nosferatu. While conducting that campaign, Alexander had been brought close to disaster at home when Thebes revolted. Yet he'd returned from defeating the Persians and in one week razed the city of Thebes to the ground and sold its population into slavery, an action that caught the attention of the rest of the Greek states not yet allied with him.

The previous year Alexander had gone after the Persians once more, crossing the Hellespont, the water barrier dividing east and west Anatolia, to the east. Alexander attacked a superior force of over 40,000 mercenaries and, according to the tales, totally defeated it while losing only 110 men.

Alexander was currently camped across the Hellespont and the rumor was that he was preparing a further expedition to the east against the Persian main army under King Darius III. With a letter of introduction from Aspasia's Shadow, Nosferatu took leave of the city of Athens and headed north to link up with Alexander and his army.

Beyond all the legends that were growing up about the boy-king, Nosferatu also knew something none of the Greeks and Macedonians who followed him did: He was a Guide, programmed by Aspasia's Shadow using the Guardian computer inside of Mount Sinai.

I✚ ✚⊕⊕K ⊕NⲒⵏ the letter from Aspasia's Shadow with the proper code word that had been imprinted in Alexander for Nosferatu to gain access to Alexander's court. However, to work his way into the inner circle of advisers took two years. There were many who did not trust him, a man whom they only saw at night, but Alexander the King was not only programmed to accept him, but learned to appreciate Nosferatu's counsel. Nosferatu knew patience, a trait he found many mortals did not appreciate. Most important, though, were his forays, when he would disappear for weeks at a time, ranging ahead of the army, hiding during the day, and scouting at night, moving like a ghost and seeing what others couldn't. He would return to the king's tent and brief the king and his staff on the terrain and enemy ahead with an accuracy that astounded all.

Nosferatu knew he could travel more quickly on his own, but he stayed with Alexander because he saw great possibilities and because he knew Aspasia's Shadow was right. The king had his sights set high, much higher than any around him realized, except for Nosferatu, to whom he would confide his dreams of conquest late at night. That those dreams had been implanted, Alexander had no clue, nor did Nosferatu see any reason to enlighten him.

The Persian king, Darius, had retreated to Babylon while Alexander continued to the east and south. Nosferatu cautioned the king that he was leaving his left flank open, but Alexander was more concerned with liberating all the towns along the coast of the Mediterranean and bringing them into the Greek fold. Nosferatu realized that even though Aspasia's Shadow had imprinted a strong desire into Alexander, the young man still retained a large degree of freedom in his decision making. More of the game, Nosferatu mused.

Thus it was that in September of 333, Darius made a bold move from Babylon, marched hard to the west into the rear of the Greek army, and cut Alexander's supply line along the coast. The first notice of this disaster they had was when those hospital cases they'd left behind appeared, wandering up the supply road, their hands amputated, the wounds sealed with pitch, babbling of the mighty Persian army they'd been given a tour of after having their appendages removed.

This was when Nosferatu saw the unique nature of the man, which he had sensed from their first meeting as Aspasia's Shadow obviously had also, expand to take control over an army. Cut off, exhausted from hard marching, drenched by torrential rains, and greatly outnumbered by the Persians to their rear, somehow Alexander managed to infuse his fighters with a sense of optimism.

Alexander personally led the charge against the Persian lines, heading straight for Darius's golden chariot. The Greeks and Macedonians broke through and Darius fled, so frightened that he left his mother, wife, and children behind to be taken hostage.

While his generals urged him to pursue Darius and finish off the Persians once and for all, Nosferatu had different advice, given the new state of affairs. Thus, Alexander marched south, capturing Tyre after a siege, then into Gaza to take advantage of the sudden power vacuum in Egypt. In short order, Alexander controlled the entire Mediterranean seacoast from Greece around to Egypt.

THE NIGHT OF the army's triumphant entry into Egypt, Nosferatu went to the Giza Plateau in the darkness. Alexander and his army remained at the mouth of the Nile, where he was to found the city named after him.

There was panic in nearby Cairo over the defeat of the Persians and the lack of any Pharaoh to fill the void. Nosferatu cared nothing for that. He went to the bank of the Nile, to the same hut he had visited so many years before. How better to learn what was new than to ask those whose job it was to watch?

When he kicked the door open, Nosferatu was not surprised to see a wizened old man sitting on a straw mat, whittling away at a stick. The man looked up at the sudden intrusion, but didn't stop whittling.

"You are a Watcher, a *Wedjat*?" Nosferatu demanded.

"I am of the order," the man affirmed. "I am a Watcher. And I am not involved in your war."

"Your name?"

"Does it matter?"

"No. But your name anyway."

"Kajik."

"Do you know who I am?"

The man's eyes narrowed. "You appear to be a One Who Waits. As I said, I only watch. You have no reason to do me harm."

Nosferatu laughed. "I am not one of them. My name is Nosferatu."

Kajik nodded, still without any sign of panic or fear. "I have heard of you. From my father. The Undead one who killed a God. Who came here and took his love away many years ago."

"You do not seem surprised to see me."

"Much has happened in my life," Kajik said. "It would take a lot to surprise me. I have seen the rule of two Pharaohs and three Persian kings. I have had six of my seven sons forced into armies—the army of whoever was ruling at the time—and die in battles against foes whom they had no reason to fight. I have seen my wife die of grief."

"And the seventh son?" Nosferatu asked. "The next Watcher of Giza?"

"Hidden away. I have taught him what he needs to know and when I am gone he will take over. But for now, I am the Watcher of Giza. I do not fear you nor do I fear death, for I have done my duty."

"I have not come here to kill you, old man."

Kajik shrugged. "So you say. Do you know some of my order now hunt your kind?"

"What do you mean?"

"There are those in my order who see your kind as an abomination that should not be allowed to walk the Earth. So they hunt you."

"I thought you were just supposed to watch?"

"That is our mandate, but some have grown weary of just watching. They search things out."

Nosferatu laughed. "It would be most unfortunate for any of these Watcher-Hunters to find me. For them, not me."

"Perhaps that is what Vampyr thought until Tyrn, what you call a Watcher-Hunter, found him in Greece."

Nosferatu leaned forward. "What of Vampyr? What happened?"

"He fought among the Spartans for many years. Rumors of a very strange man among the Greeks began to grow and were passed on by members of my orders to our headquarters. Then Tyrn began the long search. He caught up to Vampyr in Greece while the Spartans were conducting a campaign against another city and convinced the Spartans to turn on him."

"Vampyr's dead?" Nosferatu could not believe such a thing after so many years. He remembered Aspasia's Shadow speaking of Vampyr fighting to the south.

"The Spartans would not allow Tyrn to kill him. But they cut off his hands and set him off into the wilderness with no clothing or supplies. That was years ago. I think he would have died by now."

Not Vampyr, Nosferatu thought. "His hatred is too strong for him to die."

Kajik shrugged once more. "I tell you only what I know. There is much in the world I do not know."

"Vampyr killed the four remaining Airlia Gods here?"

Kajik nodded while continuing to whittle.

"Tell me something, Watcher."

Kajik stopped whittling and waited.

"You know what happened to Vampyr. Your order exists around the world."

"My order has people in many places," Kajik confirmed.

"What of the other Airlia Gods?" Nosferatu asked. "Where are they?"

Kajik carefully put the stick on the floor, then looked up at Nosferatu. "Why do you want to know?"

"You don't serve them, correct?"

"We will never serve them," Kajik said.

"Then what is the purpose of your order?"

There was a long silence in the hut, before Kajik spoke once more. "It is our mandate to watch."

"Who gave the mandate?"

"At the First Gathering, after the fall of Atlantis, those who were there gave it."

"Men. Like you?"

"Yes. Priests who had escaped Atlantis and who would not serve the Gods ever again after the great betrayal."

Nosferatu thought back to his childhood and the First Age. "Those at that First Gathering had been abandoned by the Gods. Other priests were chosen, many brought here to serve. Maybe to other places. But not those who formed your order. Have you ever considered that?"

"What difference does it make?"

"It means your order was founded out of bitterness."

"So?"

"What is born in hatred is doomed to fail."

"Who are you to say that?" Kajik demanded. "Why do you think those like Tyrn hunt you? Are you any better than the Gods?"

Nosferatu squatted so he was at eye level with the man. "Yes. Because over the years I have learned much. I just want to be able to live in peace. And have my love live. That is all most people ask, isn't it? But as long as the Gods exist, that can never be.

"So I ask you once again, Watcher, what is the purpose of your order?" Nosferatu did not wait for an answer. "I will tell you why you only watch. Fear. Your ancestors— those who founded your order—knew they could not fight the Airlia Gods, so they decided only to watch. It was a decision based on fear. They should have decided to fight them."

Kajik's dark eyes stared at Nosferatu, whatever

thoughts he had to what he was hearing hidden behind them. "Fight and die?"

"This"—Nosferatu waved his hand about the hut—"is living? I have been here before. Nothing has changed here. But the world out there"—he pointed out the door of the hut—"is changing."

"What do you want from me?"

"I have been told that some of the Airlia—those led by Artad, along with him—sleep in a place called China. Is this so?"

"Yes."

"Do you know where exactly? I was told a place called Qian-Ling but that means nothing to me."

"He sleeps underneath a mountain made by men."

"Like the pyramid?"

"That I do not know."

"What else do you know about Artad's sleeping place?"

"A Watcher-Hunter passed through here during the time of my grandfather. He was looking for more information on you and others like you. He told my grandfather there is rumor of Undead near where Artad sleeps."

Nosferatu had never considered that there would be others besides Vampyr. He was still, assimilating this startling news for several moments. Then he asked, "Where is Aspasia?"

Kajik simply pointed up.

"What does that mean?"

"He is not on this planet. He is sleeping among the stars."

Nosferatu slid his legs out from under him and sat down, feeling the weariness of the years he had already lived. Aspasia was inaccessible. It was as likely that Artad was too, even though he was in the place called China.

But that there might be other Undead there gave him hope of perhaps enlisting some allies, in addition to Alexander and his army. Aspasia's Shadow's plan might simply be a distraction, another role of the dice; but that didn't mean Nosferatu couldn't turn it to his own advantage.

Nosferatu took leave of Kajik and returned to the army. Alexander led the army north and east out of Egypt and toward Babylon. They crossed the Tigris and the Euphrates and met Darius once more in battle at Gaugamela. Once more Alexander was victorious and once more Darius fled, although this time he escaped Alexander but not death as he was slain by two of his own generals.

Nosferatu found that following an army on the march made for excellent feeding because of the number of camp followers, on whom no one kept a close eye. However, he was still dismayed at the slowness of the advance. It was four years since he'd left Greece with Alexander and they were still within the known world. He spent many of his nights wandering local villages and cities trying to learn more of the world to the east and listening for any mention of the land of China and of other Undead. But nothing.

At his urging Alexander moved forward in the winter of 331, an unheard-of thing, and captured the Persian capital of Persepolis. He burned the city, ending the Persian Empire.

With access to the Persian court records, Nosferatu found the first mention of a land that might be China. Far to the east and north of a huge mountain range. There were drawings of flying dragons and other odd beasts and tales of a strange people with yellow skin and slanted eyes. He was discouraged to see the distances drawn on the maps and the number of kingdoms still between him and his objective.

Alexander didn't care. They finished the winter outside the sacked remains of the Persian capital as his emissaries went to all the surrounding kingdoms and demanded tribute lest they face destruction. By winter's end his domain stretched from Greece to Afghanistan to Turkistan to Carthage. He was essentially the ruler of the known world.

It was to the unknown world, however, that Aspasia's Shadow's imprinting and Nosferatu's urging pushed him. Any other ruler at such a young age would have been content to govern and reap the rewards of his hard labor. But Alexander was not the ruler of his own mind.

In 326 he crossed the Indus River and invaded the Punjab.

Nosferatu could finally see the high mountains to the north, apparently impassable, blocking him—and Alexander's army—from the goal of China and Qian-Ling.

At that point what Nosferatu had long feared finally happened, the army rebelled. They had been away from home and loved ones for almost a decade in an age when the average life span was barely three decades. They refused to continue and no amount of coaxing or threats by Alexander could make them go a step farther.

Nosferatu stood on the bank of the Indus and watched as the hastily constructed fleet of Alexander set sail, to go downriver and then into the Indian Ocean and on to the Persian Gulf and eventually home.

He did not join them. He turned his face to the north and headed toward the white peaks that seemed to touch the ceiling of the sky. He would try to reach Qian-Ling on his own.

Nosferatu, who knew Vampyr well, was right. Vampyr's hatred had kept him alive when the Spartans had sent him out of their camp, naked, handless, without any supplies, and frighteningly depleted of blood. All he had was his xithos, which Acton had hung around his neck on a scabbard, saying he had earned the weapon.

Vampyr had staggered through the forest, weaving his way among the trees. A wounded animal, simply seeking some place to hide. The first day he'd burrowed under the previous winter's leaves, his body wracked with pain, real and phantom from where his hands ought to be. How could flesh that was not there cause pain? he'd wondered in bewilderment.

He had judged the humans wrongly, he'd realized those first weeks after he was maimed. They were more cunning and determined than he had imagined. He promised himself he would never underestimate them again.

It took all he had learned over the many years and the training of the Spartans for him to survive his wounds and the handicap of not having hands. He fed on children, the old, the weak, those he could overpower most easily. And he made his way south, knowing he needed to get back to his tube, to go into the deep sleep. It took him two years to cross southern Greece. Then another year before he managed to make his way on board a ship to Crete.

He found the island fragmented, the kingdom he had once ruled a distant memory that most believed never really existed. He went to the ruins of his old palace, to the hidden chamber behind the throne room. Using a stick gripped between his teeth, he set the controls, and then crawled in, managing with great difficulty to put the leads around his arms and legs. Then he went into the deep sleep, his mind filled with thoughts of revenge.

CHAPTER 8

NOSFERATU WALKED AMONG THE
stone people, a shadow in the darkness. The statues that
lined the dirt road on either side glared down on him,
their faces forever set in anger. They were a warning, a
silent message sent to those in the area to stay away from
the mountain to which the road led.

Nosferatu could see the peak looming directly ahead,
the destination that Aspasia's Shadow had told him to
seek so many years and miles ago. Nosferatu had gone
north out of India and skirted the foothills of the
Himalayas, following them around to the west, as the few
locals he talked to late at night recommended. He'd
crossed hills and vast deserts, sometimes going for long periods without feeding until finally the massive mountains
were to his right and he was moving east once more. He
came upon a well-worn trading route, one that would not
be called the Silk Road for hundreds of years, but was already in use by intrepid souls willing to attempt the dangerous journey.

He fed upon stragglers and upon those who wandered
too far from nightly encampments. His primary impres-
sion of China was one of vastness. Seemingly endless
deserts rimmed by mountains. He heard there was an
ocean to the east, but very far away.

The Silk Road ended at the city of Xian, which those he had talked to around the fire in encampments had told him to seek. A local warlord ruled in Xian and there appeared to be no centralized government, indicating to Nosferatu that the word "China" was merely a geographical, rather than political, term. He'd spent several weeks in Xian, listening at night to words spoken in darkened taverns, learning the language and feeding to rebuild his strength after his long, arduous journey.

Few spoke of Qian-Ling and then only in whispers. There were supposed to be evil demons around the mountain protecting it, and if one did get past the demons, the story was that those who went in never came out. It was not very much different than what was spoken of the Giza Plateau. When the moon was darkest he departed Xian for Qian-Ling.

Nosferatu paused between the statues and looked up. Three thousand feet high, the mountain was much larger than the great pyramid he had seen in Egypt. It was perfectly shaped, its rounded shoulders graced with terraces filled with plants and trees leading to a rounded top.

Nosferatu sensed movement in the darkness. He made himself as still as the statues. There was someone out there, stalking him. He'd been hunted before, by humans when he had stayed too long in one place and fed too often. They never stood a chance of capturing him in the dark and he always made sure to hide well during the day. But this was different. His pursuer wasn't a clumsy group armed with swords and carrying torches.

Nosferatu moved quickly to one side of the road and hid next to one of the statues. He turned his head slowly, peering about, while also listening closely. He heard a slight rustle of cloth to his right front. There. Also in the darker place at the base of a statue was a figure. Staring back at him. Nosferatu realized with a start that the other could see him just as well in the dark. He knew then that he had found another like him, another Undead.

Then he realized there was more than one. He turned his head to the left and saw another figure. Slowly turning in a circle, Nosferatu saw that he was surrounded by half a dozen silent figures, all of whom held weapons, short swords carried at the ready.

How had they encircled him so easily? He should have heard them well before they got close. Turning swiftly, Nosferatu bounded up into the air, alighting atop a statue and looking down at the encircling group. He leapt from the top of the statue to the next, landing hard and grabbing hold to keep from falling off.

He was surprised to see that the circle had moved and was gathered around the base of this statue, keeping a careful distance, but all eyes upon him.

Nosferatu held up both hands, empty palms out to show he was not armed. The circle didn't respond, simply staying in place, staring. The tableau remained frozen, as if they were statues also, for over ten minutes, then two of those who had trapped him moved apart and another, taller figure, walked between them and up to the statue on which Nosferatu was perched, halting about five meters away. Nosferatu still had his empty hands held up and this new figure mimicked him, doing the same. He appeared to be a man, of above average height for the people of the area, with long dark hair, wearing loose-fitting black pants and shirt of the shiny material Nosferatu had seen others in this land wear, a fabric the locals called silk.

Nosferatu jumped down onto the road and the man held his place. Now that he was closer, Nosferatu could see him clearly in the moonlight.

It was the eyes that told him he was indeed looking at one of his own kind. They were dark and deep and he could sense as much as see a tint of redness in them. Nosferatu felt no fear. Indeed after so many years, he felt a desire to speak with someone who shared his fate.

"Where are you from?" the man asked. He spoke in the ancient tongue of the Airlia.

"I am Nosferatu, made in the First Age of Egypt, the spawn of Osiris the Airlia God and a High Consort of the Gods."

The man nodded. "I am Tian Dao Lin. I was made here"—he pointed at Qian-Ling—"by Artad himself in consort with a sacrificial girl."

"How long have you been here?" Nosferatu asked.

"For over three hundred years I have walked the night here."

Nosferatu glanced about. "And the others?"

"They are from me."

Nosferatu was surprised. "From you? How?"

Tian Dao Lin smiled. "From me and local women."

Mating with a human. It had never occurred to Nosferatu. The hunger for blood had always ruled. And then there was Nekhbet.

"They are less than we," Tin Dao Lin said. "Only one quarter of the God blood. The eldest is almost ninety years old and close to death. Several others, older, have already died of old age."

"Do they also have the hunger?"

Tian Dao Lin stepped closer. "I do not let them feed on blood. They crave and eat human food. I do not want them partaking of the hunger." He gestured. "Come."

Nosferatu followed Tian Dao Lin, the entourage of Quarters falling in behind. They headed directly away from Qian-Ling into the countryside, arriving at what appeared to be an abandoned village, the buildings badly in need of repair.

"These people ran away long ago," Tian Dao Lin said as he led Nosferatu into the largest hut in the center of the village. The Quarters, who Nosferatu saw included only males, separated and disappeared into the surrounding huts.

"No females?"

Tian Dao Lin frowned. "I do not let female Quarters live."

"Why?"

"Because then they could mate with male Quarters and increase their power."

That made brutal sense to Nosferatu. Tian Dao Lin settled down cross-legged on a cushion and indicated for Nosferatu to do the same across from him.

"You have traveled far," Tian Dao Lin said. "It must have been a dangerous and difficult journey."

"It was."

"One does not undertake such an arduous endeavor without a very good reason."

"He who made you . . ." Nosferatu paused.

"Yes?"

"The Airlia—where are they now?"

"They sleep below ground, in the mountain-tomb."

"Can you get to them?"

"No. I have tried and, with tales of great riches, I have tempted others to try. I even sent a small band of Quarters into the mountain. All have failed and most have died in the attempt."

Nosferatu felt a blanket of weariness come down over his shoulders. To have come this far and be told so quickly his goal was not attainable was overwhelming.

"Are you hungry?"

Nosferatu weakly nodded.

Tian Dao Lin stood. "Come. There is still enough darkness. We can hunt together."

NOSFERATU SPENT a week with Tian Dao Lin, feeding and learning of his life. In turn he told the Chinese man of his travels and how things were in the Western world. Sensing that Nosferatu wasn't satisfied with being denied access to the Airlia by just words, Tian Dao Lin agreed to lead him as far into the mountain lair as he safely could.

Early one evening after rising, Tian Dao Lin led him to the base of the mountain, a half dozen Quarters trailing after them. They passed between two large boulders, each with a statue of a crouching tiger perched on top. They entered a small courtyard, thirty meters wide by fifteen long. At the far end were two large bronze doors covered in writing.

"Are there Watchers here?" Nosferatu asked, remembering how there was always one near the Giza Plateau. He quickly described that situation.

"I have not seen anyone like that," Tian Dao Lin said.

"What about Watcher-Hunters?"

"What are those?"

"Humans who hunt us?"

"I, and my people, have killed some humans who came after me, whether they were Watchers or not, I do not know."

They stood in front of the doors. "I hired some bandits to open these doors." Tian Dao Lin swung one a little bit open. "After they breached this, I killed them all to keep the place safe." He then ordered the Quarters to maintain a watch on the doors.

Tian Dao Lin slid through the open door, Nosferatu following. They were in a large anteroom. The walls were painted with many figures, similar to what Nosferatu had seen in Giza, along some sections of the Roads of Rostau.

A wide tunnel was at the end of the anteroom. Ten meters wide, it ran straight as an arrow into the bowels of the mountain. The workmanship was as superb as that of the Roads, the walls cut smoothly.

They went down about two hundred meters where two smaller tunnels, each going ninety degrees in opposite directions, split off. Nosferatu could see the writing on the walls around the split.

"Warnings," he said.

Tian Dao Lin nodded. "Yes. Watch." He walked a little way down the main tunnel. A dim red glow appeared just ahead of him. The glow became a circle, then stretched up and down, narrowing. It took a shape Nosferatu recognized: an Airlia. Pure white skin like ivory, legs and arms longer than a human's, with a large head covered with flame red hair. The burning red cat eyes looked at them as if the image could see.

"That is the image of my father, Artad," Tian Dao Lin said.

The right arm rose, its six-fingered hand extended, palm out. The image spoke in the language of the Gods, reiterating what was written on the walls: It was forbidden to enter unless one had the key. Any who tried to pass without it would die.

"And many have died," Tian Dao Lin said. "If you go farther down this tunnel, there is a beam of light that slices through flesh and bone like a knife through water. None can pass."

"And down there is where Artad and the other Airlia

sleep." Nosferatu did not make it a question, so Tian Dao Lin did not reply.

So close. Nosferatu could sense the Airlia ahead of and below him. Sleeping in their tubes. With the blood he needed to resurrect Nekhbet in their veins.

"What about this key? Any idea where it is?"

Tian Dao Lin shook his head. "None. I have searched far and wide. I fear it might even be down there, with the Airlia. I see no reason why they would leave it outside."

"What about the other tunnels?"

"The one to the left has an air shaft crossing it, very small, which dead-ends at stone. The one to the right—I will show you."

They backed up and took the right-hand tunnel. They went straight and down for a little way, then the passage-way began weaving back and forth in wide turns and descending at a steeper angle. The tunnel suddenly began to widen, then opened into a large chamber, the far end of which Nosferatu could not see. As soon as they stepped out of the tunnel into the chamber, a dim glow came alive far above their heads.

As the glow grew brighter, Nosferatu put his hand up to shade his eyes. "What is this place?"

The glow was soon as bright as the sun, and Nosferatu closed his eyes to mere slits.

"It is where they have stored much of their riches," Tian Dao Lin said.

Nosferatu could see they were in a massive cavern, the roof of which was supported by metal beams. The room had to take up the entire interior of the base of the mountain, he realized. The floor was covered with numerous large black rectangular containers.

"I have tried to get into them, but never succeeded," Tian Dao Lin said.

"Are there no guards?" Nosferatu asked. "In the Roads of Rostau there is a beast that prowls the tunnels and kills interlopers."

"Just the trap far down the main tunnel," Tian Dao Lin said. "Look."

Another red glow appeared in front of them. It coalesced into another Airlia form. The figure began to speak but many of the terms it used were unfamiliar to Nosferatu. He realized it was probably giving an inventory of what was stored there as several times it mentioned amounts and numbers and pointed at various containers.

"I am sorry," Tian Dao Lin suddenly said, catching Nosferatu by surprise.

"Sorry for what?"

"That you cannot get what you came for. That you cannot return and rescue your love, Nekhbet."

Nosferatu backed up into the tunnel, Tian Dao Lin joining him. The light from the chamber dimmed, leaving them in their darkness. They headed back up the tunnel.

"Will you stay here?" Nosferatu asked Tian Dao Lin.

"This is my home."

"Will you watch this place?"

"Yes." Tian Dao Lin knew what Nosferatu was getting at. "If there is a change, if we can get to the lower level, I will let you know. Where will you go?"

That was an interesting question as Nosferatu had no idea what his next move was to be. "I will go back to the west." He did not tell Tian Dao Lin that he planned to go into the deep sleep, as the other did not have a black tube, nor seemed to know of their existence. "I will seek out Aspasia's Shadow and try to learn more."

"He does not sound like a creature that is to be trusted," Tian Dao Lin noted.

"He seems to take amusement in the misery of others," Nosferatu acknowledged. "Still, he has an agenda that was imprinted on him by Aspasia. He sent Alexander and his army in this direction in the hope they would make it and perhaps force an entrance. I am sure he will cause more trouble in the future."

Both were startled when there was a loud bang. "The doors!" Tian Dao Lin cried out.

They raced up the tunnel to find the large bronze doors shut and the bodies of the six Quarters scattered about in front of them in the foyer room, ripped to pieces. Nosferatu and Tian Dao Lin ran to the doors and leaned against them, pressing with all their superhuman might, but they would not budge.

"Who did this?" Nosferatu demanded, as they turned back to face the main corridor.

Tian Dao Lin shook his head. "I do not know. I have been inside the mountain a half dozen times. Never has this happened."

Nosferatu knelt next to one of the bodies. The wounds were clean, caused by something very sharp.

"In the Roads of Rostau—" Nosferatu began, but he fell silent as they heard a noise above them. Both looked up to see a trapdoor swing open in the rounded dome ceiling. A glowing gold orb with black legs—a twin to the one under Giza—dropped down, hitting the floor with a clatter of metal legs on stone.

One leg lifted, razor-sharp tip pointed at Nosferatu, while another was directed at Tian Dao Lin. For several minutes everything was absolutely still in the foyer. Then the sound of boots echoed up the main corridor. Nosferatu took an involuntary step back as two Airlia appeared in the entranceway to the main corridor, long spears in their hands. They wore black, one-piece suits and looked none too pleased, their fierce red eyes glaring at the intruders.

"My lords—" Tian Dao Lin began, hands held up in supplication. His entreaty was cut short by a bolt of gold from the tip of one of the spears hitting him in the chest and knocking him backward.

Nosferatu finally reacted, reaching for the dagger in his belt when a bolt took him in the chest and his world went black.

CRETE: 325 B.C.

Vampyr came awake to darkness. He lay still for several minutes, slowly breathing, trying to regain his orientation. Coming out of the deep sleep was always a disconcerting experience. He reached up to open the tube. When the stump of his arm hit the top of the tube, it all came rushing back to him: what the Spartans had done to him; the years of making his way here, forced to live like an animal, feeding on the weak and the young.

Vampyr pressed the lid open. Faint starlight and moonlight seeped into the chamber from slight cracks caused by the earthquake so many years before. He sat up and fumbled with the leads to his arms and legs, using his stumps and a stick between his teeth. It took hours to remove them, then he exited the tube.

Vampyr held up his arms, staring at the stumps. Something was different. The flesh on the stumps of his forearms had healed and skin covered the wounds—but after over five years of deep sleep he could swear that the forearm was ever so slightly longer. Were his arms growing back? Was the Airlia virus in his blood allowing him to regenerate?

Vampyr left the chamber to hunt for someone to feed on as he considered the possibility. He went to the closest village and reached in a window, taking a sleeping child into what remained of his arms and running off into the forest before the alarm could be raised. He drained the child and buried the corpse in a shallow grave before returning to his ruined palace just before dawn. He searched for a piece of stone that matched the length of his forearms. He finally found one and took it with him into his tube, where he set the controls for ten years and reattached the leads. Then he closed the lid.

WHEN VAMPYR AWOKE ten years later, the first thing he did was open the lid to let the meager light of the chamber in. The second was check his stumps against the stone marker.

They were indeed a fraction of an inch longer. He felt hope for the first time since Acton had swung the axe. His hands would be back. Judging by how little had grown in ten years it would take a very long time, but that was the one asset he had plenty of. Without exiting to feed, he edged toward the top of the tube and with the stick reset the controls for a much, much longer deep sleep. Then he shut the lid and passed again into darkness.

CHAPTER 9

THE BRONZE DOORS LEADING INTO Qian-Ling swung open and a young woman staggered out, a boy-child less than a week old in her arms. The doors swung shut behind her and she wandered into the dark terrain around the mountain. She made it little more than a mile before she was surrounded by a group of four men who were not quite completely human.

They were the descendants of Tian Dao Lin's Quarters, who had stolen local women and intermarried, mixing their blood and genes over and over again through the centuries until what was left were these creatures who prowled the night, attacking unwary travelers, eating their flesh and drinking their blood like animals, with little intelligence left in their twisted minds.

They took the girl down in a swift charge, her screams cut off as one sliced her throat open with a stone knife. Three of the four vied for position at the spurting arteries, drinking her blood. The fourth spotted the small bundle she had carried and picked it up. He felt something move inside the blanket and, knowing the others would want this prize too, he made off into the darkness.

A short distance away he put the bundle down and un-wrapped the blanket. He looked down at the baby boy's face. He frowned, a memory and faint emotion that he couldn't quite grasp whispering in his mind. He did not, however, feed. He rewrapped the child in the blanket and headed back toward the decrepit village his kind in-habited.

He went into the mud hut where he lived with his mate, a woman who had lost her own child in birth from a genetic defect caused by too much inbreeding. He held out the bundle to her and she took it.

HE WAS SMARTER than the others. He'd known that for as long as he could remember. He was also faster, an attribute that had saved his life several times as men in the village, in their burning desire for flesh and blood during particularly lean times, came af-ter him.

He'd also accepted that he must leave. This was not a place for him, among degenerate survivors in a squalid village. But he did not go until his twelfth year, the day after the woman he had grown to call mother died.

He left in the night, as even more so than the others in the village, he could not abide sunlight. He went north and west, away from Qian-Ling. With natural cunning he sought out a weak tribe of humans, one that had suffered many defeats and was living in inhospitable land they had been forced to, slowly dwindling and starving. He entered the first night with a deer he had run down slung over his shoulders. He gave the food to the famished people.

Despite his youth and the oddness of his ways, only

being about at night, his ability to hunt and share what he brought down gained him quick acceptance. Within two years he led the tribe, and already he was wrapped in legend, The old woman who was the tribe's healer and seer claimed he was descended from the union of a gray wolf and white doe and that he was destined for great things.

He learned that these people were known as the Mongols and lived a precarious existence between the empires of China and Russia. He took the name Temujin, after a former local chief who had died bravely fighting the Chinese. He encouraged the myths that surrounded him. He began to conquer one tribe after another. His fledgling rule grew by force of arms, bribery, or expedient alliances.

After ten years, in his early twenties, he had accrued so much power that the Mongol leaders declared their loyalty to him and acclaimed him Universal Monarch—Genghis Khan.

In the year 1202 he led his people against the Tatars and annihilated that tribe, becoming master of eastern and central Mongolia. In 1206 he completed the conquest of Mongolia and was proclaimed the Great Khan. With all the tribes behind he turned his attention in the direction he had always yearned to attack: to the south and east, into China. He invaded in 1211 and overran most of northern China within a year.

Military necessities forced him to attack toward the capital city of Beijing rather than Xian, which was in the vicinity of his true goal of Qian-Ling. The Chinese Emperor sued for peace and sent a princess with an immense dowry as an inducement.

Satisfied that his flank was secure, the Khan turned his mighty army toward Xian and conquered that city easily. Then he rode at the head of his column of troops toward the mountain known as Qian-Ling. On the last day of March 1214, he reached the wide dirt road leading to the mountain.

And there he was halted and could go no farther. An invisible wall that nothing could penetrate extended around the mountain in all directions.

The Khan spent four months encamped just outside of the barrier, probing it nightly, and each time he was stopped. He had bows, spears, even the explosive Chinese powder used against the strange barrier all to no avail. Finally, the demands of keeping his empire intact forced the Great Khan to return to the east and sack Beijing to put down a revolt.

With Qian-Ling denied to him, the Khan decided he would take the rest of the world. There had been a story in the village of someone like their common ancestor Tian Dao Lin, coming from the west a long time ago and disappearing into the mountain-tomb with Tian Dao Lin. The Khan led his forces in that direction.

He conquered Turkmenistan, Uzbekistan, Tajikistan, Afghanistan, and most of Persia. He sacked the great city of Samarkand, slaughtered every single one of its inhabitants, and killed the Sultan Muhammad in 1220. He continued west, farther than any Mongol had ever been, deep into Caucasia, where he defeated a combined Russian-Turkish army. While he was doing that, the Chinese once again revolted. Realizing it was as impossible to maintain such a large empire as to enter Qian-Ling, the Khan staged his own "death" in August 1227.

A handpicked group of twelve warriors took his body to a hidden location to be buried. The night before the burial, the Khan killed all twelve and buried their bodies.

Then he mounted his horse and rode to the west, fading into history and legend.

He went to the fledgling city of Moscow, where he assumed a new identity. One of many he would have over the ages until he was finally known as Adrik.

CHAPTER 10

NOSFERATU WOKE TO FAMILIAR darkness. He was in an Airlia tube, of that there was no doubt. He had spent so much of his life in one, he could sense the dimensions of his prison. However, it wasn't *his* tube, of that he was also certain. He reached up and, as he feared, the lid was secured from the outside.

He tried to recall what had happened. China. Tian Dao Lin. Qian-Ling. The large bronze doors locked, the dead Quarters. The gold spider. Then the Airlia with the spears. That was it. His last memory. They had captured him. The feeling of despair was brought up short by the next thought—why hadn't they simply killed him? And then—was Nekhbet still alive in the deep sleep in her tube?

Nosferatu reached up and felt his neck. A shunt was in place, but he couldn't remember having been fed. So why am I still alive? And how long have I been in here? This was the first time he could recall being awake. He reached farther up and felt the crown on his head and his panic came back. How long have I been asleep?

He heard movement, someone touching the tube, then the top swung up. Nosferatu could only make out a form leaning over him. Hands removed the crown from his head and the leads to the muscle exercisers around his body. Nosferatu blinked, trying to adjust his eyes. The lighting was very dim, but it still hurt his pupils. He could tell from the form that it appeared to be a human who had opened the tube. The man put a hand on Nosferatu's shoulder and pulled him to an upright position.

Nosferatu looked around. He was in a room with a half dozen black tubes. A black wall made of some strange material was to his right. He turned back to his left, where the man that had awakened him was opening another tube. The man was short, less than five and a half feet in height. He wore a richly embroidered silk robe with images of fire-breathing dragons sewn into it. In one hand he held a spear, like the ones used to overpower Nosferatu and Tian Dao Lin.

Nosferatu was not surprised to see his fellow Undead sit up in the other tube. The man who had freed them turned back to Nosferatu. Though the man was short, his eyes indicated he wasn't completely human, as they were the red-within-red cat eyes of the Airlia. A One Who Waits.

"I am Ts'ang Chieh, court official to the most noble Emperor ShiHuangdi, Commander of all the World, the Hidden Ruler whose reign goes from rising to setting sun and beyond." He stepped closer. "ShiHuangdi was Artad's Shadow. Do you know what a Shadow is?"

"I've met Aspasia's Shadow," Nosferatu said.

"We know."

"How long have I slept?"

Ts'ang Chieh glanced at the display at the head of the tube. "One thousand, seven hundred and thirty years."

Nekhbet. It was all Nosferatu could think of as the impact of those numbers sank in. He was consoled by the knowledge that she was in the deep sleep and would not have been aware of the passage of time, just as he had not.

Of course, there was the danger of some natural disaster having overtaken her hiding place in the Mountains of the Moon, but Nosferatu knew he could not dwell on that or he would go insane.

"Who is this Emperor ShiHuangdi?" Tian Dao Lin was out of his tube, getting his legs back under him. "Emperor of what?"

"Who *was* the Emperor ShiHuangdi is the correct phrasing," Ts'ang Chieh said. "He combined all the lands to make the Middle Kingdom known to the outside world as China. We are now in the midst of a vast empire stretching from the Yellow Sea to the far mountains of the west."

"Why have you woken us?" Nosferatu asked. He realized he had jumped over the more important question of why they had been taken alive.

"You are needed," Ts'ang Chieh said. "Aspasia's Shadow is causing trouble in the West. The truce is threatened. The new Emperor, Yongle—acting on my advice and the wishes of the God whose name must not be spoken—is mounting an expedition to maintain the truce. You both will accompany it."

"For what purpose?" Nosferatu asked.

"To kill Aspasia's Shadow."

THE EMPEROR must be taking the threat quite seriously," Nosferatu said, as he and Tian Dao Lin stood next to Ts'ang Chieh on top of the harbor watch tower and peered out over the fleet. A forest of masts crowned the flotilla, which stretched as far as they could see to the mouth of the harbor and beyond. They had traveled from Qian-Ling to Nanking in style, an imperial escort guarding them the entire way.

"Three hundred and seventeen ships," Ts'ang Chieh said. "Crewed by 27,870 sailors and soldiers. The commander, whose ship you will be on, is named Cing Ho. He knows of your nature and your mission. He will get you as close to Aspasia's Shadow as he can."

"And then?" Tian Dao Lin asked.

"You kill Aspasia's Shadow." Ts'ang Chieh reached inside his cloak and removed two swords in sheaths engraved with High Runes. He extended them grip first to the two Undead. Nosferatu and Tian Dao Lin took the weapons. "But"—Ts'ang Chieh drew the word out—"before you kill him, you must find out where his lair is and enter. You must go there and kill the clone that is waiting to replace him. If you do not do that, after a certain amount of time the clone will automatically be reborn to replace him and your efforts will have been in vain. And I am certain the new Aspasia's Shadow will extract vengeance on whoever slew the previous one."

Nosferatu glanced at Tian Dao Lin. "And why should we do these things for you?"

"You are not doing them for me," Ts'ang Chieh said. "You are doing them for Artad. He let you live so many years ago when you invaded Qian-Ling. He could just as easily have had you killed."

"Why not have your Ones Who Wait do this task?" Nosferatu asked, remembering the creature that had tried to kill him in Athens.

"The Ones Who Wait suffered a terrible defeat a while ago," Ts'ang Chieh said. "It will take many years for them to regain their ability to counter Aspasia's Shadow."

Nosferatu wondered what kind of defeat and in what form, but Ts'ang Chieh had no more patience with questions or delays. "If you do not agree to perform these tasks, you will be killed right here immediately. Admiral

Cing Ho has other orders, and he will, shall we say, execute them if you stray from your mission."

CING HO'S FLAGSHIP was the largest oceangoing vessel yet built by man. Over four hundred feet long, it had a compass, a stern rudder, and several watertight compartments built into the hull for safety. It displaced over three hundred tons, making it over three times larger than the ships Columbus would sail to the New World at the end of the century.

As Ts'ang Chieh had said, they were well accommodated aboard the massive flagship with a belowdecks cabin that was all their own. The ship was a marvel compared to what Nosferatu had previously traveled on. Besides its huge size, it had nine full masts spaced out along the deck. The four-story-high rudder was controlled by an intricate system of blocks and tackles so that one helmsman could handle the wheel. Next to the helmsman was the navigator who had a compass consisting of a magnet floating in a small bowl of water.

The journey proceeded in leaps and bounds south along the coast of China, with several engagements with Japanese pirates along the way. From Canton they sailed to Indochina, then on to Indonesia, where Cing Ho confronted and defeated a large fleet of Chinese pirates who were headquartered in Palembang. He kept the lead pirate prisoner to bring him back to Nanking for execution.

With each victory, Cing Ho provided Nosferatu and Tian Dao Lin with captives to feed on in the privacy of their cabin. The two were confined to their cabin except once weekly, when they were allowed to wander the large afterdeck in the evening. Occasionally they met Cing Ho there. Nosferatu found the Chinese admiral to be quite a fascinating character for a human. He was of Arab-Mongol descent and had been captured by the Emperor's forces during the northern border wars. Upon his capture Cing Ho was castrated—a common practice with prisoners—and pressed into the army of a prince named Chu Ti. In 1402 Chu Ti rebelled and usurped the throne from his own nephew and became the Emperor Yongle. For his faithful and brilliant service, Cing Ho was made an admiral.

When Artad directed that a fleet be sent to battle Aspasia's Shadow's growing influence in the Middle East, Cing Ho was given command of the mission. Nosferatu began to realize there was more to the mission, though, than was readily apparent, as they progressed up the west side of Indochina and then on the coast of India. By defeating various pirate groups, the fleet was opening up a waterborne trade route to the west, one that would be much quicker than the Silk Road. Also, Nosferatu and Tian Dao Lin heard whispers of a special cargo on board the flagship, something that had come from the Gods themselves. Any effort to find out exactly what this cargo was drew immediate silence. It appeared that the cargo was held in a locked, waterproof room near the front of the ship, to which only Cing Ho had access.

They rounded the tip of India and entered the Arabian Sea after two years under sail. When they landed at Omuz in the Straits of Oman, Cing Ho led a large force ashore. The ostensible reason was to subjugate the local population, but he took Nosferatu and Tian Dao Lin with him, the first time their feet had touched dry land since leaving China. He ordered them to scour the local area at night and see if they could find word of Aspasia's Shadow.

For weeks Nosferatu and Tian Dao Lin went from village to village, even venturing out into the desert, all to no avail. At Nosferatu's urging they ranged north far into the desolate countryside of what would become Iran until they found an oasis where a group of Bedouins were camped.

From his journeys many years ago, Nosferatu still remembered some of the desert people's language. He and Tian Dao Lin entered the encampment just after nightfall, their wrists draped with pearls and their open palms filled with gold.

The first Bedouins they encountered were wary and would not take the offered riches; but they took the two to an ornate tent set in the middle of the camp, next to the water. Nosferatu and Tian Dao Lin entered and bowed before the old man who sat in the place of honor, and four of the desert warriors took a position between them and the old man, scimitars drawn.

"We come from the land of the Emperor Yongle, far to the east," Nosferatu said. "We bring you gifts of peace."

The old man didn't reach out to take the gifts, but indicated they should be deposited on the ground in front of the warriors. Nosferatu did as indicated and waited.

"I am Al-Fatar, leader of the Qabila of Fatar. We have heard of strange, great ships to the south. Is this how you came here?"

Nosferatu nodded. "Yes. We have journeyed far."

"Why?"

Nosferatu knew such directness was unusual for Bedouins, who had strict rules of hospitality which he had counted on. He realized it would be best to be as direct. He sat down cross-legged. "We are seeking someone. A powerful lord who is supposed to dwell between here and the land of Egypt. Since you travel much of that land, we thought you might be of assistance in this matter."

"This lord's name?"

"Aspasia's Shadow."

Al-Fatar shook his head. "I know of no such lord."

"He might go by another name," Nosferatu said.

"Then how would I be able to tell you if I knew him?"

"He is more than a man," Nosferatu said. "He has lived the lives of many men. He has walked the Earth since before the beginning of time, when the Gods themselves walked the Earth."

Al-Fatar stared at Nosferatu. "If he is so powerful, why should I tell you of him?"

Nosferatu stood. "Because I too am powerful. And I too have walked the Earth since the time of the Gods. I was in Egypt before the Great Pyramid was built. And the great fleet you have heard of is under my command."

Al-Fatar was not impressed. "Words are easy."

Nosferatu jumped, bounding over the warriors as he drew his dagger. He landed behind the old man and spun about, pressing the dagger against his throat. "Is this blade easy on your skin?"

Tian Dao Lin had also moved, attacking in a flurry faster than the Bedouins could follow. Within seconds all four warriors were unconscious on the floor. More Bedouins poured into the tent, weapons at the ready; but they came to a halt on seeing their leader's plight.

"Tell me what you know," Nosferatu said.

Surprisingly, Al-Fatar laughed. "I have never seen a man so eager to go to his death. The person you seek is called Al-Iblis. Some say he is a man, but most call him a demon. He has been sending out a call to the Bedu, wanting us to ride under his flag. Many have chosen to do so. Some say he has spells he casts over men to make them do his bidding. I have stayed here, far away from him, and will not go to his flag, so I care not what you do."

"Where can I find this Al-Iblis?" Nosferatu demanded.

"In the Sinai," Al-Fatar said. "It is said he rules from Jabal Mosa, where the prophet Moses received the law from Allah. What those in the West call Mount Sinai."

Nosferatu had never heard of the place or anyone named Moses, but he knew they could find it with that information. "What is Al-Iblis doing?"

"He is raising an army to fight in the name of Allah. To pursue a Jihad."

"What is a Jihad?" Nosferatu asked, the word not one he had heard before.

"A war of faith."

"Against whom?"

Al-Fatar shrugged. "It is not my concern, but the rumor is he wants to march on Egypt, that he seeks something underneath the Great Pyramid."

Nosferatu wondered what Aspasia's Shadow sought in Egypt. The Grail? Had he found the key to the Hall of Records? Or something else? Nosferatu nodded to Tian Dao Lin. He turned and slashed with the sword he had been given by Ts'ang Chieh cutting a hole in the side of the tent. They both dashed out the improvised exit and into the desert. Nosferatu was not surprised when there was no sound of pursuit.

CING HO LISTENED to Nosferatu and Tian Dao Lin's report in the privacy of his cabin aboard the flagship. When they were done he unrolled a map across his large desk, pinning the ends down with small lead weights. The information on it was based on intelligence gathered, not firsthand knowledge, as no Chinese sailor had ever ventured so far from home.

"The Sinai is a large place" was Cing Ho's summation, tapping the large blank space indicating a landmass between the Persian Gulf and the Red Sea. "You have no idea where exactly this mountain is?"

"No," Nosferatu said.

Cing Ho seemed troubled. "This land is not very hospitable. I believe it will be difficult to find a landfall where we can get enough provisions for the entire fleet."

Nosferatu remained silent. Cing Ho's problems were not his. He and Tian Dao Lin had even considered not returning to the fleet, but the reality was that the Chinese armada was their best possible chance to overcome whatever force Aspasia's Shadow was gathering. For Nosferatu the goal was to get Aspasia's Shadow to reveal where Horus and the other three Airlia were in the deep sleep, so he could drain the blood from at least one of them for Nekhbet. For Tian Dao Lin the fleet was his best opportunity to return to his home in China and be in favor with Artad.

"I will land here," Cing Ho finally decided, tapping a landfall on the Sinai next to the Red Sea. "However, there is something we must first do elsewhere."

Nosferatu wondered what could be a higher priority than finding and killing Aspasia's Shadow, but he kept the question to himself.

IT TOOK A WEEK to sail around the tip of the Sinai. As they approached the Red Sea, Nosferatu felt a twinge of recognition. It had been many, many years since he had sailed out of the Red Sea on a flimsy reed boat, escaping from Egypt and the Airlia Gods.

Nosferatu received a second unexpected surprise when, instead of turning to the northwest and entering the Red Sea, they cut south across the Gulf of Aden to the shore of Africa and actually turned to the east, paralleling the shore, in the same manner Nosferatu had done so many years previously. For a moment, as he saw the shore of Africa appear, he feared that somehow Cing Ho knew where Nekhbet was hidden and was heading for her; but he realized the ridiculousness of that fear immediately. He had told no one, not even Tian Dao Lin, where he had hidden his love. And why would Cing Ho—or his master, Artad—care? Nosferatu knew that the Chinese admiral was on some other mission, most likely something to do with whatever was locked in the vault near the bow of the ship.

They sailed along the Somalian coast before making landfall in a natural harbor. A small village was on the shore and Cing Ho had all the villagers put to the sword. That evening, under the cover of darkness, Cing Ho went to the forward hold and unlocked the door. A heavy wooden crate was brought out and rowed ashore. Two long poles were slid through hinges on either side. Cing Ho formed a division of two thousand soldiers on the beach, the crate secure in the middle, carried by a dozen men on each pole.

Nosferatu and Tian Dao Lin watched from the deck of the flagship as the formation moved inland. Cing Ho had not said a word to them, so by default they were being left with the fleet.

"Where do you think they are going?" Tian Dao Lin asked.

Nosferatu shrugged. "What is more important is what it is that they are carrying. It is more important than Aspasia's Shadow."

"Perhaps it has something to do with Aspasia's Shadow," Tian Dao Lin suggested.

"How can that be?"

It was Tian Dao Lin's turn to shrug. "I do not know, but Artad is obviously very wise and his reach is long."

"There is one way to find out," Nosferatu said. "You remain here. Keep up the pretense that I remain in our cabin. I will follow." The Chinese had not watched the two very carefully, primarily because jumping ship in the middle of nowhere wasn't considered a viable option.

Nosferatu had no problem slipping off the flagship undetected. It was also easy to follow the trail of Cing Ho's army inland as they cut a broad swath through the jungle. Nosferatu quickly caught up to the army. He followed for two weeks, sleeping during the day while the army marched and catching up every evening.

The terrain quickly grew more rugged and mountainous. Near the end of the second week the army entered the strangest land Nosferatu had ever seen. It was as if a giant had smashed the Earth with a large axe, leaving a massive rift in the surface. A river ran in the bottom of the rift and sharp peaks surrounded it on both sides. Nosferatu followed the army down into the rift.

After two days of difficult maneuvering north, the army came to a halt. That evening Nosferatu watched from a nearby hill as Cing Ho gathered a small group of his most trusted warriors around the mysterious box. They were lined up next to the wall of the rift and Nosferatu blinked in amazement as they turned toward the wall and seemed to disappear from view. He realized there must be an opening, perhaps a cave in the rift wall. He crept down through the Chinese camp to the spot and saw an opening behind a boulder. He could see the glow from the torches of those who had entered ahead and he followed, keeping his distance.

The small tunnel soon opened into a sloping cavern

over five hundred meters wide, the ceiling over a hundred meters high. Nosferatu knew from his time in the Roads of Rostau and Qian-Ling that this was not a natural formation but the work of the Airlia Gods. For as far as he could see the cavern descended into the Earth at the same angle. Cing Ho's party was a glowing spot about eight hundred meters ahead.

Nosferatu followed. The cavern grew even wider until he couldn't see either side. While the Black Sphinx and Qian-Ling had been magnificent in their own ways, this cavern made Nosferatu wonder at the true power of the Airlia. He felt as if he were descending to the very center of the Earth as he continued to follow Cing Ho's party down the steady slope.

He realized that the temperature, which had been cooler than the outside when he first entered the cavern, was beginning to rise. Then, far ahead, he could make out a faint thin red glowing line. As he got closer he could see that a crevice split the cavern floor. The far side of the crevice was over half a mile away. Nosferatu swung to the right as Cing Ho's party reached the crevice and came to a halt.

Sliding to the edge of the crevice, Nosferatu peered down. The walls were vertical and there was no bottom that he could see, just a bright red glow pulsating upward. He could feel the wave of heat coming from the bowels of the planet. It was a mesmerizing vision and, with great difficulty, he drew his attention back to Cing Ho as he heard the faint echo of the Chinese admiral giving orders to his men.

Nosferatu saw that there was a console, similar to the one he had seen in Qian-Ling, near the edge. Cing Ho was standing behind it, his hands moving over the surface, his face reflected in a glow. Nosferatu moved back and above the site. He could see that the surface of the console was like that on his own tube—covered with hexagonals with High Rune writing.

Cing Ho tapped several of the hexes as two of his men used bars to break open the crate. As the wood fell away it revealed a large, dull red, multifaceted sphere. Other soldiers gathered round the sphere and, at Cing Ho's command, carefully edged it toward the edge of the chasm.

Cing Ho hit another hex and a black metal pole came out of the side of the chasm. Then another. And another. The three poles stopped when they were extended about fifteen meters out. Three intrepid soldiers climbed down and balanced themselves on the poles as the other slid the red sphere over the edge. As soon as they had the sphere balanced precariously on the poles, the soldiers quickly moved out of the way.

Cing Ho continued to work the console and cables snaked out of the poles, wrapping around the sphere. Then the poles began to extend once more. As they did so they spread apart. The sphere suddenly dropped, only to come to a halt five meters below, suspended from the cables. The poles continued to extend until they had bridged the chasm and the sphere was directly in the center.

Cing Ho ordered his men back. Then he hit one last hexagonal.

Nosferatu dived to the floor as the sphere gave off a fierce red glow, bathing the immediate area with light. Cing Ho and the soldiers were so focused on the sphere that they didn't spot him. A shelf slid out of the console, and upon it rested a small black sphere that Cing Ho removed and placed in a leather satchel at his side. Nosferatu got to his feet and ran back up the cavern into the darkness.

Looking over his shoulder he could see that Cing Ho and his men were also heading back.

Nosferatu sprinted on, keeping ahead of the group. Heading upslope, the cavern seemed even larger. He had no idea how long they had been underground, but his internal sense of time told him that it would be daylight. He moved to the right, out of the direct path to the exit, and allowed Cing Ho and his men to pass.

He sat down on the smooth stone to wait. Cing Ho and his group passed out of sight. Nosferatu had no idea what he had just witnessed, but he was sure there was great power revolving around the mysterious red sphere.

Several hours later, Nosferatu heard the sound of metal on stone echoing down the cavern. He panicked, worried that Cing Ho was sealing the cavern from the outside. He dashed upslope until he could see several torches near the entrance, but quickly came to a halt when he realized they weren't blocking the entrance. They had erected a black stone, three meters high by one in width. Several men were polishing the surface smooth while another was chiseling something on it as soon as they finished a spot.

This went on for several hours, then the group departed, leaving Nosferatu in darkness once more. He went up to the stone. He could just make out the Chinese writing. He'd learned the language while on board ship and he read the words: *Cing Ho reached this place as directed. He did his duty as ordered.*

THEY MADE LANDFALL at Jidda, a small port along the Arabian coast. Nosferatu had easily beaten Cing Ho and his men back to the fleet and told

Tian Dao Lin about what he had witnessed. They discussed it at length but had to accept that they had no idea what the purpose of putting the ruby sphere in the cavern could be. They also discovered that Cing Ho had had every man who'd gone into the cavern with him executed during the march back, their bodies buried in the barren countryside.

Leaving a guard force of five thousand sailors, Cing Ho led the rest of the contingent, roughly twenty-three thousand men, ashore. He took the entire town of Jidda hostage and located Jabal Mosa by the expedient methods of torture and execution.

Finding the mountain's location was easy, but getting there would be another matter. According to the information they received, the mountain was located inland, across inhospitable desert. Cing Ho approached it as if they were simply continuing their long voyage on land. Numerous water casks were unloaded from the ships, along with other provisions, and the army set forth with several captives who claimed to know the location of the mountain at the head of the column. They marched at night, resting during the heat of the day.

Nosferatu and Tian Dao Lin rose each evening and ranged out from the long, dusty column, searching the countryside. On the fourth evening, the two crested a small hill and looked to the south and east. They could see two mountains in the distance. Looking back the way they had come, they could see a plume of dust indicating the progress of Admiral Ho's column, the lead about a half mile behind them.

Nosferatu knew without having to consult any of the captives that the mountain to the left was Jabal Mosa even though the other was taller. It was a jagged peak, with a gray cloud swirling around the top, a most strange phenomenon as the sky was otherwise clear, the stars sparkling overhead.

They waited until Cing Ho rode up to their position. The Chinese admiral stared at the two peaks for several moments in silence, then he spoke. "The locals—the desert people—they worship the mountain. They say a demon lives there."

"That would fit," Nosferatu said. "Aspasia's Shadow enjoys sowing fear."

"I will encircle the mountain this evening. Tomorrow evening we will assault it. You will follow the assault to finish off Aspasia's Shadow once we have him cornered."

Nosferatu said nothing as Cing Ho went off to deploy his large army. When he was out of earshot, Tian Dao Lin expressed what Nosferatu was thinking. "It has been too easy."

Nosferatu continued to stare at the cloud-crowned peak. "Thus far it has. I think that will change tomorrow evening."

AS DAWN BROKE, Nosferatu and Tian Dao Lin sat on the hill, their bodies draped in robes, turbans wrapped around their faces, protecting their eyes. Through the layers of cloth both could see the dust raised by the Chinese army as it moved forward toward Jabal Mosa. Bugles relayed commands, keeping the advance coordinated. By early afternoon the mountain was surrounded by a cordon of troops.

"There is something strange about the mountain," Tian Dao Lin said. "One can understand why the local people believe it is haunted."

The unnatural cloud that swirled around the peak had not dissipated all day and yet remained. There wasn't any sign of life on the slopes of the mountain even though Cing Ho made no attempt to hide his preparations for attack.

As darkness fell, the thousands of torches that the Chinese soldiers had carried with them were lit, encircling Jabal Mosa with a ring of fire.

Nosferatu sniffed the air. "Something is not right."

Tian Dao Lin was looking about, left and right. "We're not alone. Humans. Close. Behind us."

Nosferatu saw nothing, but he could smell the sweat of men. He stood when a half dozen figures appeared, bows with drawn arrows in their hands. Nosferatu and Tian Dao Lin drew their own weapons, prepared to give battle.

"Hold." The language was that of the Airlia, followed immediately by something in Arabic to the warriors. The speaker strode forward.

"You must have come close to Artad," Aspasia's Shadow said, coming to a halt in front of the two Undead. He looked past them at the circle of fire and laughed. "But you did not slay him it appears. You have been gone a very long time." He looked at Tian Dao Lin. "Another half-breed. By Artad?"

Tian Dao Lin nodded. "Artad is my father."

"It is rather amazing that the Airlia have been viewed as Gods for so long considering how they seem to want to consort with inferior species." He gestured back the way he had come. "Come with me."

"Where?" Nosferatu held fast.

"Come with me or die here and now."

Nosferatu and Tian Dao Lin bowed to the inevitable and irresistible and followed Aspasia's Shadow as he made his way down the hill. More Bedouin warriors appeared in the dark, completely surrounding them. Peering about, Nosferatu realized there was a massive army of

Bedouins surrounding the Chinese. How so many had managed to move up unnoticed he didn't know, but if anyone could do it here, he knew it would be the desert people.

Aspasia's Shadow seemed to disappear behind a boulder and when they followed, they discovered a door, similar to the guarded entrances to the Roads of Rostau, that opened on the back side of the boulder. They entered along with a guard of a dozen Bedouin warriors. As soon as they were all inside, the door slid shut.

The corridor was dimly lit by recessed lighting of a form Nosferatu had never seen before. They descended, then reached a long, straight tunnel of smoothly cut stone. They went along the tunnel for quite a while and Nosferatu realized they were passing underneath the encircling Chinese troops. Soon the tunnel began to ascend and they entered a large hallway with wood doors along both sides.

Aspasia's Shadow halted in front of one of the doors. "Now you will see my power." He opened the door and walked down a short corridor. A second door, this one of black metal, slid open at his approach. "Stand here," Aspasia's Shadow ordered, indicating the entryway.

Nosferatu and Tian Dao Lin went to the indicated location and looked into the strange room. Aspasia's Shadow went to the center of a hemispheric chamber. He pulled a sword out of a sheath on his side and slid it into a dark red crystal directly in front of him. A golden field emanated from the pommel of the sword, covering Aspasia's Shadow and reaching the walls. Nosferatu felt it pass over his skin with a crackle, the same feeling he'd had sometimes at sea during a storm when lightning played along the masts of the ship.

The walls came alive with a view of the terrain surrounding Jabal Mosa. It was as if they were standing on the top and able to look in all directions. The ring of approaching Chinese troops was readily apparent, with every fifth man carrying a torch.

WHAT N⊕SFERATU and Tian Dao Lin couldn't see was the fifty-foot black metal pole that extended up out of the top of the mountain. Mounted on the very end was a golden sphere, which was hidden inside the black swirling cloud covering the peak.

ASPASIA'S SHAD⊕W directed his gaze toward a section of the incoming Chinese line. His hand was on the pommel of the sword. He squeezed the grip.

A B⊕LT ⊕F LIGHTNING arced from the golden sphere to the spot Aspasia's Shadow was looking at. It hit with a tremendous explosion and sent a surge of electricity through the ground. Those within fifty meters of the impact point were killed outright by the explosion. Anyone outside of that range but within two hundred meters was electrocuted by the power coursing up from the ground.

N⊕SFERATU AND Tian Dao Lin watched in amazement as Aspasia's Shadow shot bolts along the front of the Chinese line, killing hundreds, then thousands. The attack came to a halt, then the troops began to turn and run, unable to face an assault from what appeared to be the Gods themselves.

Aspasia's Shadow laughed as he continued firing. "Who is the commander of this force?" he demanded.

"An admiral named Cing Ho," Nosferatu said.

"Do you see him?" As he asked, Aspasia's Shadow twisted the sword's handle and they saw a close-up view of a section of the panicked troops, then the view rotated slowly, circling the mountain, pausing when Aspasia's Shadow realized he had found the command group. A bright red banner fluttered, embroidered with a dragon. In front of it stood Cing Ho, shouting commands, sending couriers off to the troops, trying to keep them from fleeing. As Aspasia's Shadow zoomed in on the commander, they could see he was holding up a small black sphere in one hand as if presenting it to someone.

"That is not good," Aspasia's Shadow murmured.

"That is he," Nosferatu confirmed. "But beware," he added.

Aspasia's Shadow let go of the pommel and turned to Nosferatu. "Beware what?"

"Beware what Cing Ho has in his hands."

"I recognize it," Aspasia's Shadow said. "It is a command module." Aspasia's Shadow looked at them. "What does it have command of?"

Nosferatu smiled for the first time. "Why should we tell you? You plan on killing us, don't you?"

Aspasia's Shadow looked back at the image of Cing Ho. The admiral's forehead was covered in sweat and his hands were shaking. He held the black sphere with both hands and was staring up at the peak of the mountain from which the lightning had come.

Aspasia's Shadow cursed. "I cannot fire at him—the power surge might activate the sphere. And whatever it controls. Tell me and I will give you what you want. The blood of an Airlia. And I will let you leave here alive. I give you my word on it."

Nosferatu wasn't certain how much Aspasia's Shadow's word was worth, but he knew there was no choice. He had a feeling no one wanted Cing Ho to activate the black sphere. It was obvious that even the admiral was afraid of what he held. "Before we came here, Cing Ho led an expedition into Africa. Far inland, where a deep valley cuts into the Earth. He went into a cavern, cut out of stone, much like this place. Obviously by the Airlia. At the very bottom, over a flaming chasm, he emplaced a glowing red sphere. It now hangs over that chasm. I believe he can drop the red sphere with the device he holds in his hands."

Aspasia's Shadow cursed once more. "Artad! Always a move ahead." Aspasia's Shadow shifted the view on the walls to the 360-degree display. Cing Ho had regained control of his forces, but the soldiers were refusing to advance. He still held the command module in his hands. Aspasia's Shadow looked at Tian Dao Lin. "Do you speak his language?"

"Yes."

Aspasia's Shadow reached into a pocket and pulled out a six-inch-long black rod with a green button on one end. He tossed it to Tian Dao Lin. "When you push the green button, your voice will sound as if it comes out of the mountain itself. This Cing Ho will hear you. You will say what I tell you to. Do you understand?"

"Yes."

Speaking in Chinese, Tian Dao Lin translated Aspasia's Shadow's words into the device and they echoed off the top of the mountain:

"This is the voice of Al-Iblis, ruler of Sinai, descendant of the Gods. The truce has been restored. Return whence you came and never return and I will disband my forces. And I will not seek the weapon beneath Giza if you do not activate what you have emplaced."

Nosferatu watched the screen. Cing Ho was staring up at the mountain, listening. His troops were cowering, first from the lightning assault and now from the God-like voice speaking their language.

Cing Ho lowered the command sphere and bowed every so slightly in the direction of the mountain, then began issuing orders. The Chinese army started to withdraw.

ASPASIA'S SHADOW led them along a corridor inside the Jabal Mosa complex. He did not seem particularly upset by what had just occurred. "Stroke. Counterstroke. So it has been for millennia. So it will continue until both sides awaken and finish this damn war."

"What weapon is buried under Giza along the Roads?" Nosferatu asked.

Aspasia's Shadow laughed. "It is none of your concern, half-breed." He opened a door and they walked into a chamber filled with a half dozen black Airlia tubes. He went to the closest one and laid a pale hand on the top. "Horus's body is within. As I told you, he is dead, but I have kept the corpse in stasis." He went over to the side of the room and opened a black box, retrieving a syringe and two glass flasks.

Nosferatu felt the pang of hunger, even though he had fed just two nights earlier. Aspasia's Shadow swung up the lid of the tube, revealing an Airlia body inside. Nosferatu recognized Horus and was suddenly flooded with memories—of being a child playing in the sand under the bright sun; of being trapped and bled for centuries; of his fellow half-breeds being killed; of Nekhbet imprisoned on the top of the Black Sphinx.

Aspasia's Shadow slid the syringe into Horus's neck. Dark red blood, almost black, slowly flowed along the tube into the first flask. "Unlike human blood," Aspasia's Shadow said, "because of what it contains, Airlia blood remains viable even if the body is dead. You can take this with you." He finished filling the first small flask, then did the second. He glanced at Tian Dao Lin. "I suppose you desire some too?"

Tian Dao Lin nodded.

"Get another flask."

Tian Dao Lin did as ordered and Aspasia's Shadow filled it. Then he removed the syringe and he returned it to the case. Aspasia's Shadow shut the lid and put the flasks in a wooden case, which he handed to one of the silent Bedouins.

He led them out of the room, along the tunnels to the surface. Once they exited the interior of the mountain, Aspasia's Shadow took the case from the Bedouin and gave it to Nosferatu. "Take these and go. Do not ever return here."

CRETE: A.D. 1425.

Eleven hundred years. Vampyr had originally considered setting the tube for an even thousand, but decided to throw in the extra hundred years just in case. It had been long enough. His hands were back, all the way to the tips of his fingers, the skin smooth and flawless. He held them in front of his face, marveling at the feeling, at being able to grasp things. It was amazing how something he had taken for granted for so long had become so important.

It was time to venture out into the world once more, to inflict pain and suffering on those who had done the same to him so many times in the past. First, though, he would try once more to rule an empire. He had learned a bitter lesson about power from his time with the Spartans.

Crete was too isolated. The first thing he would do, after feeding, was buy transport off the island to find a fertile land for his terror.

CHAPTER II

TRANSYLVANIA: A.D. 1462.

"THAT IS ASPASIA'S SHADOW," Nosferatu said as he pointed across the field behind the center front of the Turkish army. He was standing next to Vampyr in the center of the Hungarian force that faced the Turks.

Vampyr was dressed head to toe in black armor, with a full visor helmet on. Strapped to his side was his Spartan xithos. Nosferatu had learned in the month he had been in Transylvania that this was how Vampyr always appeared in daylight, which, along with certain brutal practices, had led to his reputation as prince of darkness. Nosferatu himself wore a gray hooded cloak and a face mask to protect his skin and eyes. It was early morning and the Turkish army commanded by Aspasia's Shadow had been approaching since dawn.

For thirty-seven years Nosferatu had nursed his anger toward Aspasia's Shadow. After leaving Mount Sinai, Nosferatu had split from Tian Dao Lin. His Chinese friend had headed west to link up with what remained of Cing Ho's fleet and go back to China. Nosferatu had journeyed from the Sinai into deepest Africa to recover Nekhbet's tube from the Mountains of the Moon, a most arduous journey. But all had been for naught when he opened Nekhbet's tube, brought her awake, and gave her the blood that Aspasia's Shadow had given him. It had had little effect and she'd been drawn and tired, aging almost in front of Nosferatu's eyes. They realized he'd been duped by Aspasia's Shadow and given human blood instead of Airlia. Together they'd made the difficult decision once more to put her to sleep in the tube and leave her on the mountain.

Seeking revenge, Nosferatu had heard rumors of a dark lord gaining power in Hungary and he'd guessed that Vampyr was the subject of the rumors. Listening to people speak in port cities he learned that a prince called Vlad Tepes had establish a strong domain in the midst of much political turmoil in Eastern Europe. He'd united many of the warring factions, extending his power from Transylvania over most of Hungary. Nosferatu had traveled there, throwing himself on the mercy of his old comrade, seeking an alliance against Aspasia's Shadow.

In his loneliness after so many centuries Vampyr had welcomed Nosferatu into his castle at Tirgoviste. As Nosferatu had hoped, the combined threat of two Undead together in one place and Vampyr's growing power had drawn Aspasia's Shadow's attention. Unfortunately, they had not expected such a massive and swift response. The Turks Aspasia's Shadow had under his command outnumbered the Hungarian army three to one and Nosferatu could sense the uneasiness among Vampyr's troops.

"Lord Vlad Tepes." Vampyr's commanding general went to one knee in front of him, calling him by the name he had assumed since working his way into a position of power in Transylvania. Translated, the name meant Vlad the Impaler. The Turks called him Kaziglu Bey, the Impaler Prince.

"Yes?"

They were deployed on the east side of the Danube, blocking the Turkish army's invasion route into the heart of Hungary. Initial intelligence reports had not indicated that the opposing army was as large as what was currently deployed in front of them, but Nosferatu knew that Aspasia's Shadow had unnatural ways of recruiting soldiers to his cause. The two armies were drawn up parallel to each other on a large two-mile-wide field that sloped from rough hills in the east to the broad Danube in the west. To the rear of the Hungarian army was a narrow pass, less than a hundred meters wide.

"We cannot hold this line," the general said, keeping his eyes downcast.

"You can hold it until you die," Vampyr corrected him. Nosferatu noted movement near Aspasia's Shadow, then a flag of truce was displayed on a long spear.

"Look." Nosferatu tapped Vampyr on the shoulder. "We should go discuss the matter with my old friend."

Vampyr spurred his horse and galloped down the small hillock on which he had set his command group, Nosferatu following. Soldiers leapt to get out of their way as they raced forward. Aspasia's Shadow came from the Turkish lines, dressed in the fine armor expected of a high prince. They met halfway between the two lines.

"Does the sunlight hurt?" Aspasia's Shadow greeted them as he lifted his own helmet visor, revealing his pale face.

"Only if I allow it to," Nosferatu replied. Neither he nor Vampyr lifted their visors, as was the custom during a parley.

Aspasia's Shadow looked past them, taking in the Hungarian forces. "You cannot hold against me."

"How many of your men are Guides?" Nosferatu asked. "How many have you corrupted?"

Aspasia's Shadow laughed. "Just my primary commanders. And speaking of corrupting"—he looked at Vampyr—"your manner of rule is quite notorious."

"I rule through fear," Vampyr acknowledged. "It is what works best."

Nosferatu had heard rumors of Vampyr's brutality, but having only been there a short time, he had yet to see it firsthand. The stories he'd heard seemed so outrageous that he dismissed most as having to do with the fact that Vampyr fed off live victims brought to his castle.

"You have been building up your strength for over a decade," Vampyr continued. "All of Eastern Europe knows you plan to move north and west to conquer."

"You know that the Grail is no longer hidden in the Roads of Rostau?" Aspasia's Shadow asked, a surprising twist to the conversation.

Nosferatu shrugged. "Some say it is in England, where you fought Artad's Shadow so many years ago. Others say the Watchers have hidden it. I have even heard the Watchers took it back to Giza. Another tale says that the one called Merlin carried it far to the east, into the high mountains so no man could get to it."

"I think it is in England," Aspasia's Shadow said. "So I decided to go there."

"With an army at your back?" Vampyr asked.

"Better than going alone," Aspasia's Shadow said with a smile.

"You betrayed me," Nosferatu said.

"Surprise, surprise." Aspasia's Shadow laughed. "And how is your love Nekhbet doing?"

"You did not give me the blood of an Airlia. You switched it. You gave me human blood. It did nothing for her. When I brought her awake, she was weakened and sick, not alive as she should have been."

"For someone as old as you are," Aspasia's Shadow said, "you are rather naive."

Vampyr held his horse in place with some effort. "The Eldest has always been love-struck. But now you deal with me."

Once more Aspasia's Shadow looked past them at the army. "You will not hold me."

"Perhaps," Vampyr said. "We shall see."

"Then I suppose we will have to fight," Aspasia's Shadow said. "I've let you live too long anyway."

"So be it," Vampyr said. He turned his horse and as he did so, he signaled to his general. Nosferatu turned to follow and saw that the front of the Hungarian army began to fall back, the rear echelons having already been pulled back as they talked to Aspasia's Shadow.

With great haste, the Hungarians retreated, catching the Turks by surprise. By the time Aspasia's Shadow fully realized what was happening—that Vampyr was not going to do battle with him here—the bulk of the army was through the pass. Vampyr left a special unit to hold the pass as long as possible, five hundred knights whose families he held hostage in his castle. Nosferatu listened as Vampyr promised the knights if they held the pass to the last man, slowing down the Turks, he would free their families. If any of them retreated, he promised that not only would the coward die, but so would his family. It put chains of fear into the five hundred and they turned to face the Turks with the frenzy of the doomed.

Vampyr led his remaining army north, burning everything they passed, leaving nothing, not even a blade of grass for Aspasia's Shadow's horses to feed on. Reaching Tirgoviste, Nosferatu was stunned by what Vampyr had prepared and he realized the stories he had heard were true.

On the large plain in front of the castle was a man-made forest. Over twenty thousand eight-foot-high stakes had been driven into the ground. The upright end of each wooden pole was sharpened to a point. At Vampyr's signal, Turkish prisoners captured in previous battles were driven from their holding pens onto the plain. Working efficiently, apparently having had considerable practice, teams of soldiers used a rolling crane to lift a prisoner by his tied hands. They then threw a loop over each ankle as he cleared the ground. The crane was turned until the prisoner was positioned directly over one of the poles. With a soldier on each ankle lariat pulling to either side and down, the prisoner was lowered, impaled on the stake until it was far enough into his body that he could not get off. The ropes were released and they moved on to the next prisoner. They could impale a man every minute and there were over twenty crews at work.

The screams began and did not stop.

"What are you doing?" Nosferatu demanded.

"You are indeed a fool," Vampyr snapped. "Aspasia's Shadow is right. I am amazed that you have lasted this long. How do you think I keep these people under control?" He did not wait for an answer. "Fear. It is the primary motivation of humans. It is how the Airlia ruled in Egypt." He gestured. "A man can last up to six days impaled, depending on the angle the pole makes on its way through the body as gravity slowly pulls him down."

Vampyr leaned close to Nosferatu. "And the smell of the blood. It is so sweet. I have found traces of the Airlia God blood once in a while. Very faint, but every so often there is some. I drink from those."

Nosferatu wondered if his old comrade had lost his mind, having lived so long. Vampyr had not spoken of the time after leaving Egypt so many years ago or how he had survived. Nosferatu knew how heavy the weight of the years could be on the mind. He had not shared with Vampyr his own adventures or what had happened to him under Qian-Ling. Most especially, he had not told the other about Nekhbet and where she was hidden.

It took twenty-four hours for all twenty thousand prisoners to be impaled. The screams of the dying echoed off the walls of Vampyr's castle, reaching down to the cell where Nosferatu tried to get some sleep during the day.

The Turkish army arrived on the third day. They heard the screams before they crested a hill and saw what was causing it. The sight that greeted them was more horrific than any had ever seen.

And stalking among the stakes was Vampyr, sniffing, searching for any pole with blood soaking down it that contained even the least part of the Airlia virus. In over twenty years of impalement, he had found four people with very faint traces. He'd had them immediately removed from the stake and brought into the castle, where he drank their blood.

Nosferatu stood on one of the turrets of the castle and watched, his desire for vengeance lost amid the horror he was witnessing. He realized that Vampyr was no better than Aspasia's Shadow or even the Airlia.

Even Aspasia's Shadow and his handful of Guides could not overcome the horror the Turkish army faced. The army began to disperse, fear giving wings to men's feet. Within an hour the invading force was racing to the south, spreading the word of the terror that dwelt in Transylvania and was known as Vlad Tepes.

Yet through the chaos, Nosferatu could see one solitary figure who remained on a distant hill, staring down at the forest of the dying. Even at this distance he knew it was Aspasia's Shadow. And he knew that he would never know peace as long as the Airlia or their minions such as Aspasia's Shadow or the Ones Who Wait walked the Earth. He also knew that he could not take the path that Vampyr had, trying to use humans as pawns in the fight— he would let time defeat Aspasia's Shadow and the Airlia.

Nosferatu slipped away that night, riding hard to the south. He had decided he would make his own Haven in the one place he had been where humans did not go: the Skeleton Coast. And he would bring Nekhbet there and wait. It was what he did best.

MOSCOW: A.D. 1533.

Ironic. It was a concept that the man who had been anointed Great Khan by the Mongols was finding more and more applicable to human affairs. He now went by the name Ivan and had been in Moscow for over a century, gathering power. The previous tsar, also an Ivan, had been the one finally to defeat and stop paying tribute to the Golden Horde, the descendants of the Mongols that the Khan had led out of the west so many years before. For that he had been known as Ivan the Great.

In a palace coup the new Ivan had replaced the old Ivan, but the people did not add "the Great" to his name, but rather "the Terrible," as he ruled Moscow and the burgeoning Russian Empire with an iron fist covered in blood. Ivan the Terrible's greatest troubles came from the *boyars*, Russian noblemen, who knew that there was only so much power to be had, and the more the tsar had, the less there would be for them. This was a different type of power struggle for Ivan than when he had been the Khan, and he used different tactics. To fight the *boyars* Ivan developed ranks of government bureaucrats who owed their jobs, and thus their loyalty, to him. He also took land from the *boyars* and gave it to generals loyal to him.

Russia's power grew as the years of his rule stretched on. He pushed Russia's borders south and west into Siberia. He opened commercial trade routes with England through the treacherous White Sea. He brought foreigners in for technical and military advice, something later monarchs, especially Peter the Great, would imitate.

None of these efforts, naturally, was what gained him the name appendage of "the Terrible." He earned that because of his nature. He was only about at night and, of course, in dark chambers of the Kremlin, he fed on the blood of criminals brought to him. He routinely ordered mass executions at whim. Perhaps most disastrous, he began a system of serfdom, tying workers to landowners, something that would boil over with stunning results centuries later.

He continued in this manner, his rulings growing more and more outrageous, his murderous decrees growing broader and more capricious until one morning, after he had left the throne room, the captain of the palace guard led a dozen of his bravest men in an assault on the room deep under the Kremlin to which Ivan the Terrible retired every time the sun rose. They carried flickering torches to light their way in the dark warren of tunnels, swords to slay the tsar, and chains to weigh the body down, as the plan was to throw him in the river.

They broke down the door to the room where they had determined the tsar hid every morning and were briefly stunned to see a stone coffin resting on a pedestal. Since there was no other way out of the room, and they had seen Tsar Ivan go in, they had to assume he was inside. Throwing off their shock, they wrapped the iron chains they had brought for the tsar's legs and arms around the coffin and locked them in place. They were rewarded with the lid lifting the inch of slack that was in the chain and their tsar screaming dire threats at them, demanding that they remove the chains.

Having committed themselves, they knew they could not turn back. They dragged the coffin out of the room as the tsar continued to scream at them. They pulled it along the tunnels built under the Kremlin by the tsars, and those before the tsars, as escape routes in case of exactly what was happening at that moment—a coup—or invasion. They reached a deep, narrow shaft that went down over 150 feet. It was the remains of an attempt years earlier to reach water before someone realized the Moscow River was not even that far away laterally and a tunnel was dug to that water source.

The captain of the guard had the men place the coffin on the lid of the well. This was better than the river, he decided, thinking of the long walk back to the surface.

They tipped the coffin on edge. It wavered, then turned vertical, sliding down out of sight, just a bit smaller than the circumference of the shaft. Seconds later the thud of the coffin hitting the bottom of the shaft reverberated up to them.

THE PRESENT

CHAPTER 12

The Skeleton Coast, West Africa

"GENTLEMEN, ARE WE IN AGREE-ment?" Nosferatu sat down in the chair at the head of the table and shifted his gaze between the two men.

"I will do my part," Tian Dao Lin said. Both then turned and looked at Adrik.

"I can recover that which the KGB has," Adrik said. "What is your timetable for all of this?"

"The X-craft launches in three days. It will take it about twelve hours to rendezvous with the derelict mothership and drain the bodies. Then it will land at an airfield close to here. At that time I will begin processing the blood. Ninety hours."

"That is not much time to get someone up Everest to recover the blood from the Ones Who Wait," Tian Dao Lin said.

"No, but it is possible," Nosferatu replied.

"I will make it happen," Tian Dao Lin averred.

Nosferatu stood. "I will see you gentlemen back here in four days."

Puget Sound, Washington

Four days. Vampyr stared at the intelligence report that had just been forwarded to him, then walked over to the large bay windows in his mansion overlooking Puget Sound and the lights of Seattle beyond. It was a magnificent view, one that he had enjoyed for the past ten years, ever since purchasing his own private island in the Sound at an outrageous cost.

Money meant nothing to Vampyr. His assets were under so many different names and umbrella corporations that it would take a roomful of accountants several lifetimes to figure it all out, which was appropriate in Vampyr's view, as it had taken him the equivalent of many lifetimes to accumulate it.

He did not pursue money for itself, but for what it could bring, which was a form of power. There were many forms of power and Vampyr, since his time in Sparta, had dedicated large amounts of his time to studying them all.

He had used his money to hide himself, most particularly during the recent world war in which the humans, most surprisingly, had defeated the Airlia. In all his long life Vampyr had never anticipated that the humans would be capable of such a feat. He had prepared for one side or the other of the Airlia to gain the upper hand if they ever came out of their deep sleep underneath Qian-Ling or on Mars but the human victory was totally unexpected.

The Grail was lost. Lisa Duncan had made sure of that, taking it and the second mothership down with her into the array on Mars. In Vampyr's opinion, a most brave but stupid action. He did appreciate that she had stopped the Airlia from getting a message out to others of their kind, but losing the Grail was a tremendous blow. It had always been his primary plan to recover the Grail once it was located and use it to gain the immortality the high priests had chanted about since Atlantis.

Now he felt like he had come full circle. It was all about blood. But Airlia blood now. He knew exactly what the Eldest, Nosferatu, wished to do. But he had learned one thing over his many incarnations among the humans—power could only be wielded by one. While the Eldest was so focused on bringing back Nekhbet, Vampyr did not trust him. And then there was Tian Dao Lin and Adrik. Four was three too many in Vampyr's opinion.

He turned from the large, bulletproof windows and went over to the large globe in his study. The walls of the room were lined with books, many of them ancient, original texts that scholars would weep with envy just to be given a glimpse of. They were not for show, as Vampyr had read all of them.

Vampyr placed his hands on the globe and slowly spun it.

Everest. Moscow. And in the derelict mothership in orbit.

Nosferatu and the other two were moving. Vampyr knew that power, like chess, was all about move and countermove. And allowing one's opponent to set his own destruction in motion.

Patience. Four days was but a blink of the eye in the eternity that Vampyr had lived, but he knew it was long enough.

Time to move a few pieces.

CHAPTER 13

Mount Everest

THE HIGHEST POINT ABOVE THE surface of the Earth is the peak of Mount Everest. At 29,028 feet high, it is the highest and most inaccessible place on the surface of the planet. The perfect place to hide the key to the Master Guardian, which controlled all of the Airlia computers—the legendary sword of Arthur: Excalibur.

The race to recover it had been brutal. On one side had been Mike Turcotte and Professor Mualama. On another, two Navy SEALs turned into Guides by a Guardian computer and questing for the key in order to bring it to Aspasia's Shadow. On the third front, Chinese military forces led by three Ones Who Wait, human-Airlia clones who served Artad. Even on Turcotte's end all had not been as it appeared, as it turned out that Mualama had been corrupted by a Swarm tentacle and had tried to destroy the sword, only to be thwarted by Turcotte at the last moment.

In the end, Turcotte had emerged victorious, literally the last man standing on the mountain, Excalibur in his hand, and that had allowed Yakov, inside the last mothership hidden in Mount Ararat, to gain control of the Master Guardian, and thus all other guardians, allowing the world to win World War III and compel the alien forces to leave.

Littered on the slopes of Everest were the bodies of those who had failed in this quest: SEALs, Chinese, Mualama, and—last but not least—the three Ones Who Wait. They mingled with the bodies of 160 climbers who had died in their attempt at summiting over the years. Most of those bodies lay in the "death zone" above 25,000 feet.

Everest was not considered a particularly difficult climb in terms of technique, but the collection of avalanches, crevasses, winds up to 125 miles an hour, storms, temperatures that went down to forty degrees below zero and oxygen depletion make it the deadliest place on the planet. In the death zone the air holds only one-third the oxygen present at sea level. As a result high-altitude pulmonary edema (when the lungs fatally fill with fluid) and high-altitude cerebral edema (when the brain, starved for oxygen, swells) are common, often causing death unless the person is quickly brought down the mountain, something that is practically impossible as the death zone is above the reach of even the best helicopter's altitude ceiling.

High overhead was a spy satellite launched by the Russians. Its mission was to monitor southwest China. Within its zone of observation was Everest. Under orders relayed covertly from Moscow, the high-resolution camera turned its attention to the slopes of Everest and began quartering the snow-covered terrain. Since Turcotte had been the only one to come off the mountain alive, no one knew exactly who had fallen where.

It took over four hours, but a complete image of the mountain had been accomplished. The data was digitized, then transmitted to Moscow military headquarters, where it was forwarded—with a healthy kickback of cash going the opposite direction—until it ended up in the hands of the one who had requested it.

Adrik sat behind his desk and stared at the file marker on his computer screen. It had cost him one phone call and over 1.6 million US dollars to get this imagery. He didn't even bother to open the file and look at what his money had bought. Instead, he had it electronically transferred to Hong Kong. Then he sent the file to a second destination.

Earth Orbit

It was the largest object in Earth orbit, far eclipsing the collection of pods that made up the International Space Station. The mothership was over a mile long and a quarter mile wide at the center, coming evenly to points at both ends. In the forward portion there was a huge gash in the black metal where Mike Turcotte had set off a nuclear charge supplemented by an Airlia fuel pod inside a cargo bay. Floating inside the bay were also mangled Talon spacecraft—Aspasia's fleet from Mars, which had come to recover the mothership. In one fell swoop Turcotte had managed to destroy most of one side of the millennia-old Atlantean Civil War.

Now the mothership floated dead, a symbol of mankind's victory over alien forces. Inside the Talons were dozens of Airlia bodies, preserved in the cold vacuum of space. And inside their frozen veins were the scant remnants of the virus that Nosferatu and his comrades sought.

Hong Kong

Nima Namche wasn't used to the ill-fitting suit he was wearing or the low altitude. Even though the anteroom he was waiting in was on the forty-fourth and top floor of a skyscraper in the center of Hong Kong, it was still at least three miles lower than where he lived, in the Khumbu Region of the Himalayas. He was a Sherpa, one of the mountain people, and his motivation for coming to Hong Kong was a simple and ancient one: money.

A Sherpa, Tenzig Norgay, had been at Sir Edmund Hillary's side when he became the first to summit Everest and they had been part of every expedition ever since, or at least the ones that were known about. Namche knew that others had climbed Everest for reasons other than summiting, but among the Sherpas those climbs were not spoken about openly.

He'd been approached by a well-known Sherpa whose job it was to coordinate guides for expeditions— except this proposal had been very different. Namche was given one hundred thousand US dollars simply to fly to Hong Kong, an unheard of sum, with the promise of another nine hundred thousand US upon acceptance of the climb. Who he was to guide and when he was to do it were two questions he hoped to have answered soon.

So far, answers had been in short supply. He'd been met in the airport by two very pale men wearing expensive suits and sporting dark sunglasses who had simply taken his one, rather decrepit piece of luggage and escorted him to a waiting limousine. He'd sat in the back with the two men, who had not offered a single word of greeting or even acknowledged his presence, their attention focused on the exterior as if they were concerned about being attacked.

They'd led him into the lobby of the building, past the security guards, and to a private elevator. When the door had opened, one of the two had indicated he should exit and upon his doing so, the door had shut, leaving Namche alone in this room.

There was a large stainless-steel door directly ahead that Namche had approached, but decided against knocking on. He doubted any sound would carry. So he sat and waited, something that did not overly bother him considering the strange reception.

He started at a slight hiss. He was amazed as the steel door slid to the right without making another noise. Namche got to his feet and tentatively approached the doorway.

"Come in." The voice was Chinese, the words English.

The interior of the room from which the voice had come was dark, and Namche paused in the entryway, trying to get his eyes to adjust. All he could see at the moment was a wooden chair with a single beam of light oriented on it.

"Sit there," the voice ordered.

Namche walked to the chair and sat down on the edge, trying to peer ahead to see who owned the voice. His seat in the beam of light, however, defeated any possibility of his eyes adjusting to the darkness or penetrating the room's interior beyond the cone of light he was in.

"You have summited Everest six times."

Namche did not think it was a question but he nodded anyway. "Yes, sir."

"Each time you guided another to the top."

"Yes."

"I do not need you to summit. But I do need you to climb within forty-eight hours and take someone with you."

Namche immediately began shaking his head. "It is the off-season. The weather will not allow climbing for at least another month, and that is only to base camp. And then—"

"Silence."

Namche fidgeted on the edge of the chair, fearing he was in the presence of a rich madman. He'd seen some of those who hired Sherpas to help them get to the top—men and women who had money to spare but could barely climb off their cots, never mind up the great mountain. They expected literally to be carried up there. And Namche had friends who had died trying to do just that. No amount of money was worth that. He had always picked carefully those he'd guided.

"The party consists of only one person. You must get him to these spots."

Namche turned in surprise to his right as a three-dimensional image of Mount Everest suddenly appeared, hovering in the air. There were three red dots flashing. Namche immediately recognized the locations. The first was along the northeast ridge approach, a most difficult route. The other two were close together on the Kanshung Face, a place where no one went because it was not on either of the two approaches to the summit. It was hard to tell because of the flickering image, but Namche had to wonder what the dots represented, as he knew the Face was almost sheer for over a vertical mile. Among Sherpas, the top of the Kanshung Face was a place of legend where none he knew dared approach.

"Forty-eight hours is impossible," Namche said, still marveling over the holographic image. He had been to the summit and lived in the shadow of the mountain all his life, but he'd never seen it presented like this. "Acclimatization takes at the very minimum two weeks at base camp or else—"

"There is no need for acclimatization," the voice said. "My man is ready to climb. And you will get as high as you can using the most advanced helicopter in the world. This helicopter will drop you off at 17,000 feet right here." A dot glowed on the image. "My man just needs you to lead him the last bit to these places."

"Why?" Namche hadn't meant for it to be so blunt, but it was all coming so quickly and the situation was so strange. He had no idea who he was speaking with.

"Because we are paying you one million dollars to do so."

Namche wasn't sure what to say to that. It was more than he could ever hope to make in a lifetime. And he knew he didn't have many more climbs left. He had already cheated the fates too many times. He glanced at the image. The legends said there had been strangers who'd climbed Everest in the distant past and put something on the mountain at the top of the Kanshung Face. Something special. Namche's curiosity was warring with his fear.

"And because my name is Tian Dao Lin and I am telling you to do it."

Namche almost leapt off the chair in fright. It was a name mothers used to frighten their children to stay safe in their beds at night. A name that brought fear even as far away as Nepal and Tibet. The light level in the room increased, a dim glow coming from recessed strips around the top edge, and the bright light above his chair began to dim. Namche blinked, as his eyes slowly adjusted. Finally, he could see a large teak desk. The surface was covered with papers and scrolls. And behind the desk a tall chair. And in the chair what appeared to be a man, with liver spots on his bald head, but the face and eyes were unnatural.

It was the eyes that riveted Namche. He had been in the Himalayas all his life. He had met the old wise men who followed the path of Buddha, men who could do remarkable things. But he'd never seen eyes like these. They glowed with a red fire and fixed him to the seat with their stare.

"Do you understand?"

Namche could only nod.

A door to Tian Dao Lin's left rear opened and a man walked in. He was thin, his face like the edge of a knife. His skin was pale white. He went to the side of the desk and stood rigidly at attention.

"This is Tai," Lin said. "He is the man you will guide to those three bodies."

The last word barely registered on Namche for a moment, then it hit home.

"You may wait outside," Tian Dao Lin said.

Namche got to his feet numbly and walked out of the door. Tai remained standing, still as a statue.

Tian Dao Lin turned his seat toward Tai. "You understand what you are to do?"

"Yes, Father."

Tian Dao Lin reached into a drawer and pulled out a small wooden flask. The exterior surface was intricately carved with many Chinese symbols, the interior lined with animal gut to make it waterproof. "I give you the gift of my own blood. It will allow you to survive the climb, but you must be swift."

"Yes, Father."

Tian Dao Lin handed Tai the flask. "Do not drink until you are ready to begin the climb."

Kouros, French Guiana

With the decimation of the American shuttle fleet, the most active spaceport on the planet's surface was no longer Cape Canaveral in the United States, but Kouros in French Guiana. Set on the coastline of the South American country, Kouros was originally the launch site picked by the European Space Consortium.

The reasons the European Space Consortium chose to locate their launch facility on a different continent were several and practical. Europe's population density was too great to safely put a launch site there. Also, the politics of which country would get the site was a problem none had wanted to wrestle with. From the engineer's point of view, there was also the question of latitude, as all of the participating European countries were rather high up on the planet, making a launch less advantageous.

Kouros was on the ocean, which meant a launch took place mostly over water. It was near the equator, making possible the use of centrifugal acceleration of the planet's rotation, the so-called catapult effect, to help launch payloads. The ESA ran Kouros more as a business than a nationalistic endeavor like NASA and the American space program. As such, one of its goals was to try to make money; because of this, anyone who anted up enough cash had access to both the facilities and launchpads and even rockets if they paid enough. The Russians had even gotten in on the deal, providing Soyuz rockets as platforms for commercial satellite launches.

A state-of-the-art satellite preparation complex had been financed by Arianespace, the ESA, and GoStar, a private company that, unknown to most, was financed by Vampyr. The EPCU, Ensemble de Préparation des Charges Utiles, was a massive complex, covering over ten square kilometers, with buildings occupying four square kilometers of that area. It held three twenty-meter-high "clean" rooms connected by corridors eight meters wide by twelve high. Components moved along the corridors on hovercraft, ensuring smooth and efficient transportation.

For the first time in its short history, the EPCU was being used for only one task. In three of the four buildings were specially designed components that had just finished their final testing. They were part of a revolutionary concept from GoStar that had been in development for over eight years and finally neared completion.

From Building 4, a maneuvering-and-thruster assembly was loaded onto a hovercraft and floated down the corridor to Building 1, where it was set on the center platform. From Building 3, an environmental-and-shield assembly was finished and also moved to Building 1 and fitted to the M&T assembly. And most important, in Building 2, the crew compartment had just been finished. It had been hovered to Building 1 where, like the last piece of a puzzle, it was connected to the other two assemblies.

The X-Craft was ready.

Technically the first flight was scheduled to be launched in two days and was labeled simply a test flight to make sure the craft was functional.

It was to be anything but that.

Moscow

At the knock on his office door, Adrik looked up from his computer screen.

"Enter," he called out.

The man who entered was short, wiry, and impeccably dressed. Petrov had traded his military uniform and the blue beret of the Spetsnatz, the Russian Special Forces, for tailored suits over six years earlier and had never looked back.

"Sir." Petrov may have traded camouflage for suits, but his manner was all military as he stood ramrod straight in front of Adrik's desk.

The office was dark, lit only by recessed lighting above rows of bookcases that lined all the walls. They were on the first level of the most modern office building in Moscow. The books on the shelves would have made a collector weep with envy. First editions dating back hundreds of years, they were an eclectic gathering for a mind that had grown bored with the world around him many centuries earlier.

Other than the recessed computer screen, the desktop was clear. Adrik sat in a high-backed, black leather chair. There were two halogen lights behind the desk that pointed forward, fixing Petrov in their glow, while Adrik was hidden in shadow.

"Have you ever been in Lubyanka?" Adrik asked.

"Yes, sir."

Usually Adrik liked Petrov's lack of verbosity. He detested those who spoke and said nothing. At the moment, though, he needed a little bit more from his subordinate. "When?"

"Several times in my career, sir. During my time in Spetsnatz we worked closely with the KGB and SVD's paramilitary people."

"Have you ever been in the tunnels underneath Lubyanka that connect with the Kremlin?"

"No, sir."

"You will be. There's something down there I need you to get for me."

"Yes, sir. And that is?"

"Blood."

Airspace, Polar Region

Vampyr's jet was taking the shortest route from Seattle to Moscow, flying over the top of the world. He sat in the rear, with only the glow from a large flat-screen display illuminating the cabin. Through one of his defense contractor companies, he had access to the United States military's secure Interlink system. He also had the proper code words to bring up data from just about anywhere in the system.

Vampyr accessed Space Command, headquartered underneath Cheyenne Mountain outside Colorado Springs. That was the unit responsible for tracking all objects, man-made and otherwise, in orbit around the planet. He brought up the data on the derelict mothership. He projected its orbit and was pleased to see that it was stable.

He stared at the image of the Earth floating on the screen with the mothership's orbit projected in red for a few seconds. Then he accessed the Space Command database and checked to see if the mothership's orbit would intersect at any time in the near future with the orbit of any other object.

On the screen the paths of anything that would come close to the mothership flashed, then disappeared as the computer determined that there would be no collision until the screen froze showing a green track intersecting with the red one of the mothership. Green indicated a future orbit for something not yet launched.

Vampyr ran the code for the orbit.

TL-SAT-7-7//MISSION-COMMERCIAL//GOSTAR//KOUROS

It was as he had expected. GoStar was a company that was under Nosferatu's control through various other holdings. When he tried to find out more about the specific payload, he discovered that Space Command didn't have that information. As Kouros was a privately run launch site, it had no obligation to provide it. Vampyr could guess well enough without it, having tracked Nosferatu's development of the X-Craft for years. He'd even covertly steered a few scientists in his fellow Undead's direction to aid in the research and development.

Satisfied that all was going as he'd projected in that area, Vampyr shifted his attention elsewhere. A contact in the Hong Kong police department who kept tabs on Tian Dao Lin for him had reported the arrival of the Sherpa and his departure on Tian Dao Lin's personal jet with one of the Chinese Quarters. Destination: a staging area close to Mount Everest. Again, as expected.

Last, he decrypted the latest message from Adrik. The youngest Undead had only gone to the meeting at the Haven because Vampyr had told him to. Vampyr smiled coldly when he thought of the Russian. Another fool who fancied himself quite cunning. Adrik owed his very existence to Vampyr. After all, it was Vampyr who had rescued him from his stone coffin underneath the Kremlin so many years ago, less than a week after the palace guard had dumped him into the shaft.

What had apparently never occurred to Adrik was how Vampyr had been able to find him. The Russian had accepted Vampyr's explanation, that he had heard of Adrik's rule and wanted to join forces with him. The Russian had never entertained the idea that it had been Vampyr who had enticed the palace guard to revolt—not that they had needed much enticement—so that Vampyr could be lurking in the shadows to rescue him, and thus have him in his service.

Vampyr had let Adrik suffer in the stone coffin stuck

in the shaft for a week, stopping by occasionally to hear his screams—enough time to make the gratitude for rescue that much stronger. Certain of Adrik's secret loyalty, Vampyr had gone his own way, traveling to the West, first to England, then on to the New World to make his fortune, while Adrik had reincarnated himself once more in Moscow, now heeding Vampyr's advice not to seek obvious power, but rather to gain it in the shadowy world of the criminal.

Vampyr read Adrik's report. He was disappointed but not surprised that Adrik had delegated the mission into the tunnels under Moscow to recover the blood. After Adrik's experience, not even the lure of eternal life could bring him to enter those tunnels again.

Vampyr sent a message back to Adrik with further instructions. Satisfied, he leaned back in the chair and closed his eyes.

The Skeleton Coast

Nosferatu walked into observation room and looked through the one-way glass at the sterile blood lab. It was getting more and more difficult to obtain clean blood from the continent. The AIDS rate in South Africa was closing on 50 percent of the adult population, a number the rest of the Western world had yet to comprehend in its horrific totality. Elsewhere in Africa it fluctuated between 25 and 40 percent. The best scientists were projecting that at the current rate the continent would be close to being depopulated in two generations.

Nosferatu had to admit that Adrik did have a point. Left to their own devices, humans could be extremely destructive and horrific in their treatment of their fellowmen.

Drug companies in America and Europe had the medicine needed to keep most of the infected people in Africa alive, but they made the cost so prohibitive that few could afford it. Profit over life. It was an equation that Nosferatu had seen many times before. On the other hand, though, he had also seen human behavior that defied such cold logic and showed the best of the species.

Inside the lab, the specialist that Nosferatu had hired at an extravagant wage was checking each bag of fresh blood flown in from Cape Town. Each pint cost Nosferatu over five thousand dollars and though it was supposed to have been screened at a hospital in South Africa, almost a third had to be discarded either because of the HIV virus or other infectious problems.

The equipment in the lab was the best available on the current medical market for screening blood, but Nosferatu knew from the data that it wasn't good enough for what he needed to achieve once he acquired the Airlia virus.

There was one place where such equipment had been designed, based on Airlia machinery in the mothership: Dulce, New Mexico, where Majestic-12 had sent part of its classified programs, the ones having to do with biological and chemical operations. Dulce had also been pulverized by foo fighters. The Americans had begun excavating the rubble, but that effort had been sidetracked by World War III. Nosferatu's informants had reported that excavation had been put on hold, while America focused on rebuilding and helping other countries devastated by the recent war, particularly South Korea.

Nosferatu stirred uneasily. When the other two fulfilled their parts and brought the blood to him, he needed to be ready. He was concerned about Vampyr. The second Eldest was angry—he had been angry as long as Nosferatu had known him. His actions throughout the ages had been horrific at times. Nosferatu still remembered the forest of impaled Turkish prisoners. That was the last time he had encountered his comrade from the cells along the Roads of Rostau. He had heard rumors of the others' actions over the years; but Vampyr had faded into the shadows, becoming a legend among the humans, especially after one of the humans penned a book about their kind. Nosferatu had always suspected that some of the information about vampires was leaked by the Watchers, as within the myth there was quite a bit that was accurate.

Nosferatu picked up the secure satellite telephone and made two calls. One to Kouros, confirming the time and date of the launch. The second was to the United States to a contact he had used there before.

Nosferatu desperately needed the plan to succeed. Because it was the only way to bring back Nekhbet.

CHAPTER 14

Moscow

YELLOWING ARCHITECTURAL
plans covered the tables in the warehouse. Some dated
back as far as a hundred years, when the tsars still ruled in
the Kremlin. Many were from 1939 to 1945, when a
flurry of digging for protection against the invading Nazis
had occurred. The vast majority, though, dated from the
beginning of the Cold War through the end, over forty
years of burrowing deeper and deeper under the capital
city in response to America's development of increasingly
powerful nuclear weapons targeting Moscow.

Petrov was wading through the plans, reading, making
notes, and searching for a room that existed only in rumor
so far—where the KGB had stored a large supply of blood
taken from the SS at the end of the war and done its own
blood work.

The warehouse was surrounded by guards under
Petrov's command, mostly ex-Spetsnatz men, enjoying
the fruits of capitalism that the Mafia had to offer them.
In addition to having large legitimate holdings, Adrik was
one of the most powerful of the Mafia bosses in Russia.
Petrov didn't quite understand why his boss still dabbled
in crime when so much money came in from the legitimate side of the house, but he knew better than to ask
questions. Adrik was an enigma to start with, a man who

had been on the scene as long as Petrov, and anyone he had met, could remember. Old-timers with white hair who had fought in the Great Patriotic War knew of Adrik and described him exactly as he appeared now. It was as if the man never aged.

Petrov had heard other rumors about his boss. That Adrik never went out in the daytime. That he brought in young girls every week or so who were never seen again. Sometimes young boys. Virgins, it was whispered, with medical tests to prove their health. Petrov didn't particularly care about the rumors. He cared that he was paid well for his work and that Adrik obviously had the power to keep other Mafia groups and the government at arm's distance.

One of the guards challenged a man at the door to the hangar, allowing him in only after an extensive examination of the case he carried and a careful search of the man himself for weapons and explosives. Petrov looked up from the old map showing tunnels running from Lubyanka to the Kremlin and watched the man approach. He was old and walked with a limp. He carried a battered leather satchel that he placed on the table across from Petrov.

"My name is Kokol," the old man said. "I was called by your benefactor to give you assistance."

Petrov waited as Kokol opened the satchel and lifted out several bound documents. The covers of each were made of some strange material and the pages between were old and faded, written by hand in a fine script. Petrov stiffened when he saw the swastika stenciled on each cover along with the SS insignia. Kokol saw his reaction.

"I took these from a bunker under the Chancellery in Berlin at the end of the Great Patriotic War." He indicated the binding material with disgust. "Human skin. From the camps. The pigs."

Kokol flipped open one of the books. "These are medical reports. The SS doctors did much testing, things that you could not do under normal circumstances. They would put naked people into vats of water and lower the temperature, making observations how the body reacted and how long the people took to die. The most extensive testing for hypothermia ever conducted.

"They did other things." Kokol paused, his old hands resting on the pages. "Blood. That is what your master seeks."

Petrov frowned at the man's choice of words.

"Adrik. I knew him in the war." Kokol waved a hand, indicating his white hair and lined face. "Look at me and look at him. He was the same during the war. He has not aged a day since. Why do you think that is?"

"It is not my business," Petrov said.

"You work for him," Kokol countered. "If it is not your business what nature of creature your master is, then what is your business?"

Petrov glanced around, making sure none of his men were within earshot. "What do you mean creature?"

Kokol sighed. "After all that has happened in this past year, with the aliens, one would think people's minds would be more open."

"Adrik is—" Petrov began, but Kokol held up a hand interrupting him.

"Adrik is not human." Kokol said it flatly. "He may look like a man, but he is most certainly not."

"Who—what is he then?"

Kokol tapped the document in front of him. "He is someone seeking the blood drawn by the SS during the Great Patriotic War. According to this, the SS secretly had their doctors in the camps test the blood of many select prisoners."

"Looking for?"

"A special strain. They did this at the behest of someone who was a very high-ranking member of the Nazi Party, someone in the SS. The specifications were to focus on people with red hair; those with pale skin; those in good health but at an advanced age belied by their appearance. What was collected was sent to Bavaria, to the castle there where the inner circle of the SS met at Wevelsburg." Kokol turned some pages, uncovering a manifest. "As the war progressed, most of it was transported, along with many other artifacts collected by the SS, to Berlin, to be deposited in the large vault under the Chancellery."

"If you got the books, who got the blood?" Petrov asked, although he had a very good idea.

"I was army intelligence, NVD. The KGB was there also. There was even a brief firefight between our two units as we fought over the Nazi corpse." He tapped the book. "This is part of what we got. The gang from Lubyanka got the blood."

"And what did they do with it?"

Kokol nodded toward the schematics spread out over the table. "Put it in one of their holes under Moscow. And from what I understand they continued the search, bringing prisoners down there from Lubyanka and draining them of their blood. It was said you could hear the screams echoing out of the earth all the way into the Kremlin itself."

Petrov was tired of the old man's stories. He had a simple mission and wanted to achieve it. He didn't care why Adrik wanted the blood, any more than he cared why Adrik wanted young girls and boys brought to him in the darkness. But something Kokol had said sparked a curious suspicion in him.

"Adrik drinks their blood, doesn't he?"

"Whose?"

"The children that are brought to him. He has them tested. We thought it was for AIDS and other diseases for sex, but it's for the cleanliness of the blood. It is how he has lived so long." Petrov looked at Kokol sharply. "How long *has* he lived?"

Kokol shrugged. "I do not know and I have no desire to ask. I heard of Adrik when I was a young puppy assigned to the NVD in the thirties. His was a name to inspire fear back then. And even the old dogs who worked there, Stalin's pit bulls who were part of the Revolution, *they* had heard of him when they were young puppies. And they, men who had killed millions and laughed, they feared him."

Petrov considered this. "Do you know where the KGB stored the blood?"

Kokol closed the binder with a thud. "There was a man who ran the Alien Archives for the KGB, then the FSB. His name was Lyoncheka."

" 'Was'?"

"He was killed during the recent events."

"Who replaced him?"

Kokol reached into a pocket and pulled out a slip of paper. "Here is his name, rank, position, and office."

Petrov took it and read the name. "I think I will visit Comrade Pashenka."

Kokol tapped the binders. "Do you want to read these?"

"I don't read German and I don't care," Petrov said. "I have a job and I will do it."

"It's that simple?"

Petrov smiled without humor. "Yes." He paused. "But leave the books anyway."

Kouros

The X-Craft was rolled out of the launch assembly building toward the launching pad. An Ariane 5 rocket waited on the pad, with a crane nearby, ready to lift the X-Craft onto the nose of the rocket. A large red digital clock placed near the pad read: 45:00:00. As the carrier holding the X-Craft exited the doors of the assembly building, the official countdown to launch began and the first second clicked off.

Tibet

Tian Dao Lin's power base in Hong Kong had long tentacles, reaching through Beijing and thus to all areas of China. Pethang Ringmo was a small village of fewer than one hundred and the last civilization before one stepped off into the northern shadow of Everest. It was where the Ones Who Wait had launched their assault on the mountain in the attempt to gain Excalibur not long ago and it was where Tai brought Namche to begin their attempt to recover the bodies of that failed assault. They flew into the closest airfield on Tian Dao Lin's personal jet, and then switched over to a French-made helicopter that was waiting for them—a craft especially designed and modified for high-altitude operations.

It was a frozen place in a frozen land. To the southwest the horizon was filled with mountains that in any other place would each be spectacular, but dwindled next to

Everest. From the north, Everest appeared as a triangular peak, the top of which was shrouded, as usual, in clouds.

Namche stood for several moments staring at the mountain, then he said a silent prayer. His companion had not uttered a single word during their trip. Namche was used to tourists who babbled and asked uncountable questions.

"Everest," Namche said, not sure if the man even knew which of the peaks was their goal, given they were eighty miles away and the very top was cloud-covered. "Changtse there to the right along with Lho La. To the left, Nuptse. All over 7,500 meters in altitude."

Tai remained silent.

"I have never climbed from the north," Namche said, getting that worry out in the open. "Always the south. The north is more difficult, more technical. The path we must take is even the more difficult of the two northern routes. Most take the West Ridge, via the Rongbuk Glacier. We will be taking the East Ridge. Very steep. Very dangerous."

Tai broke his long silence. "How soon can we leave?"

"Dawn."

"And then how long?"

"To the first spot? Six hours. If the helicopter can get us as high as our employer says it can. The second—it would be very difficult to make it and back down before dark. We would most likely have to camp on the mountain and try the following morning."

"We shall see."

The Skeleton Coast

Nosferatu had not left the Haven in many years. He had spent the time plotting and preparing but now it was time for action. He'd pushed the others and now he had to push himself. He did not want to leave. Since the beginning, little good had come to him when he'd traveled out into the world.

He took one last trip down to the vault where Nekhbet lay. He put his hand on the front of the tube, in a place where the acid from his skin over the millennia had worn the imprint of his fingers and palm.

"Soon. Very soon, my love. We will be together."

He left the crypt and went up an elevator to where a helicopter waited on the cliff top.

CHAPTER 15

I**T** HAD **T**AKEN **T**HREE PH**O**N**E** CALLS for Petrov to get all the information he needed on Pashenka. Within an hour Petrov had managed to assemble a dossier complete with photos on the man. He was high-level FSB who made more money selling information to the Mafia than he did from the government. He'd even had dealings with some of Adrik's organization at midlevel.

The Mafia connection meant that Petrov could most likely get the information he needed from the FSB official with a bagful of money. However, while that would be the easiest way, Petrov decided not to take that path. Everything he had learned so far had gotten his mind working and he knew he was on the trail of something more valuable than cash.

Petrov was seated in a panel van across Lubyanka Square from the FSB headquarters, waiting. According to his informants, Pashenka left work every day exactly at 1600 hours, crossed the square and went to a trendy bar next door to the Mir store. Such predictability indicated that Pashenka had long ago lost his tradecraft, something Petrov kept in mind as he watched the man exit the front doors of Lubyanka at 1602 and head across the square.

Pashenka wore an expensive suit, far beyond the means of even a high-level FSB official. The clothes, however, did little to hide the thuglike body they covered. The FSB man was built like a slab of beef, large, but softening around the edges. His face was red, indicative of heavy drinking, but the eyes were those of a man who enjoyed wielding power and inflicting pain.

"Go," Petrov said, the mike wrapped around his throat transmitting the sound to the driver in the front of the bulletproof van. There were two other men in the rear of the van with Petrov, his most trusted subordinates, both dressed in black fatigues, with body armor covering their backs and chests. They pulled black balaclavas down over their faces as the van moved across the square on an intercept course with the FSB agent.

Petrov leaned back in a captain's chair that was bolted to the floor, a pistol held loosely in one hand. They had done this many times and he anticipated no trouble, but it never hurt to be ready. The van slid next to Pashenka, the driver tapping the brakes lightly to slow it to about five miles an hour, slightly faster than walking pace, as the two men across from Petrov slid the side door open. One jabbed Pashenka with an upgraded cattle prod, sending an incapacitating jolt of electricity through the FSB man's body, while the other looped a length of thick rope over Pashenka's head, then jerked it tight as it settled just below his shoulders.

Both men hauled on the rope, lifting the flopping body off the cobblestones of the square and into the van in less than two seconds, sliding the door shut. The driver accelerated and they were moving along an alley off the square within ten seconds. Behind them a small cluster of pedestrians stared at the escaping van in shock, but by the time an alarm was raised, it was long gone.

Petrov looked down at Pashenka as one of his assistants took a syringe and injected the FSB man with a very strong muscle relaxant that guaranteed the captive would be conscious but incapable of any action stronger than breathing, talking, shaking his head, and wincing with pain for several hours.

Pashenka blinked his eyes as the effect of the electric prod wore off and he tried to focus on his immediate surroundings. By the time they pulled into the warehouse that Petrov was working out of, Pashenka was fully conscious but the drug was also fully functional and he was unable to move his limbs.

"I am a senior member of the FSB," Pashenka sputtered. "You have made a very large mistake."

"If you answer the questions I pose truthfully, I will let you live," Petrov said. "One lie, no matter how small, and you will never be seen again."

He gestured to his subordinates and they grabbed the FSB agent, dragging him to a heavy wooden chair bolted to the floor. They threw Pashenka into it and secured him with leather straps around his chest, legs, and arms.

Pashenka's eyes shifted, moving about the warehouse, taking in the armed guards and their top-of-the-line equipment. "Who do you work for?"

Petrov shook his head. "I said I would be asking you questions, not the other way around."

"The FSB will be looking for me. I am due at a meeting in—"

Petrov rolled a stool to a spot five feet in front of Pashenka and sat on it. "The FSB will miss you, but they have no idea where you are, and frankly, let us accept that they will not search that hard for you. Your only option if you want to live is to answer my questions."

"What do you want to know?"

"What do you know of Adrik?"

Pashenka's red skin went pale. He began shaking his head ever so slightly, a movement Petrov mimicked. Pashenka stopped shaking his head and swallowed hard before answering. "Adrik is a very dangerous man. I have never seen him, but that is what I have heard. He runs many businesses and is also connected with organized crime."

"I can read the newspaper and know that," Petrov said. "I want to know what the classified FSB file on him says."

"That file was most likely destroyed."

"Why?"

"It was at Section IV."

Petrov had never heard of that agency and he had worked countless missions in concert with the KGB and FSB during his time in the service. "What is Section IV?"

"You mean what *was* Section IV," Pashenka said. "It was the branch of KGB, then FSB, that dealt with the alien issue."

Petrov felt a surge of excitement. He'd known this was big. "You said 'was.' What happened to Section IV?"

"Its headquarters were in a large underground bunker on Novata Zemlya. It was attacked and severely damaged recently by one of the alien factions during the war."

"Why would Adrik's file be with Section IV?"

"It was suspected he was one of the Ones Who Wait. Half-human, half-Airlia clones who worked for Artad."

Petrov thought of the dark office in which he always met his boss. The white skin. The rumors. "You use the past tense—so he isn't?"

"No. He's something different."

"What?"

"An Undead."

Petrov leaned forward. "And what is that exactly?"

"We don't know," Pashenka admitted. "All we know is he has been alive for a very long time thanks to access to some aspect of the alien technology or biological or chemical material of the aliens. Some say he actually is part Airlia. His file dates from the very beginning of Stalin's secret police—and there were notes in there that predate that, from the time of the tsars. There is even one report that speculates that he was a tsar—Ivan the Terrible, no less. The fact is that no one knows how old he is or who he has been over the years."

Petrov abruptly switched the subject. "The tunnels under Moscow. I was told you know much about them."

Pashenka blinked. "The archives are my responsibility and they lie under the city."

"Is there a place in the archives where blood is stored? Blood taken from the Germans at the end of the Great War."

Pashenka hesitated. Petrov pulled back the hammer on his pistol, the sound echoing across the hangar. "Yes," Pashenka said. "There is a room where blood is stored."

"You will take me there this evening."

Mount Everest

"I have never seen anything like this." The words were barely audible, ripped from Namche's mouth by the brutal wind and dashed apart over the deep gorge to their right. As soon as he finished speaking, Namche slipped the full face mask back on, leaving not a single speck of his skin exposed to the elements. He could tell Tai was laboring in the thin air. The Chinese was half-doubled over, staring down at the climbing garments frozen into the ridgeline. The fact that there was no sign of the body inside the garments had been the cause of Namche's comment.

Namche had seen many bodies on the mountain. It was virtually impossible to bring one back down, so the over two hundred who had died in the past century trying to reach the summit all lay where they had fallen, or, at best, covered with a cairn of rocks piled on by their climbing companions. The freezing temperatures preserved the dead, but here there was no sign of whoever had worn the clothes.

Namche looked up to the southwest, toward Everest. A plume of snow blew off the peak, but it wasn't bad, perhaps winds of twenty to thirty miles an hour. Strong anywhere but there. They'd choppered up to 17,000 feet at first light. The helicopter had labored in the thin air, but it had gotten them a good way toward this spot.

Tai stood and followed Namche's gaze upward. "We must go to the other two."

"And if they are the same as this?"

"Then we have failed."

Namche frowned. "I do not think you will be able to go any higher."

Tai reached inside his jacket and pulled out the carved flask. He unscrewed the lid, pulled aside his mark, and drank deeply, draining it. Namche was shocked to see the blood around his lips as Tai pulled the flask away. Tai blinked several times and his chest heaved for a few moments, then he nodded. "I can make it to the bodies."

Besides his conditioning, the other thing that concerned

Namche was the bulky pack on Tai's back. He didn't know what was in it, but it was large with a six-foot-long piece of eight-inch-thick PVC pipe secure on either side, not making for easy climbing. The pipe had already become entangled in the safety line several times.

It was not his problem. Namche turned into the wind and tugged on the rope connecting the two of them. "Follow me."

Airspace, Atlantic

Nosferatu was the only occupant in the cabin of the Gulfstream jet. He had all the shades pulled and the lights off. Despite the darkness, he could easily read the latest report from the team he had hired in the United States. They were ready to move as soon as he landed.

The Americans had excavated a large part of the Dulce underground complex, but then work had ceased during the Third World War and had yet to be resumed. According to the report there were guards, a platoon of infantry, working in shifts at the site; but other than that, nothing to stand in his way.

He also had reports from Tian Dao Lin and Adrik. The two were still in the process of accomplishing their tasks, but all seemed to be going according to plan.

Despite his well-honed capacity for patience, Nosferatu could not stop a small surge of adrenaline from coursing through his veins. After so many millennia of waiting, what he had dreamed about could become a reality in just a few short days. Nekhbet would be back at his side. And they would be immortal.

Nosferatu realized that the hand that was holding the

reports was shaking. He blinked, feeling a stinging in his eyes, and when he brought his hand up to wipe his face, it came away with a faint red smear. He realized he was crying tears of blood.

Moscow

Petrov had his assault and recovery teams loaded into three vans marked with proper insignia indicating they were part of the SVD fleet. That would ensure that the police would ignore them no matter what they did and also precluded interference from the SVD as most agents would assume the vans belonged to another section and were on legitimate operations. Petrov loved turning bureaucracy against itself. They drove along the Moscow River until they reached the base of the hill on which the Kremlin crouched.

"Here," Pashenka said.

With a flick of a finger, Petrov indicated for the driver to stop the van. He looked about. The streets surrounding the Kremlin were practically deserted this late at night. Petrov put a small earpiece in and wrapped a mike around his throat. He did a comm check and was immediately rewarded by the sound of all twelve members of his teams succinctly checking their mikes in order as he had trained them.

He wore unmarked black fatigues, over which he had strapped black Kevlar body armor and on top of that was a combat vest. He had an AK-74, the upgrade of the venerable AK-47, but chambered with a higher velocity, smaller 5.45 mm round, for his primary weapon. He would have preferred something else, perhaps a German HK-95, but he knew they had to keep the appearance of being SVD as long as possible and the AK-74 was the armament of that organization.

"Let's go."

Shoving Pashenka ahead of him, he went out the side door of the van. Four of his men moved up the slope toward the wall of the Kremlin, spreading out, weapons at the ready. Two more covered each flank and the last four covered the rear. The drivers stayed with the vans, armed with proper papers to deflect anyone stupid enough to inquire why they were parked right outside the Kremlin so late at night.

They arrived at a portal in the redbrick wall, blocked by a steel gate. Petrov assigned two of his men, both armed with sniper rifles with night-vision scopes to take up flanking positions, covering both the portal and the vans.

Pashenka fumbled with his wallet, finally producing a plastic card that he pushed into the electronic lock. He then entered a sequence of numbers. The light went from red to green, and the gate slid open.

Petrov entered a small alcove with him, to be faced by another door. Pashenka used a different card and a different code on its lock, and the door rumbled open, revealing a descending stairway. Petrov put out a hand as Pashenka started to enter. He tapped the side of his head, then slid down a set of night-vision goggles. The rest of his team did the same. Then he signaled with two fingers and gestured down. Two of his men slid past, descending into the darkness.

"Clear to another door," his lead scout reported. "It's sealed with a retinal scanner to one side."

Petrov grabbed Pashenka and guided him down the stairs, the rest of the team following. Overhead Petrov could see lines of fluorescent lighting, but the power was off. They reached a solid steel door. Pashenka leaned over the retinal scanner and the laser projected a beam across his eyes, reading the pattern. Petrov thought the presence of such a sophisticated device was indicative that he was on the right track. Even at Lubyanka they still relied on name badges with photos for access, each checked by some old, about-to-be-retired agent who could barely read the names.

The steel door slid open, revealing a descending corridor. The floor was gray and the walls were painted the same flat color. Petrov pulled up the night-vision goggles as the corridor was dimly lit by recessed lighting. As soon as the last member of the team was in the corridor, Pashenka turned to the control to shut the door behind them.

"No," Petrov said. "Never close an escape route." He detailed a pair of his men to stand guard, then looked ahead. The corridor went straight as far as he could see. From the papers he had perused and Kokol's briefing, he'd learned that the first tunnel built under the Kremlin had been finished during the time of the tsars as an escape route in times of extreme trouble. Obviously it had not been used when they really needed it, Petrov thought as he gestured for his two point men to move ahead. He followed right behind, with Pashenka at his side.

Kokol had described how during World War II, Stalin had begun by building a large bomb shelter directly under the Kremlin as the Nazis approached Moscow. He'd also had bunkers dug under other government buildings and connecting tunnels bored out.

However, the rudimentary bunkers, designed to provide survival against Stuka dive-bombers, were obviously inadequate against nuclear weapons. So the government dug deeper and deeper, burrowing into the earth below Moscow in the foolish hope that perhaps the government could survive a direct nuclear attack. That there would be nothing on the surface to govern had not seemed to occur to anyone.

Pashenka paused before a side door. "We are under the palace."

"How deep?" Petrov asked, as it appeared to him they had been moving relatively level.

"Eighty feet or so." Pashenka opened the door. The tunnel beyond was older and smaller. Beads of moisture glistened, illuminated by naked lightbulbs attached to an electric cord bolted to the ceiling.

They moved about one hundred meters before reaching another door. Unlike the previous ones, though, this door was wooden, with metal bands across it. Petrov noted an electronic eye to the left and above the door.

"Who is watching?" he demanded of Pashenka.

"One of my people," Pashenka said.

"You did not tell me this." Petrov signaled to his men that they should be at the ready.

"He can be trusted. I just hope the repairs have been completed."

Petrov wanted to laugh, but held it in. No one could be trusted in Russia these days. "Repairs?"

"The bottom of the elevator shaft and the tunnel at the bottom were destroyed recently by traitorous activity."

Pashenka waved at the camera and the door opened with a click, followed by the hiss of the hydraulic jack.

Petrov's first two men dashed through, moving to covering positions inside on either side. Petrov shoved Pashenka through, staying behind him, AK-74 at the ready. They faced a sheet of bulletproof glass that bisected the room. A door, also made of bulletproof glass, was to the right. A man sat behind a desk on the other side, a video monitor in front of him. He had an AK-74 in his hands.

"Sir, who are these people?" the man demanded of Pashenka.

"Section IV," Pashenka said. "They have authorization."

"May I see the papers, sir?"

Pashenka stepped closer. "You know better than that. This comes directly from the Chairman. I take full responsibility."

The man shrugged. "I had not heard they reconstituted Section IV. I am surprised, that is all." He pressed a buzzer. The glass door swung open. Pashenka walked through, followed by Petrov.

"Is the elevator fixed?"

"Yes, sir."

"The tunnel at the bottom?"

"Most of the debris has been removed. It is passable."

"Good," Pashenka said, pulling a key on a chain from inside his shirt. The man did the same. They walked to opposite sides of the room to two boxes, where they inserted the keys. Pashenka counted to three and they both turned.

Steel doors in the back of the room opened, revealing a freight elevator. Pashenka walked onto it. Petrov signaled for two of his men to stay behind, then entered the elevator with the rest.

With a jerk, the elevator began descending.

Petrov felt his ears pop. "How deep?"

"A half mile."

"Are the archives there?"

Pashenka shook his head. "No. They are very, very deep. This is just the first step."

The elevator halted with a slight jar. The doors rumbled open. A dank corridor, lit with hastily rigged work lights beckoned. There were piles of rubble dotting the pitted floor here and there.

"Who tried to gain access?" Petrov asked as they got off the elevator.

"The Ones Who Wait."

Petrov had read of the various alien groups. "Why were they trying to infiltrate the archives?"

"I do not know," Pashenka said. "My boss, Lyoncheka, went with them and was killed. A Section IV operative named Yakov and an American escaped with something."

Petrov knew the name Yakov. It had been all over the news. "The Yakov who went to Mars and helped defeat the aliens?"

"Yes." They reached an intersection and Pashenka halted, then consulted his handheld. "This way." They turned right.

Petrov considered putting a bullet in Pashenka's brain, taking the handheld, and leading the men there himself, but he knew that might be precipitous. If Pashenka retained any of his tradecraft he would have a cutout built in, where he would be needed for an important leg of the journey that wasn't programmed into the handheld.

They made three more turns at the same level, then suddenly they were at the head of a wide tunnel that slowly curved clockwise and descended. It was large enough to drive a truck down and off to the left a long ramp ascended, just as large. He left one man at the intersection, then they began to go down.

Petrov noted what appeared to be air shafts spaced along the inner wall. He assumed there was a central vertical shaft that supplied air to these lower levels. Pashenka was counting to himself, then suddenly halted before the first door they had encountered on the right. By his pace count, Petrov estimated they'd walked over a mile in a descending circle.

"This is it," Pashenka said. Then he cursed.

Petrov looked over his shoulder and saw the reason: The outer edges of the door had been welded shut.

Petrov snapped an order and one of his men ran up. He tossed off his backpack and pulled out a welding torch and fired it up.

THE SILENT ALARM brought a squad of soldiers running into the courtyard of the Kremlin, under the command of a senior captain, where they were met by a senior FSB colonel on the premier's protection detail. The colonel was standing there in full battle gear as if he had anticipated the alarm. Colonel Kokol was an old man, but still in good shape. The cane he had used when he visited Petrov was no longer visible and the limp was gone.

"What is it, sir?" the FSB captain demanded, still struggling to put on his combat vest.

"Infiltrators in the tunnels, sir."

"Where?"

"They tripped an alarm on Level Six, Section Eight."

"What's there?"

"Old KGB archives," Kokol said.

"Strange," the captain said. "They didn't trip any alarms getting into the tunnels. How can that be?"

"Because someone let them in," Kokol said. "One of our men, Pashenka, was kidnapped yesterday afternoon right out of Lubyanka Square. He has access to the tunnels."

"Any idea where exactly he's going?" the captain asked without much hope.

Colonel Kokol smiled broadly. He brought his small handheld device and showed it to the captain. It had a six-inch oval display and there was a glowing dot with some numbers next to it. The dot was almost exactly in the center.

"Pashenka's bugged?"

Kokol nodded as he read the data. "I was prepared for this. They've moved since they tripped the alarm." He pointed down. "Just about right below us and over eighteen hundred meters down."

The captain turned and pointed at an eight-foot-wide column that came out of the ground and extended up about fifteen feet. "Main ventilation shaft for the Kremlin underground complex. Goes straight down just about two thousand meters."

"We'd need an awfully long rope to rappel down that far," Kokol said, as they walked over to the shaft. Several soldiers were already unscrewing plates from the outer surface. Another was opening a small chest bolted to the ground nearby.

"There was concern about a swift way to get deep if all power was cut and missiles were inbound," the captain said. "Elevators wouldn't work, and taking stairs or even the ramp would be too slow."

Two panels came off the side of the tube, revealing two brass poles bolted to the side of tube. The captain went over to the chest and reached in, pulling out two devices. They had handholds with straps that wrapped securely around the wrist. Facing outward were clamps that would go on the brass poles and levers controlled by the hands determined how much pressure they applied to the pole.

"Jumars," the captain said as he held them up. He wrapped the straps around his wrist, making sure his hands were secure inside the devices. Colonel Kokol hesitated only for a moment, then got his own set.

Together they walked over to the tube and looked down. Lonely lightbulbs lit the tube every fifty feet or so, leaving sections of darkness between.

"I am willing to allow your rank to proceed me," the captain said.

Kokol demurred. "I would prefer to watch your expertise with the equipment first, so I might learn the proper way to do this."

The captain laughed and stepped onto the narrow ledge around the inside top, sidling over to one pole. He clamped the jumars down on the pole and tested the pressure, squeezing his fingers against the pads they rested on. He glanced over at Kokol, no sign of laughter on his face now. The colonel nodded.

The captain carefully released the pressure and began to slide down.

PETROV CHECKED HIS watch but displayed no sense of impatience, knowing it would do no good. The man was working as fast as he could. The flame went out and the welder stood. "It's clear to open."

Two mercenaries began unscrewing the door, which seemed to consist of a single large threaded metal disk, about five feet in diameter. It moved easily and they had it unscrewed in less than fifteen seconds. It slowly rotated away from the entrance on hydraulic arms.

It was dark inside. Petrov pulled down his night-vision goggles and turned them on. He waited until the green glow came alive, then poked his head in the opening. He saw a large chamber, the far end of which wasn't visible in the night-vision goggles. Petrov blinked as he recognized the forest of vertical objects filling the chamber—human beings impaled on stakes set in the floor.

"Hold here," Petrov ordered as he stepped over the threshold in the chamber. There were hundreds of mummified bodies dangling on stakes run up through the centers of their bodies within view. Directly in front, less than ten feet away, was a heavy wooden chair, bolted to the floor. Leather straps were looped over the arms and legs, indicating that whoever had occupied the chair had not done so willingly. The chair faced the forest of dead. Looking up, Petrov saw that rails lined the ceiling with small trolleys with chains dangling from them. He immediately understood that was the way each body had been conveyed to its stake, then lowered onto it.

Ingenious. Petrov had seen many horrible things in his time and he had watched much torture. He could envision the process here. A victim was interrogated in the chair, facing all the bodies, some probably still alive and writhing on the stakes, while the victim could witness his pending fate, probably with an offer of being spared if he spoke. Petrov imagined most spoke, even making up things if they weren't really guilty, which was often the case. Regardless of what he said, the prisoner was lifted out on the chains and pulled to his final resting place and the next victim was brought in and strapped down.

How long had this been going on? he wondered. He looked at the closest body. The skin was stretched tight, the body mummified. The naked body was shriveled tight as if every fluid inside had been drained. Petrov felt a start as he remembered why he had come there.

He moved farther into the room, up to the chair. Directly on the other side was something he had not seen at first. A large wooden cart with a metal device on it and large glass bottles on the lower level. Rubber hoses led from the metal device to the cart. It took him a few seconds before he realized the device was a pump. And there were more thin rubber hoses on top with large-gauge needles on top. There was writing in German on both the bottles and the metal device. A swastika was stenciled on the side of the cart.

There was no mistaking the device's purpose: to forcibly draw blood from a victim.

So where was the blood?

"Get in here," Petrov ordered. His remaining commandos entered, all with night-vision goggles on. It was a tribute to their training that not a word was said.

"We need to find a cache of blood," Petrov said. "Search the room."

The men spread out.

"ARE WE THERE yet?" Colonel Kokol hissed. His forearms were aching and the last halt had taken all his energy to compress the pads against the pole.

The captain glanced down at the tracking device hung around his neck, craning to be able to see the display. "Close."

Kokol glanced at the small grate between the two poles. They'd passed one about every thirty feet on the way down. Each had a small six-inch-wide ledge in front of it. "Should we exit?"

Kokol waited for the captain's answer as the junior officer tried to angle his head to get a better read on the screen. The colonel's old forearms supplied the answer in the absence of anything from the captain. Kokol swung his feet over onto the ledge, then completely released his hold on the poles. His arms swung free and he used his teeth to release the wrist straps on the jumars.

"We are exiting, then?" the captain asked.

"*Da*," Kokol muttered as he tried to see through the grate. He saw the ramp, but nothing else.

The captain joined him. Together they pushed out on the grate and it popped loose. Kokol stuck his head out and saw nothing either way, so he slid through. However, when it was the captain's turn, the weight lifter's shoulders wouldn't make it through, no matter how hard he tried. As the captain strained and twisted, Kokol cocked his head to catch a sound floating up the ramp. Voices.

"I've got contact just below," Kokol hissed to the captain.

"I can't get through," the captain muttered, stating the obvious.

"There must be a maintenance entrance at the bottom," Kokol whispered. "It's not that much farther down. Get there, then come up the ramp. I'll hold from above."

The captain pulled back and looked up. "My strike team is on its way down. Wait for reinforcements before you do anything."

"Certainly," Kokol said.

The captain clamped onto the pole and began heading down. Kokol turned back to the ramp and waited, AK-74 at the ready.

THIS HAD TO BE IT—sixteen crates loaded on four-wheeled carts. There were faded swastikas stenciled on the outside and writing in German. Petrov used his knife to pry up one of the lids. Nestled in straw inside were rows of bottles similar to the ones on the lower level of the cart. Inside each was a dried, coagulated reddish mass that Petrov assumed had once been blood.

He ordered his men to wheel the carts out.

K●K●L HEARD +HE squeal of unoiled machinery coming his way. Then he spun to his right as he heard a muffled curse. A soldier was struggling to get through the air vent and join him.

Kokol put his finger to his lips, then turned to face back down the ramp, the butt of his AK-74 tucked tight into his shoulder. The sound was getting closer and he couldn't figure out what was making it. Having fought in many wars, from World War II to the present, he decided to make himself a smaller target and went down to one knee.

The soldier managed to make it through and joined him as a second one appeared in the grate. Kokol sighted in as the muzzle of a weapon appeared, followed by the man wielding it, dressed in black. He saw Kokol just as the soldier yelled out for the man to drop his weapon.

The man did neither, bringing the weapon to bear instead, and Kokol squeezed the trigger of the AK-74 twice in rapid succession. The first bullet hit the man in the cheek, ripping a gash along the side of his face while the second hit right between the eyes, sending him flopping back down the ramp.

The reply was instant and fierce as automatic weapons let loose and high-velocity rounds tore up the ramp, bouncing off the walls and ricocheting all about. A round hit the soldier coming out the grate in the back of his head, killing him instantly and leaving his body jammed in the hole. Kokol dived to the ground and fired several rounds even though he could see no targets, figuring the ricocheting would work just as well the other way.

He heard a strange grunt, a sound he had heard before—a last breath of air being expelled as a bullet tore through lungs—and glanced to his left to see the other soldier sink to his knees, then fall face forward, blood seeping out of a wound just under his armpit where his vest didn't cover.

Kokol rolled twice, putting himself behind the man's body and resting his submachine gun on top of him. Several more rounds hit the body and Colonel Kokol emptied the rest of his clip, silently counting to himself, so that when he fired the last round, his finger hit the release, the magazine fell and he slammed another home without making the mistake of firing on an empty chamber and wasting precious seconds.

Where the hell was the captain? The firing from below suddenly ceased and Kokol heard voices, someone issuing muffled orders. Were they retreating? Regrouping?

The answer came swiftly as three hand grenades came flying through the air. Colonel Kokol rolled, pulling the dead body on top of him as the first one went off less than ten feet away. The concussion hit him, followed by two more, like body blows from a mule, but the dead SVD man absorbed the shrapnel. The last wave slammed Kokol's head against the inner wall, knocking him out.

PETROV JUMPED IN the van with the blood, as his mercenaries fired back at the security forces on the outskirts of the Kremlin wall. He pressed a detonator, and two of his own people's cars exploded, behind his van, taking out several police cars with them, blocking the way, and allowing enough of a diversion for his van to disappear into the warren of alleys.

He had the blood. The issue he had now was what exactly to do with it. He was not sure any longer that turning it over to Adrik was the most prudent course of action—at least not without a substantial finder's fee.

CHAPTER 16

Mount Everest

NAMCHE RUBBED THE FROST OFF
the eyepieces of his oxygen mask and checked his global
positioning receiver. According to the data he'd been
given, they were close to the other two bodies.

"Not far," he shouted, the words muffled by his mask.
He wasn't certain whether Tai heard him or not. The
other man was leaning against the side of the mountain,
obviously exhausted. Namche wondered if he would still
be paid the remainder of his fee if Tai died and had to be
left on the mountain.

They were approximately two thousand meters from
the top of Everest. To the right was the Kanshung Face, a
practically vertical mile-long stretch of rock on the north
side of Everest. From the display he had seen in Hong
Kong, it appeared to Namche that the two bodies they
were after had been on top of the Kanshung Face and
fallen. Instead of plummeting all the way to the bottom, it
appeared as if the rope connecting them had caught on a
spur of rock jutting out from the face and they were frozen
in place, an adornment to Everest's deadliness. He looked
in the direction, trying to see through the blowing snow.

"There," he yelled, pointing. The wind had shifted direction briefly, exposing the Face. The bodies looked like
white lumps on the rock wall about fifteen meters away.

This time Tai acknowledged he'd heard by nodding.

Namche climbed up, checking over his shoulder to make sure Tai was following. They gained another thirty meters in altitude, then Namche halted. He pulled four pitons off his climbing rack and used a small hammer to pound them into the mountain, making sure they were in place. Then he secured a fifty-meter length of doubled rope to all four.

"You stay here," he yelled to Tai.

Tai nodded once more.

Namche tied himself off to the fifty-meter doubled rope, gathering the slack. Holding the loose rope in one hand and his ice axe in the other, he edged over a meter, arriving at the left side of the Kanshung Face. Reaching as far as he could, he slammed the point of his axe into the ice that covered the Face. Then, using that as his leverage point, he scrambled out onto the Face. He dug the toes of his crampons into the ice and began making his way across. It was precarious climbing and Namche didn't allow his mind to dwell on the numerous lethal possibilities.

He moved quickly, staying in no position for more than a few seconds, afraid the thin sheet of ice would give way. He glanced down and saw he was now above the bodies. It was clear that their rope had caught on a small spur, less than eight inches long, that poked out from the mountain. Namche knew he'd have one shot at this.

Namche let go of the mountain and fell. As he went down he slammed the point of the ice axe into the mountain to slow his descent and to be ready for when he reached the bodies, which occurred in less than two seconds. His axe caught on the dead climbers' rope and slid along until he reached one of the bodies, where it jammed against the attachment point of the rope on the body. Namche came to a jarring halt, breathing hard.

Using short nylon slings, he made sure both the dead men were attached to the rope he had brought. Then he leveraged the ice axe underneath one of the bodies, trying to break it free from the mountain. It detached with a last crack of ice, sliding down until it reached the end of the rope, where it jerked to a halt, then swung to the left, coming to a halt just below where Tai was.

Namche did the same with the second, except this time he made sure he was attached to the body. Once more he fell free for a couple of seconds, then he and the body swung over and came to a halt.

Namche put in more pitons, securing the bodies in place as Tai climbed down.

"What now?" Namche asked. He assumed Tai was there to collect something from the bodies. Perhaps a family heirloom? Or to perform some burial rite? Namche was surprised when Tai began lashing the two bodies tightly together.

"We cannot carry them down," Namche said.

Tai ignored him. He opened his pack and took out what appeared to be a very thin blanket, which he wrapped around both bodies. Namche had seen that kind of blanket before—it was an emergency heater, designed to be used to rapidly raise someone's core body temperature. Numerous thin wire conductors were woven into the material and attached to a power source, in this case a pair of lithium batteries Tai had in his pack. Once the blanket was tight around the bodies, Tai turned it on.

This confused Namche even more. What was the purpose of thawing out dead men?

As the blanket poured heat into the frozen flesh, Tai pulled something else out of his pack. A syringe and several plastic blood bags.

"What are you going to do?" Namche demanded, although he was beginning to get the idea. But the reason behind these apparently insane acts escaped him.

Tai continued to ignore him. He reached under the blanket and checked the exposed flesh of one of the bodies by the expedient method of poking it with the syringe. Apparently the body wasn't quite ready yet as Tai turned his attention to what was left in and on his pack. He removed the two pieces of PVC pipe and unscrewed the ends. He pulled out a complicated mass of extendable titanium poles and Kevlar cloth from each. They connected together at an anchor point.

Tai turned back to the body and poked it with the syringe. The point punctured the skin and he searched, trying to find a vein. When he located one, he attached a small battery-powered pump to the line and began draining the blood from the body. Namche watched in horrified fascination. Tai drained the first body into four bags. Then he did the same to the second.

Namche watched, confused as to the purpose of Tai's actions and what would happen next. As soon as Tai had the second body drained, he packed the blood bags into his rucksack. Then he unhooked his harness from the safety line.

"What are you doing?" Namche reached forward to grab him.

Tai connected a snap link on the back of his harness into the anchor point of the strange tube-and-cloth contraption, looked at Namche, smiled, and then jumped out into the clear air in front of the Kanshung Face.

Namche stared in shock as Tai free-fell. Then the poles on his back snapped out, spreading, deploying the high-strength cloth. A half mile below Namche's position, the hang glider locked into place and Tai grabbed the controls, banking to the north and west, disappearing from view in the blowing snow.

Kouros

Final checks were made, no glitches were found, and the countdown now moved into its final phase. A night launch was a bit unusual for Kouros; but Nosferatu had insisted, and since he was paying top dollar, the officials at the facility had been only too happy to agree. He was in launch control, in the VIP lounge, watching the procedures. He had been forced to pay a considerable amount of extra money to keep the launch information from being released, a particularly difficult task given this was the first manned launch ever performed outside of the American or Russian programs.

The overly attentive lackeys of the ESA were beginning to bother Nosferatu. Waiters hovered at his elbow, offering him champagne, and the luxurious buffet laid out at the rear of the room bustled with activity. He brusquely ordered everyone out of the suite.

The Ariane 5 booster, the X-Craft on top, was fixed in spotlights. A beautiful sight to Nosferatu, who had been at the forefront of spaceflight for many years, ever since the beginning. It was another of his objections to the Airlia—how they had hamstrung the human attempts to get into space. It was amazing that man had managed to make it to the moon and walk on it, an effort that had been rewarded with an intense push by the Ones Who Wait to make sure the space program went backward rather than forward. While science fiction writers had predicted that man would be much further ahead by the

turn of the millennium, the reality had been a great dis-
appointment.

The X-Craft design was simple but functional. He'd begun work on it many years previously and kept it as secret
as possible to prevent interference from the Ones Who
Wait. Over the years he'd brought in the best and brightest
to work on certain parts, but he'd kept overall control of
the development compartmentalized so that only the tiniest handful of people knew the big picture. Money had
been no object.

The X-Craft was a delta wing craft, more arrowhead-
shaped than the American space shuttle, and smaller. Its
cargo bay could hold only one-quarter of what the American shuttle could, but it was one-tenth as costly to produce
and fly. The crew consisted of a pilot and copilot. Addi-
tional personnel could be put on board if a crew pod was
inserted in the cargo bay. For the moment, the cargo bay
was empty except for two EVA space suits and special
equipment they would need once they reached the derelict
mothership.

Nosferatu had test X-Craft models flown in Australia
and even achieved two successful landings of the craft
that was now on top of the booster, flying it up on top of
a 747 and releasing it. The Ariane 5 booster was proven
with many successful liftoffs. As far as Nosferatu could
predict, everything should work perfectly.

He was less certain of Vampyr's actions.

His thoughts were interrupted by the final seconds of
the countdown. The rocket ignited and began to lift.
Nosferatu slipped on a pair of sunglasses to protect his
eyes as the flame seared the night sky. He watched the
rocket accelerate upward until he could no longer see it.

Time to move on to his next task.

Hong Kong Chek Lap Kok Airport

"You are not welcome here."

Vampyr had had a feeling that he would not be warmly greeted in Hong Kong. He was standing on the tarmac at the new Hong Kong International Airport, an island set apart from the mainland. His jet was behind him in a secure area, bathed in the flashing lights of security vehicles. The man who had greeted him with those five words wore the blue uniform of the Hong Kong police. There was some rank insignia on his collar but Vampyr had no clue what they meant.

Vampyr had a pack slung over his shoulder. Inside the pack were some goodies he had rigged—just in case. He had walked into too many strange situations not to prepare for the worst possible scenario.

"You are not welcome here," the official repeated.

Vampyr decided to ignore him as he saw someone approaching, a man dressed in a very nice suit that must have come from one of the most expensive stores in Hong Kong. More important, everyone in uniform who saw him approach immediately adopted body language that indicated this was a man with real power.

"I am Chon. Deputy governor of Hong Kong. How may I be of assistance?"

"He"—Vampyr nodded at the man in uniform—"says I am not welcome."

"A misunderstanding," Chon said. "Things have been most in flux recently as I am sure I do not have to tell you. We in Hong Kong have a long history of welcoming guests regardless of outer circumstances."

Chon had been on Vampyr's payroll for over twenty years. He held his high position through Vampyr's influence. He had had only one task all those years—to keep tabs on Tian Dao Lin.

Chon snapped a command in Chinese. The area immediately around them was suddenly clear for a distance of twenty meters. Chon glanced to the right, along the east–west runway. The sun was hovering above the western horizon, a landing 747 silhouetted against it. "We do not have much time before dark. Come with me." With that Chon turned and headed for the helicopter he'd arrived in.

Vampyr followed. The blades were powering up for takeoff as they boarded. The chopper lifted and headed toward Hong Kong proper, over forty kilometers away.

Since Chon hadn't bothered to put on the headset on the ceiling over his head, Vampyr assumed he didn't want to talk while in flight. They landed on top of a tall building set among a cluster of skyscrapers. Chon got off and headed immediately for a door without looking back. Vampyr followed. They descended a flight of stairs, then went into a room containing a large desk and bay windows with a commanding view of Hong Kong.

"Please be seated," Chon said. Then he took the seat behind the desk and hit several buttons. Steel shutters dropped over the windows, cutting off the view. Vampyr placed the backpack next to the seat, facing the door behind them.

"This room is now Tempest proof," Chon said.

Vampyr knew that meant it was supposed to be secure from all forms of bugging. Tian Dao Lin was a very powerful man in Hong Kong, perhaps the most powerful. Some said he ultimately was in control of all the Triads. He also owned many legitimate businesses, just like Vampyr, Nosferatu, and Adrik. The most dangerous aspect of Tian Dao Lin, as far as Vampyr was concerned, was his inner core of Quarters. More than any of the other three Undead, Tian Dao Lin enjoyed breeding with human women and bringing offspring into the world. Even Vampyr feared being attacked by a pack of Quarters.

"What is the latest?" Vampyr finally asked.

"One of the Quarters, named Tai, paraglided off Everest earlier today. He is on his way here with a package."

Vampyr nodded. Tian Dao Lin had succeeded in recovering the blood of the One Who Waits. The end had begun.

"Do you know when he arrives?"

"In four hours."

"Will we be able to intercept?"

Chon looked uncomfortable. "I have not yet been able to determine where Tian Dao Lin's lair is. Every time we try to follow his people, they manage to lose us. He is most careful, and if one gets too close, then his inner circle makes that person disappear."

Vampyr had anticipated Chon's failure. "I am trying to discover the location by other means. Still, have your men try to follow the blood when it arrives. I want both the blood and Tian Dao Lin."

Moscow

Colonel Kokol felt the point of a needle enter his right arm but didn't have the energy to react. He focused all his remaining power on opening his eyes. Once more he was greeted by the captain's face looming over him.

"There is a problem. We did not stop them from removing what they stole from the archives. They escaped."

Kokol forced his eyes open. He was lying on a cot in a mobile operations center. He could see soldiers and police scurrying about. For the moment, the two of them were left relatively alone. "What happened?"

"After they knocked you out—and left you for dead under the body of the soldier—the infiltrators made their way up the ramp, then through other tunnels and out the exit they came in. The Moscow police and SVD security tried to stop them and suffered heavy casualties in the process."

"What did they take?"

"It appears a stock of old blood taken by the Russians from the Germans from Berlin at the end of the Great Patriotic War."

"World War II," Colonel Kokol muttered. "Who did this?"

"We have video from the entrance—they killed the guards on their way out, along with Pashenka, the SVD man who let them in. Police files indicate they are Mafia under the control of—"

"Adrik," Kokol completed the sentence. Everyone had heard whispers of the head of the Mafia in Moscow. Nothing happened at this level in the city without his blessings.

"Yes."

"Would blood stored like that still be viable?" Kokol wondered. "Why would they steal it?"

"I do not know, but twelve men are dead, so it must be important."

Colonel Kokol swung his feet to the side and tried to sit up. The attempt caused a hiss of pain to escape his lips but he managed to get upright. "Do the police have a line on where we can find Adrik?"

"Yes. They've always known where his headquarters is. No one has ever had the power or the will to attack him."

"We'll see about that," Kokol said, pulling a SatPhone out of his pocket.

Earth Orbit

With a slight burst from a forward thruster, the X-Craft decelerated as it entered the large cargo bay of the mothership. Another burst brought it to a halt, floating just above the deck and among the battered Talon spacecraft that had been knocked out of commission by the nuclear blast combined with the power of the ruby sphere that Turcotte had brought there from the cavern in Ethiopia. A hatch on the side of the X-Craft opened with a puff of escaping air and both suited crewmembers exited, carrying large plastic cases in the zero gravity.

They split, going to different Talons. Each went inside, to the first Airlia body they saw, and opened the case, revealing syringes, blood bags, and the same type of battery-powered pump that Tai had used.

They quickly got to work, poking each body in different places to draw the little remaining blood that hadn't drained out into space.

Moscow

Vampyr's reach was indeed long.

Kokol's SatPhone rang and he listened for a moment, then held it out for the captain. "It is the premier."

The captain stared in disbelief and took the phone. He listened for about a minute, his only replies "Yes, sir," then closed the phone and handed it back to Colonel Kokol.

"And?" the colonel asked.

"We attack and destroy Adrik." The captain spun on his heel and shouted orders. Soldiers jumped into vehicles and they raced into the city toward the modern office building that held the Mafia leader's office.

Colonel Kokol, having survived World War II, the Cold War, and the end of the Cold War and the bitter departmental infighting after it, along with being Vampyr's spy in Russia on Adrik for over half a century, decided to watch the assault from the command truck three blocks away. It had direct video feeds from each of the assault units, from cameras mounted on the team leaders' helmets.

"Your optics are excellent," Kokol observed, as they watched the teams surround the building.

"A gift from the Americans," the captain said. "They're supposed to be used by counternuke teams to keep track of our nuclear material and weapons."

Kokol watched as the teams stealthily approached all the known entrances to the building, listening as the captain counted down to the breach.

At zero all the ingress points were hit.

Kokol was shaking his head within five seconds as no opposition was apparent on any of the screens. "It's too easy. Something's wrong."

The teams had breached the perimeter of the building and were working their way in. Still no shots fired. Nothing.

Colonel Kokol turned to the captain. "I would pull the teams. Now."

Two of the teams were working their way up stairwells, the elevators out of order as they cut the power to them. Three other teams were doing room-by-room searches of lower-level offices.

The captain leaned over Kokol's shoulder. "I cannot pull them out. We must have revenge. Watch. We have other equipment from the Americans. Most efficient and useful." He rattled something into his mike. One of the men with a camera stopped at a computer on a desk and pulled something out of his pack. It appeared to be a handheld organizer with a lead going to a floppy diskette, which he shoved into the A drive on the computer.

"We can take everything off the hard drive in ten seconds," the captain said proudly. "It is being transmitted right here." He pointed at a computer next to the monitors.

"I'm telling you that you've got a problem," Kokol said. "The place is abandoned."

"What?"

Kokol stood, looking across the monitors as the teams progressed deeper into the building. "Get your men out. Now!" He yelled the last word.

"I don't—"

"Do it," Kokol said. He turned to the captain. "Adrik is prepared for an attack. You've encountered no resistance, which means he's letting you in. If he's letting you in, then it can't be good." Even as he said the words, Kokol knew it was too late.

This was confirmed as a flash filled one of the video monitors, immediately followed by the feed blacking out. In rapid succession the other four feeds did the same.

The command and control van lifted off its right tires as the blast wave hit it, followed by the roar of the explosion. The van slammed back down, still upright, as debris from the explosion hit the side.

Kokol knew the entire team was dead. He felt it run through his body as surely as the shock wave had hit the van.

"The computer." Kokol tapped the dazed captain on the shoulder.

"What?"

"Check the computer."

"For what?"

"The download. What they tapped."

The captain slid the seat over to the nearby computer as chaos reigned inside the command van, everyone shouting into radios trying to figure out what had happened. He looked at the screen and saw the small emblem indicating the information that had been transmitted by the team member just before the explosion.

Kokol doubted anything of value would have been picked up, but over two dozen men had just died, and he owed it to them to look. The hard drive data came up. He quickly scanned through it. Daily calendar. Interoffice memos. Shipping. Time clocks. Phone logs.

Kokol backed up. He scanned the shipping logs for the last two days carefully. Kokol smiled when he spotted a rush shipment to Hong Kong.

He pulled out his phone and dialed a number, giving the address to the person on the other end.

Dulce, New Mexico

Nosferatu and the team of mercenaries he had hired had taken off in two Huey helicopters with US Army markings from an abandoned airstrip in southern Colorado, where they had been awaiting his arrival. They were flying due south, low to the ground to avoid radar.

The town of Dulce was just south of the Colorado–New Mexico border, between the Carson National Forest and the Rio Grande National Forest. The terrain was full of mountains covered with pine trees. The town was on the forward slope of a large mountain. On the back slope was the entrance to the secret lab that Majestic-12 had established shortly after World War II.

The experiments there had been as varied as the human imagination, according to what Nosferatu had been able to learn, although much of it was still shrouded in secrecy. The United States government had done work on mind control using memory-affecting drugs and electronic dissolution of memory. Some of the work came out of Airlia technology and some from German scientists captured at the end of World War II and impressed into US service under Operation Paperclip.

This lab was also where Majestic had shipped the Guardian computer they discovered in Temiltepec in South America, the device that had corrupted the members of Majestic who had come in contact with it, giving them its programmed instructions to fly the mothership.

The team leader called out a time warning, indicating they were less than five minutes from the target. With a slight smile Nosferatu watched the men in the cargo bay don night-vision goggles. Human technology had finally started to catch up with a capability he'd had for thousands of years.

Nosferatu knew that the small security force posted at Dulce had no reason for concern. Their first indication of trouble came when the aircraft landed and the first thing off were flashbang grenades that stunned and blinded them.

Nosferatu had insisted on taking down the security force without killing them, and the mercenaries had agreed, seeing no point in committing murder if it was avoidable. They seized the stunned guards and quickly secured them. Nosferatu then exited the helicopter and followed one team down into the dig site.

The engineers who had worked on the site had dug a shaft straight down through the pancaked levels of the base, with an occasional side tunnel. A large crane holding a metal cage served as a makeshift elevator and Nosferatu climbed on board with four of the mercenaries as another took the controls of the crane.

The basket was swung over the shaft and lowered all the way to the bottom. This was where General Hemstadt had been running highly classified biological experiments for Majestic-12 before being co-opted by the Mission. The higher levels had taken most of the force of the foo fighter's power beam. This level was relatively intact, as the intelligence reports Nosferatu had purchased indicated.

There was some debris, but they were able to move. They were in a hall that extended about sixty feet, ending in a dead end. There were several doors to the left and another corridor turning to the right. There were name plaques next to each door on the left indicating that those rooms were quarters for Sublevel 1 staff. Nosferatu passed right by all of them, taking the right turn at the end of the corridor.

He was in a ten-foot-long corridor that ended in a double set of doors with biological warning signs posted on them. Nosferatu walked up to the doors and pushed them open. A rough concrete floor angled down to a large cavern carved out of the mountain. The ceiling was twenty feet high and the far wall a hundred meters away.

There were several dozen large, vertical vats in the room. They were empty, but Nosferatu knew they had once held bodies. He looked to the right, where, according to his report, the Guardian computer had been stored. There was an empty space there now.

Nosferatu walked forward, past the tubes. Set off to the left was a bank of machinery set on two carts. What he had come for. At his signal the mercenaries began wheeling out the blood machines.

Hong Kong

Vampyr's absolute stillness caused Chon great anxiety. He felt the weight of his failure to locate Tian Dao Lin's lair. And five minutes earlier his men had called to report—as he had feared—that they had lost the trail of Tai and the blood in the back streets of Hong Kong, where Tian Dao Lin's power was absolute. Two of the trailers had been shot and killed, indicating the level of seriousness of whatever was happening.

"Sir—"

"Yes?" Vampyr waited.

"Perhaps," Chon began, but he stopped when Vampyr's SatPhone rang. Vampyr listened for a few moments, then hung up without saying a word. He wrote an address on a piece of paper and slid it across to Chon. "What is there?"

Chon read it. "An office building downtown. The Pacific Rim Bank Building."

Vampyr stood. "It is time to pay Mr. Lin a visit."

"Are you sure—"

Vampyr's glare caused Chon to bite off whatever he was about to say. He grabbed the phone and barked orders.

The faint beat of helicopter blades echoed down from the roof.

Vampyr turned for the door.

"It will take a few minutes for—" Chon began, but he didn't finish the sentence as the windows and steel shutters imploded, sending shrapnel flying through the room. A piece of metal caught Chon in the chest, ripping through, severing his spinal cord and killing him instantly.

Vampyr reacted instinctively, diving to the floor unscathed. He rolled away from the windows as he caught a glimpse of figures rappelling in on ropes suspended from the roof. A half dozen figures dressed in black with black balaclavas covering their faces were in the room. They all ran toward Vampyr.

Vampyr rolled under the first, at the same time pulling a short sword—his xithos from so long ago in Sparta—out of its sheath and getting to his feet, assuming a ready stance, the point of the ancient sword directed toward the intruders. One jumped at him and he swung, the blade slicing cleanly into the man's shoulder, then diagonally through his body, coming out the opposite hip. The two pieces fell to the floor.

Everyone in the room halted. The remaining five bracketed Vampyr, keeping their distance from the sword.

"Where is Tian Dao Lin?" Vampyr asked.

No one replied and no one moved. Vampyr had never been a big believer in standoffs. He jabbed at one of the intruders facing him, then spun, sword extended and lopped off the head of the other. He began to advance on the others when the door to the office crashed inward and four more figures dressed in black jumped through, taking up positions. They were followed by an old man wearing loose-fitting black silk with red dragons on each sleeve. He took in the situation and held up a hand.

"Stop." The old man took a step into the room. "Vampyr."

Vampyr shifted the point of the xithos toward the old man. "Tian Dao Lin."

The old man nodded. "You were foolish to come here. You should have taken Nosferatu's offer." His Quarters took up flanking positions, slightly to the front of he who had made them.

"Nosferatu is weak and a fool who has been besotted by love all these years," Vampyr said.

"Perhaps," Tian Dao Lin said.

"Join with me," Vampyr said.

"At the moment I see no reason why I should," Tian Dao Lin said. "I have some of the blood and Nosferatu will have the technology needed. You have nothing."

"I have Adrik on my side. With you, we will be able to get whatever we want from Nosferatu." Vampyr backed up slightly, to a point where he was near the front of Chon's desk, his backpack lying against the metal front.

Tian Dao Lin shrugged. "So he has been spying for you. I assumed Adrik was hiding something. The last report I had was that he had recovered what he needed to also."

"He has. And he is with me, not Nosferatu." Vampyr made a show of sliding the xithos into its scabbard, while, unnoticed, his other hand slid into his pocket.

"You still have not made a proper proposition," Tian Dao Lin said.

"True," Vampyr acknowledged.

"Then I will have you killed." Tian Dao Lin turned for the door.

Vampyr leapt backward, clearing the desk, and falling to the floor on the far side. Vampyr squeezed the detonator in his pocket.

The roar of the claymore mine secreted in his backpack was instantly followed by the sound of thousands of steel ball bearings ripping into the far side of the room, tearing through plaster, wood, and flesh and bone. Vampyr felt the air being sucked out of his lungs from the proximity of the blast on the other side of the desk and the shock wave moving away from him.

He drew his xithos as he got to his knees and peered over the desk top, his ears ringing. Blood, viscera, and parts of bodies littered the room. Two of the Quarters were moving, moaning in agony. Vampyr got to his feet. Cautiously he walked around the desk, being careful where he stepped. He lopped off the heads of the wounded Quarters with two swift strokes. He spotted a blood trail leading out of the doorway and rushed forward.

Vampyr's lips split in an evil grin as he saw Tian Dao Lin trying to drag himself away along the floor of the hallway, his left leg almost completely severed from his body.

Vampyr went up to his fellow Undead and placed his boot on the practically severed appendage, causing the Chinese to scream in agony.

"You will survive this," Vampyr said. "Indeed, the leg will grow whole again. But it will take many, many years. I know. But if you ally with me now, and come with me to the Haven, it will go much more quickly."

Tian Dao Lin could only nod.

"Where is the blood you recovered?" Vampyr asked, leaning forward, putting extra pressure on the wounded leg.

Tian Dao Lin hissed. "In my helicopter."

Vampyr sheathed his xithos. With one hand he picked up the wounded Undead and slung him over his shoulder. "Let's go then."

Earth Orbit

The two astronauts made their way across the scorched deck of the mothership's hold and climbed into the airlock on the X-Craft. They carried with them all the blood they had gathered from the Airlia bodies. As Nosferatu had predicted, there wasn't much, but what they did have was pure Airlia blood. They placed it in the X-Craft's hold.

They sealed the airlock, secured the cases, and took their seats. With a few gentle puffs of power from the thrusters, they maneuvered the craft out of the hold and into space.

CHAPTER 17

The Skeleton Coast

NOSFERATU WAS JOINED AT THE round table by Adrik. In the center of the table were four flat-screen monitors, one facing each of the chairs. They displayed the blood lab, where the supply Adrik had brought from Moscow was currently being worked on.

"Your headquarters was destroyed?" Nosferatu asked, his eyes on the screen.

Adrik nodded. "Yes. The FSB assaulted it."

"Why?"

There was a short silence, then Adrik shrugged. "I'm not certain."

Nosferatu shifted his gaze from the screen to his fellow Undead. "I know you think me a fool. But I am the Eldest. I know you've met Vampyr. You've communicated with him. Do you know it was he who tried to kill you in Moscow and got the FSB to assault your headquarters?"

"I thought he might be behind it," Adrik acknowledged.

"Vampyr has no honor," Nosferatu said. "He is just like you. When you were Genghis Khan you had no honor. You killed all who stood in your way, sparing none. Vampyr did the same in his various incarnations. What did you expect from him?"

"I have honor," Adrik disagreed. "I am bound by it."

"How so?"

"Vampyr saved me. When my palace guard revolted and entombed me underneath the Kremlin, he rescued me from a horrible fate."

Nosferatu laughed, bringing a flush of anger to the other's face. "Has it not occurred to you to ask why he was so fortuitously in Moscow at just the time your guard revolted and entombed you?"

Several seconds of silence passed.

"Even if you have honor," Nosferatu said, "you do not have love. It is a trait of the humans, not the Airlia. It is what allowed them to defeat the Airlia here and elsewhere. It is more powerful than the Airlia virus that runs through our veins."

Before Adrik could say anything, Nosferatu's SatPhone chimed. He pulled it out and snapped it open, listened for a few seconds, then shut it. "Tian Dao Lin's plane is in the air coming this way. He will be landing shortly. And my X-Craft will also be landing soon."

Space

The X-Craft was flying upside down to the planet, the crew checking their flight path with observations of the planet's surface "above" them. Sure they were in the correct orbit, they then fired the maneuvering thrusters and the craft went tail over front, until the belly was facing the planet. Then it began to descend.

The Skeleton Coast

One of the scientists in the chamber turned toward the camera and gave a thumbs-up.

"They have processed what you brought," Nosferatu said. He looked at Adrik. "Would you like to go first?"

Adrik glared back. "It is for the Eldest to go first."

"Good decision," Nosferatu said, "but that is not what will be." Nosferatu stood. Adrik stared at him, waiting. "If you would indulge me, I propose that the first be Nekhbet. She has not seen the light of day in over five hundred years."

Reluctantly, Adrik nodded his agreement.

Nosferatu left the conference room and headed for the subbasement lair to bring his beloved to the blood room and back to life.

Earth Orbit

On board the X-Craft, the pilot lifted the nose to get more lift as it entered the atmosphere. At the same time, the copilot watched the crosshairs on the computer screen in front of him. The copilot hit a key, putting the system on automatic release. A red digital countdown appeared in the lower left corner indicating they were slightly less than four minutes from the airfield.

On Approach to the Skeleton Coast

Vampyr looked across the cabin at Tian Dao Lin as they were challenged by Nosferatu's security force, requesting the proper code word to land. A tone was sounding in the cabin, indicating that a ground-to-air missile radar was locked on the jet. The Chinese was very pale, the loss of blood from his leg wound extensive. Vampyr had had one of his mercenary doctors put a tourniquet on the wound and the bleeding had stopped but Tian Dao Lin was barely conscious.

"Answer," Vampyr ordered, as one of his men shoved the microphone in Tian Dao Lin's face.

Tian Dao Lin whispered the proper code word. The warning light went out.

Crowded into the rear of the jet were two dozen of the best mercenaries that Vampyr's vast fortune could buy. They were armed with the latest weapons, and all had night-vision goggles on, as the only light in the cabin came from a single red night-light.

Vampyr looked at a computer screen on the small conference table in the center of the cabin. "Perfect," he whispered as he saw the signal representing the X-Craft appear.

The Skeleton Coast

Nosferatu held the clear plastic tubes in his hands, feeling the warmed blood flowing through them and into Nekhbet. It had taken two minutes to completely drain her of her old blood and replace it with a partially frozen solution that cleaned out her system and kept her in stasis. Her entire body had been cooled down to a point where her cells were just about inactive.

Now, as the new, Airlia-rich blood flowed into her, the technicians began raising her temperature. The process proceeded rapidly to minimize the time when she was between her old and new blood. Within sixty seconds the four intravenous lines had completely flushed out the solution and filled her with the new-processed blood.

Nosferatu let go of the empty lines and leaned over her, waiting. Her eyes flickered, then opened, confusion reigning for a few moments until she could focus. Then her face split in a wide smile.

"My love," she whispered.

Nosferatu leaned down and kissed her lightly on the lips, then helped her sit up. He wrapped his arms around her tightly, her head on his shoulder. "It has been a very long time, but you are now immortal, as I will be soon."

As Nekhbet held his hand, he took her place on the table. The technicians moved quickly and smoothly, sliding the intravenous lines into his veins as the rest of the blood that Adrik had brought from Moscow was prepared for insertion.

The lead doctor picked up a needle containing sedative to inject into one of the lines to knock Nosferatu out. The Eldest shook his head. "We don't have time."

"What do you mean?" Nekhbet asked.

"Trust me," Nosferatu said, before he felt the chill of the solution pushing out his old blood hit his veins and the world went dark.

Nosferatu came to knowing that Nekhbet was standing by the table. He did not know if it was the power of the pure Airlia blood in his veins or her presence or the combination, but it was the most magnificent awakening he had every experienced.

He felt the warmth of her hand on his and opened his eyes to drink in her loveliness. He was surprised to see the concern on her face, and then looking past her toward the observation room he saw Vampyr standing there, staring down at the two of them. In his hands he held up a large case, and Nosferatu knew it held the blood Tian Dao Lin had recovered. Vampyr disappeared from view.

"There has been an attack," Nekhbet said. "I heard explosions and firing."

Nosferatu sat up and swung his feet to the floor. "I expected our old friend to show up."

Nekhbet gave him a hand as he got to his feet. He was growing stronger by the second but his system had still experienced an immense shock. The door to the chamber opened and Vampyr walked in, flanked by two men with submachine guns.

"I want you out of the room," Vampyr said. He pointed up at the observation window, where four more men with submachine guns could be seen. "They will ensure you do nothing while I undergo the procedure. You will be killed if anything goes wrong."

When they reached the observation chamber, they found Adrik with his hands cuffed behind his back, seated near the wall.

"So much for allies," Nosferatu noted.

Adrik cursed.

Nosferatu felt as if every nerve in his body were on fire. He cared little for Adrik's predicament. He wrapped his arms around Nekhbet and held her tight.

VAMPYR ST⊕⊕D UP and stretched, flexing his muscles. He pounded a fist on his chest in triumph. He stormed past the technicians and down the corridor to the observation room, where Nosferatu sat with Nekhbet and Adrik.

"When does your X-Craft land?" Vampyr demanded.

"Why do you care?" Nosferatu asked in turn. "You have had your blood."

"I have several very influential friends—humans—who would like to join the ranks of the Undead. Using the blood that would have been Adrik's and Tian Dao Lin's, I can make a handful of them half-breeds, Undead. They will serve me then."

"I am the Eldest—" Nosferatu began, but Vampyr cut him off.

"You are weak. You have spent all this time pining for her—" He indicated Nekhbet. "Well, now you have her. You can stay here in your hole with her forever as far as I am concerned. You saved me in the beginning, so I will grant you that, even though you betrayed me later." He turned to Adrik. "I owe you nothing." He pulled out a pistol and fired without hesitation, hitting Adrik in the center of his forehead, sending brain and blood splattering the wall behind him. He fired the rest of the clip, nine bullets, hitting like jackhammers, smashing into the limp body.

Vampyr went to the body and from a pocket pulled out a small vial of black sandlike material. He looked up at Nosferatu and smiled. "I took this off one of those who hunted me." He sprinkled it on Adrik's body. Within thirty seconds it was gone, except for the clothes.

Vampyr stood. "Now the next step."

Nosferatu took a step toward Vampyr, the mercenaries swinging the muzzles of their weapons to cover him in response. "Can we leave?"

Vampyr shrugged. "You may go where you want. Just do not get in my way. It is the Fourth Age. My Age."

THE PIL🌑+S 🌑F the X-Craft could barely make out the long landing strip. It was painted to mimic the surrounding desert, and only the faint straight lines on the edges allowed them to discern it. They gave up control to the ground computer that guided them along their flight path.

NOSFERATU PULLED a lever, and the overhead door above the helicopter began sliding open. He and Nekhbet were wrapped in dark cloaks, their faces covered with cloth and their eyes protected by dark, wraparound sunglasses. He'd always known he might have to evacuate the Haven, and the Dauphin helicopter hidden in the underground chamber was one of the preparations he'd made.

He and Nekhbet made their way across the hangar floor to the chopper. Nosferatu got in the pilot's seat while Nekhbet sat next to him in the copilot's. He fired up the engines and, as the blades slowly began to turn, Nosferatu pulled out a small handheld that gave him a link to the computer controlling the X-Craft. He checked the status. It was two minutes out.

"What are you doing?" Nekhbet asked, as he handed her the device.

"I am the Eldest," Nosferatu said. He pulled back on the controls and the helicopter lifted out of the hangar into the night sky.

VAMPYR SAT in the conference room, surrounded by his mercenaries, watching the X-Craft appear on the video monitors. The powerful men he had negotiated with were on their way here also. With the alliances he had arranged, Vampyr had no doubt that he would achieve a new world order, with him at the head, an Immortal with a cadre of Undead around him.

"PRESS THE RED BUTTON," Nosferatu said.

Nekhbet did not ask why. She did as he said.

THE PILOT OF the X-Craft cursed as it banked slightly out of the designated approach, an alarm rang through his headset, and several warning lights flashed on the console. He hit the button that would switch the craft back to manual control but nothing happened.

He and his copilot screamed in unison as the nose of the craft dipped below glide parameters. The craft hit directly above the Haven.

VAMPYR SURVIVED. The heavy wooden conference table had taken the brunt of the force as the explosion tore through the underground base and into the room he was in. With one arm he shoved the table off his body and took stock. His other arm had a compound fracture, white bone sticking out of the punctured skin. Breathing was difficult, and he realized he had several broken ribs.

With his good hand, he reached across to his other hand and jerked hard, his body spasming from the pain as he realigned the broken arm. The Airlia virus was already at work, repairing the damage.

Vampyr smiled grimly and staggered to his feet, silently promising vengeance against Nosferatu. This was but a delay in the inevitable.

◆ ◆ ◆

N✛SFERA✛U AND NEKHBE✛ stared at the flames that shot up from the top of the cliff from the safety of the helicopter. Nosferatu had them in a hover two miles away, off the coast. He turned and began moving away from the site, paralleling the coast.

"Do you think he is dead?" Nekhbet asked.

"No," Nosferatu said. "Even if he was killed by the explosion, the virus will bring him back to life."

"He will come after us."

"No, he won't," Nosferatu said. "When we took off from the hangar, we crossed an electronic beam that began a countdown." He glanced down at the chronometer on the control panel. "Just about—now."

Behind them the Haven, and the cliff, was consumed in a fireball as a small tactical nuclear weapon went off, vaporizing the compound, and Vampyr.

EPILOGUE

THE SUN WAS CONSUMED BY THE western desert, slowly disappearing. Shimmering heat rose up as the sand gave back what it had accumulated during the day. Shortly after the last golden ray was gone, two wraithlike figures rose from the ground, brushing the sand off their dark cloaks.

"Which way?" Nekhbet asked. They were three hundred miles from the Haven, having flown straight across the desert before the fuel ran out. Then they'd run from the chopper for several more hours before burying themselves at daybreak to rest.

Nosferatu had never felt so alive. He wasn't certain whether it was the one hundred percent Airlia blood that ran through his veins or Nekhbet's presence at his side. And he didn't care to ponder the question, simply accepting that it was. Finally. After millennia, what they had dreamed of while chained underneath the Giza Plateau was a reality.

Nosferatu stretched his arms wide, taking in the stars above and the land ahead. "There is so much in the world I want to show you. Things we never even imagined all those years we talked in the darkness."

Nekhbet laughed, the sound picked up by the wind and blown across the desert. "Then let us see them."

She took off running, her feet lightly touching the sand.

Nosferatu pulled back his hood, revealing his dark eyes and pale skin, and watched her slender form racing away, then he set off in pursuit.

ABOUT THE AUTHOR

ROBERT DOHERTY is a pseudonym for a best-selling writer of military suspense novels. He is a West Point graduate and served as a Special Forces A-Team leader before writing full-time. He is also the author of *The Rock, Area 51, Area 51: The Reply, Area 51: The Mission, Area 51: The Sphinx, Area 51: The Grail, Area 51: Excalibur, Psychic Warrior* and *Psychic Warrior: Project Aura*. For more information go to www.BobMayer.org

Don't miss the next exciting book
from bestselling author

ROBERT DOHERTY

AREA 51
LEGEND

◆◆◆

Coming in 2004